THE
LOST SESSIONS

Also by Sebastian Beaumont:

Thirteen
The Juggler

THE LOST SESSIONS

SEBASTIAN BEAUMONT

MYRMIDON

Myrmidon
Rotterdam House
116 Quayside
Newcastle upon Tyne
NE1 3DY

www.myrmidonbooks.com

First published in the United Kingdom by Myrmidon 2022

Copyright © Sebastian Beaumont 2022
Sebastian Beaumont has asserted his right under the Copyright, Designs and Patents Act 1988 to be identified as the author of this work.

This novel is entirely a work of fiction. The names, characters and incidents portrayed in it are the work of the author's imagination. Any resemblance to actual persons, living or dead, events or localities is entirely coincidental.

A catalogue record for this book is available from the British Library.

ISBN 978-1-910183-29-8

Set in Sabon LT Std by Ellipsis, Glasgow

Printed in the UK by CPI Group (UK) Ltd, Croydon, CR0 4YY

All rights reserved. No part of this publication may be reproduced, stored in a retrieval system, or transmitted in any form or by any means, electronic, mechanical, photocopying, recording or otherwise, without the prior written consent of the publishers.

This book is sold subject to the condition that it shall not, by way of trade or otherwise, be lent, resold, hired out or otherwise circulated without the publisher's prior consent in any form of binding or cover other than that in which it is published and without a similar condition including this condition being imposed on the subsequent purchaser.

1 3 5 7 9 10 8 6 4 2

For Vidyadhara
and all who dare
to truly
let go.

One

There were two impacts. The first was when Will's bicycle hit the side panel of a car that had slewed across the pavement – a dark purple Ford Mondeo, in a colour he'd once heard described as aubergine. He couldn't remember seeing a driver. The gap between the first and second impact was filled with motion. Will was propelled over the handlebars and the sensation of movement through the cool, dark, drizzly air was somehow timeless. It had no beginning or end, made stranger still by the impression of being weightless. And then he struck a pale grey period lamppost with his forehead; a massively brutal collision against unyielding iron. His instant emotional response was of bafflement and anguish, while his intellect observed what was happening with detachment. Not interest, but merely a kind of noticing.

Pain wasn't a part of it just then. There was a voice inside him, hollow with shock, that said, very quickly, *It's okay, it's okay, I'm okay, I'm okay,* while the observing part of himself noticed that this was absolutely not the case. And then he was on the pavement, in a pool of light from the lamp, feeling dazed, with a man leaning down beside him, sounding shocked and upset, saying something that he couldn't catch.

Will sat up, saying, 'I'm okay, I'm okay.'

By the time he looked across, the car had gone. The man, distraught, knelt down beside him on the wet pavement.

'Are you hurt?' he asked, aghast.

'I'm alright,' Will told him, hesitantly.

'We should get you to hospital right away. I'll call an ambulance.'

'No, I . . . only live . . . round the corner. Do you want to help me up?'

The man did so, and they stood for a few calm moments, looking down at Will's broken bicycle, with its buckled wheel and bent front forks.

'That was appalling! How could anyone do that and then drive off?' The man shook his head. 'I didn't get the registration number, mate, I'm sorry.'

'I'm alright,' Will said again. 'A bit dazed. But alright.'

'I can't believe you're conscious – or even alive, the way you went over like that. I think we should get you to hospital. You're bleeding quite badly.'

'My wife is at home,' said Will. 'I'll get her to take me.'

The man looked dubious. Drops of rain were beginning to drip from his dark fringe, catching light from the offending lamp.

'Don't worry, I live just up here,' Will gesticulated vaguely in the direction of Clapham Common. 'By the florist.'

Liquid started to trickle into Will's left eye and to drip

down onto the pavement. He couldn't tell whether it was rain or blood. The man pulled a glove out of his pocket.

'Here,' he said, 'hold this against your forehead. I'll walk you home. What about the bike?'

'Leave it,' Will said. 'If someone wants to steal it, they can have it.'

The man picked it up and hefted it over his shoulder. 'Can you walk? Do you need support?'

Will put his hand on the man's shoulder and they took a few steps in silence. Will then let go but wobbled immediately as his body veered drunkenly to one side. The man grabbed his elbow to steady him. After a couple of blocks, they came to the road where Will lived. He was in the ground floor flat of Number 12, a typical late-Victorian London semi that had been converted into flats in the 1970s and was now in need of some updating. He fumbled for his keys, one hand still pressed to his head as he held the glove there. The man took out his phone.

'Look,' he said, 'give me your number. I'll text you my details. The police will probably need a statement from me.'

Will nodded and fumbled to get his phone. 'Better give them to my wife,' he mumbled, giving up.

He managed to find his keys and the man took them and unlocked the door. They looked in at the warm light of the hall and heard the distant sound of some music in the kitchen.

'Thanks,' Will said.

The man steadied him as Will staggered slightly.

'Come on,' he said, 'let me give you a hand.'

Will allowed himself to be helped into the hall and called out, 'It's okay, I'm okay!'

Lara immediately hurried into the hall.

'What's happened?' she cried. Clearly his attempt at a re-assuring tone had failed completely. He stood, blinking, as he tried to gather his thoughts.

The man introduced himself to Lara and began to explain what had happened.

'Come into the kitchen so I can have a look at you,' Lara told Will.

'I think I might be the only witness,' said the man. 'I'll come in and leave my details.'

Lara thanked him.

'And I'd get your husband to hospital if I were you.'

'Your glove . . .' Will handed it over as the man was giving Lara his number.

He looked at the blood-sodden material and smiled. 'At least you're alive. Don't worry, I can let myself out.'

Lara thanked him again and then took Will into the bathroom where she tried to clean him up.

'Oh God,' she said, 'look at you! Oh, Will, your poor face . . .'

The ridges on the lamppost had left three parallel, horizontal contused stripes on Will's forehead. The lower one ran across a little above his eyebrows, the second was in the middle of his forehead and the third just below his hairline. His eye was beginning to close as it swelled. Will could feel fury welling up unannounced and inchoate, and he pounded the edge of the basin with his fist while Lara was getting some cotton wool.

'Aaach!' he cried, not with pain, but with an excess of emotion that simply burst out.

After Lara had bandaged him, they went to the police station. Lara wanted to go straight to A&E, but Will insisted that they go to the police first and the hospital second. He grew petulant and irritated as Lara tried to persuade him otherwise, which made her smile.

'You're acting like a little kid,' she told him, 'I've never seen you annoyed like this before.'

The red-faced desk sergeant was congenial enough. He took Will's statement impassively, asking one or two questions about the exact location, but other than that wrote down a brief description of the accident with a nonchalance that was oddly reassuring.

'At least you have a willing witness,' he told Will.

As the man read back the statement and gave Lara a crime number, Will stumbled over his words of thanks, and the sergeant looked past him at Lara.

'I'd get him to hospital, right away, if I was you. He's beginning to slur his words, which is never a good sign in someone who's sober.'

Two

Before Lara, especially through his childhood and adolescence, Will was aware of a sense of lovelessness, which manifested in him as a kind of sadness, or melancholy. It was as though on some level he didn't even know what love was, as though he had never experienced this apparently universal emotion. Maybe it was a specific deficiency in him, like a missing limb. Later, when love had dramatically impressed itself upon him, he couldn't understand how he had managed to cut himself off from the conscious experience of this vital emotion. The pain that causes us to close down, and the courage that it takes to open up, are a mystery – a miracle, almost, in a secular kind of way.

His paternal grandmother, a rather eccentric Scot from Stirling, had a convenient way of explaining oddness and dysfunction. She would say of someone, 'Mibbie he was dropped on his heid as a bairn?' This explained practically anything. There was an incident with some local youths and the use of knives. 'Mibbie they were dropped on their heids as bairns?' The local minister's wife had a nervous breakdown. 'Mibbie she was dropped on her heid as a bairn?'

It would seem that her father, Will's great grandfather, really had been dropped on his head at birth causing injury to his delicate skull. Every difficulty thereafter, and apparently there were many, was explained in this way.

'Perhaps she was dropped on *her* head as a bairn,' Kitty, Will's sister, had said.

Will had sometimes wondered if perhaps he'd been dropped on his head, too. Perhaps he had brain damage that rendered him incapable of love?

Did he experience love from his mother? Intellectually perhaps he could say yes, but she was distant and emotionally unavailable and so it didn't feel like love somehow. The thought of love as described in literature was very different from what he experienced. Did he love her? What an unbearably complicated question that was! To say no was to admit to something that might crush him completely. He was full of emotion, with a rich internal landscape of hope and curiosity and sadness and all the other feelings that a young man might have, but if he said to himself *I am loveless* it sounded true.

His father? Well, he liked his dad, but that didn't feel like love either – at least not as he understood it.

In his late twenties, when he trained as a therapist, the subject of his lovelessness came up often with his own therapist. By that time, he'd learned that it was not true, but the incident through which he was forced to acknowledge 'love' for the first time had not involved his parents, nor any kind of sexual attraction or desire. And, even as his thirtieth birthday was beginning to loom, he was still affected by the shadow of his now-distant conviction.

'I couldn't feel love for my mother,' Will had told Felix, 'not the way I saw it portrayed in novels. It was as if that emotion had been invented as an eccentric and pointless fiction. I've tried to give myself up to relationships with women. That's an understatement, by the way. I think I'm a generous person and I've been happy to give everything that I can, but there was always something missing. In me, not them.'

'You are wounded,' Felix told him. 'Love is too much of a risk for you to feel.'

'Here's hoping therapy will help. At least a wee bit.'

'You have to heal yourself, Will. No one is going to do it for you.'

Will met Lara in his first year of training as a therapist. He was twenty-eight and she was twenty-six. She was a trained dancer and choreographer and ran one-on-one therapeutic movement sessions at the Claygate Centre, where he'd got his honorary counselling placement. She also ran dance classes at a couple of studios in town. Later, she admitted that she'd been attracted to his vulnerability and stoic air of bearing up in the face of tragedy. She was also interested in his awkward physical presence. He was fit – he ran regularly and cycled several miles each way to work, college or to his placement – and yet there was something hesitant about the way he moved.

'You're trapped inside your skin,' she'd said to him one

day. 'Come and see me for a chat, and perhaps we can unlock something. I'm not too booked up at the moment, so there's always the odd hour here and there when I'm free.'

And so he went to her, and she 'worked' on him. This led to several tearful episodes on Will's part, which felt cathartic but didn't change the fact that he didn't really seem to fit the world physically. The world seemed to be a set of obstacles that weren't as easy for him to negotiate as they obviously were for others.

He realised that their relationship was becoming serious, although it was still not sexual, when Lara booked out a regular weekly slot and didn't charge him for it. This was just as well, given how broke he was. And the time they spent together was intimate – how could it not be when it was to do with movement, alignment and a physical manifestation of what was too difficult for him to put into words.

After he'd seen her for seven or eight sessions, she left a card in his in-tray that said, *The mind can be deceitful, but the body never lies*. This gave him a sense of vertigo. Love was such a mystery to him and he felt the danger of it threatening to overwhelm him. What would happen if he fell in love? What would happen to his identity? He'd found out in the most poignant way that he was capable of love, but he'd yet to authentically fall in love with a woman and for that to last, and the prospect of it was incredibly scary.

The next session, they kissed, and for Will something was bridged. That previously unconnected chasm between his body and his emotions. When they made love it made sense in a new way. He could hear Lara's voice saying, 'The body never lies', and there was a truth in his connection with her that led to an extraordinary liberation from the inhibition that he'd previously felt – of being damaged.

He could sense in Lara that she was also beginning to be healed by their liaison. From the start, she alluded to a relationship with a dancer that had recently ended. He'd been tricksy and deceitful. She finally opened up about it one evening when they were talking about vulnerability.

'I love your honesty,' she told him. 'I am working in a world where that level of honesty is often missing. In fact, I decided last year to never go out with another dancer again. It made me feel too vulnerable. I could never find anyone I could trust. They all cheated on me in the end. I don't mean sleeping with other people, either – although that was part of it. It was the deceit involved and the way that lies crept in to cover things up that couldn't be mentioned or discussed. In fact, it happened so often I'd almost come to the conclusion that it was me that was the problem, rather than them.'

Her smile then had something so beautiful in it that Will ached a little when he saw it.

'And then,' she said. 'I met you.'

Lara's trust in him felt healthy and invigorating. It was great to have something to live up to, something worthwhile.

Lara was as tall as Will. The word that came to mind when he first met her was *steady*, but that didn't encompass her astonishing physical grace, and he realised later that this use of *steady* was with regard to her psychological rather than her physical presence. *Poised* might have been a better word. She inhabited her body so well and could demonstrate posture easily, and explain it in such a way that he could grasp what she was trying to convey. She would smile at him as they worked, a mischievous smile that contained a hint of sadness, as though life was beautiful but inevitably bittersweet. She had mid-length dark hair with a slight curl that fell forward across her face when she looked down and across at him. It was glossy and thick and, when he first met her, smelled of chamomile with a faint hint of almond. How odd, he thought later, that she ended up with someone so physically awkward.

It became clear that a word like *vulnerable* would also have described her, even *frail* at times. As their relationship developed, he saw that her choreography reflected this. In fact, it was here that he first noticed her fear of being hurt, in the yearning quality of her expansive movements and in the protective way she would fold her arms across her body. He could see that she'd been burdened with doubt about relationships and it made him determined to make this one work.

She had a simple beauty that had no arrogance to it, and that was an attractive combination given her particular emphasis on movement and being in touch with her body.

'Falling in love' was not something for which he'd been prepared. Previous relationships had always stopped short of that, so he didn't notice its tendrils enter and creep through his system like cilia. However, there was no denying that it fitted his therapeutic journey. As part of his training, he had to be in therapy for the two years of his course, and this was the arena in which he could explore the fact that he'd previously, and unconsciously, used his status as a Tragic Young Man to devastating effect with women. Of course, there were still women who wanted men to be strong and perhaps even emotionless, but there was no doubt that Will presented something that was attractive to many women – athletic, but susceptible to melancholy and with an aura of misfortune that had the underlying, unspoken statement of *Don't even bother to try. You can't fix me.*

The result of this had been a series of failed relationships, entered into with hope and curiosity by both parties, but which ended when the woman in question realised the truth of that unspoken statement: *you can't fix me*. They couldn't. And why? Because Will's pain was not simple pain, crying out for healing, but a yearning for a kind of maternal holding that none of them were able to provide. He couldn't see this need in himself and so he couldn't see that he was withholding something, something fundamental, from both himself and his partners. In fact, by the time he started his training as a therapist, he had become so wary of relationships that he might easily have shied away from Lara's interest in him, just as she was shying away from others. Coming into a relationship, then, was a healing experience for both of them. They were wounded in different ways and could see the beneficial effect each was having on the other.

Lara offered him the chance to explore his pain, so that he could see it in a more helpful perspective, not so related to self-pity. He could stand there in front of the full-length mirror with her beside him and look at them as a pair. His athletic physique and pale, freckled skin counterpointed Lara's colouring, a Scot to her Adriatic ancestry. His sandy hair was thick and ruffled, no matter how he tried to tame it, and from the first she encouraged him to grow it long.

Their relationship blossomed, though for Will the 'L word' was still something from which he shied away when he thought of relationships. It was a complicated word in other respects, too. He had three clients most of the time in his placement, although that increased to four, five and sometimes even six as time passed, and he gave them all what he believed to be unconditional positive regard. Was that a kind of 'love'? Yes, of course it was. He did not deny his clients' pain, or try to avoid it, and he certainly cared what happened to them. But why was it so difficult to use that word?

Lara moved on from the Claygate Centre at this point, having found more lucrative work in the studios of the West End, where her abilities as a teacher were more appreciated and from where she could pick up bits and pieces of work as a choreographer. They stopped being work colleagues and became, quite suddenly, a couple, which was scary and delightful for both of them.

It was comforting sitting in A&E with Lara. As they waited to be seen, Will realised that most of his cognitive functioning was stripped down. He kept on wondering if things had gone into slow motion, but it wasn't that. It was as if only the part of his brain that was necessary for survival was conscious. The rest was simply not there, leaving him with a feeling of partial awareness of the world. The odd thing about this was that he couldn't be sure *what* was absent. This would have been more interesting if it wasn't for the fact that a cracking headache was beginning to develop. And all the time, part of him was noticing this.

He remembered his maternal grandfather after he'd had a stroke, saying, 'It's peculiar, Will. I know that a part of me is missing, but I don't know which bit.' Will had been disconcerted when his grandfather had gone on to say, 'Do *you* know what's missing? Your mother and father say I'm being ridiculous, but maybe you've noticed something and are brave enough to tell me.'

Will, who was twelve at the time, wasn't brave – or cruel – enough, but he might have said, 'You've lost the bit of you that makes you *you*.' Instead, he said, 'I know what you mean but I can't put my finger on it.' This had satisfied his grandfather who had murmured, 'Aye, neither can I. It's very peculiar.' He died the following week.

Will glanced over at Lara. 'I'm not going to be able to see my clients tomorrow, am I?'

Lara laughed. 'No. Not for a few days, I expect. Do you have an early start?'

Will couldn't remember. He knew it was Friday the following day but he had no recollection of what was in his diary.

'I'll give the practice a ring and tell them that you are well and truly out of action for the time being,' Lara told him. 'If you phone them, you'll worry them. You sound like a zombie.'

Will felt panicked at the prospect of missing work. It had taken him four years to build up a decent list of clients and it seemed a cruel betrayal that he was injured in this way. His current experience was of being separate from the world, distanced from it rather than present and engaged. What if this went on for weeks? What if all his clients left?

'It would be different if I had flu, or some other illness,' he told her, 'because I'd have a good idea how long it would last. But part of my thinking has gone missing. It's like I can see this moment, but nothing around it. I can't think of yesterday, or tomorrow – they seem to have disappeared completely.'

Lara smiled. 'I could leave a message saying, "My husband won't be working with clients this week because part of him has gone missing".'

Will was checked for pulse, reactions, pupil dilation, response time and his ability to squeeze the nurse's finger. The nurse, who was ornately pierced, dressed his wound and smiled at him.

'These lamppost stripes are rather unusual,' she said, 'and quite attractive in a Goth sort of way. It's a shame to cover them up. I know a few people who might pay good money to look like that – minus the black eye. I don't think they'll scar, though, unless you rub something caustic into them.'

'I think I'll let them heal without tampering with them,' he said.

She smiled with something that looked almost like pity at passing up this opportunity. 'There's less harm done than it looks. You're going to have a great black eye, but I don't think we need to keep you in overnight, seeing as you've got someone with you who can keep an eye on you.' She turned to Lara. 'Take this leaflet and make sure you do what it says. Will was fortunate to strike his head at the angle he did. At another angle he might have broken his neck.' She patted Will's arm. 'Lucky for you, foreheads are pretty good shock absorbers. Take the dressing off tomorrow, and let the wound get some air. Go to your GP on Monday to get yourself checked out or come back here at any time if you get any unusual symptoms.'

That night, after consulting the leaflet, Lara woke Will every hour to make sure that he was asleep rather than unconscious. Apart from being bad-tempered about being woken up, he was fine. In the morning, however, he felt groggy and headachy, and so Lara took the day off work, too, to keep an eye on him with a view to taking him back to A&E if necessary. She also booked him in to see an osteopath that she'd used once or twice herself. At that point Will seemed to be aching pretty well everywhere and she wanted to have him checked over.

He wanted to go to the police station in the morning to report the accident, and when Lara told him that they'd already done so the night before, he found he had no recollection of it at all. Lara seemed concerned at this. She looked up *head injuries* on the internet and came back to tell him, rather triumphantly, that this lapse in memory was caused by a moderate concussion.

'Which is a noun,' she told him. '*A* concussion. You have a concussion.'

His shouting at her when she'd suggested going to the hospital first was a common symptom of head injury, as was memory loss.

'Your general irritation gave me a glimpse of what it must be like to be married to your sister,' she smiled.

'The thought of that makes me feel exhausted,' Will said, and rolled over.

There had been an arrangement to spend Saturday walking in the countryside with Will's younger brother, Jamie, and his boyfriend, Joel. Lara phoned to cancel this and then went off to potter around the flat while he slept the day, and then the weekend, away.

'It's alright,' Lara told him at 8.45am on Monday, when she was leaving for work, 'all your clients are cancelled until further notice. Didn't you say you had a supervision planned in for this week? It's probably a good idea to cancel that, too. Take it easy today and go and see Dr Lucas at 10.45. I sorted the appointment for you online and I've set the alarm for 10.00, so that you can get up in plenty of time. Then you're booked to see my osteopath, Mandy, at the Cliffe practice at midday. I've put details and alerts for both into your phone.'

She sounded casual, but he could see that she was worried.

And so began what Will referred to as his twilight week. For the first three days he slept twenty-two hours a day, which was astonishingly easy, and would have been almost pleasant and gentle if it hadn't been for the headache and the muscle pain in his neck, shoulder and across his ribs that provided a constant backdrop to his experience. Mandy had been positive about the alignment of his skeleton, though she worked on his aching muscles and booked him in for a follow-up appointment the following week to check that his neck was settling down. His brain continued to dampen input. It took some in. Rejected most. He enjoyed Lara's return from work and the simple meals that she cooked, before he slipped back into a comforting lethargy, followed by sleep.

The one thing he hadn't expected was that, by half way through the third day, amidst the woolly-ness of it, it was all becoming so intellectually challenging. What did it mean, that a part of his consciousness was 'absent'? What did it mean that he no longer had a sense of who he was? After all, he could say: 'I am Will Thomas. I am thirty-four years old. I am a psychotherapeutic counsellor. I am married to Lara Thomas and I live at 12a Oxney Road, London.' But this didn't seem to really capture the *me*, and that was the challenging thing; he didn't feel like *me* anymore. But what was it that was missing?

He was aware, for example, that if he went to make a cup of coffee, he experienced the room differently. It was as if his brain was only allowing in information that was specifically relevant to the task at hand. All else was screened out – to keep things simple and restful, he assumed. This was highlighted on the Tuesday, the fourth day after his accident when, in one of his brief periods of wakefulness, he ventured outside to get some chocolate and discovered how dangerous the world seemed. The newsagent's was on the other side of the high street, which was busy, and which Will had often crossed to get a paper. On this occasion, however, the task of crossing the road was hugely complicated by the fact that traffic was approaching too fast for his slowed-down thinking processes to easily register, and cars seemed to flash frighteningly almost out of nowhere. In the end, Will realised that he would have to walk down to the next block and cross over at the pedestrian lights.

His sight was technically unimpaired, if you didn't count his half-closed black eye, so it wasn't a fault with his vision. It was as if he had no peripheral *cognition*, which was surreal and disturbing, not only because he found so much of what he was experiencing confusing, but also because this strangeness contained no *me*.

He tried to explain this to Lara, but it wasn't easy.

'Of course you're you,' she said. 'A little more needy, perhaps, but that's hardly surprising given what's happened.'

She laughed when he tried to explain further and said, 'When this is over, you'll laugh at it, too.'

What a balm her laughter was, and more healing than anything else that she was doing for him. In fact, her steady cheerful presence managed to help him keep from worrying about the financial implications of taking time off work. They weren't flush with money and there wasn't a great deal of security for them.

There was something in the unchanging quality of his experience over those first few days that drove him, fairly quickly, to the computer and the internet, to the website that Lara had already bookmarked. Like so much diagnostic information and advice on the internet, it could be more worrying than comforting. Technically, a concussion of Will's kind was described as a *mild traumatic brain injury*, and although the medical use of the word *traumatic* was different in flavour from the psychotherapeutic one, it was just as complex and disturbing.

A concussion mostly cleared up of its own accord, except when it didn't. This major sleeping, his headache and the fact that he couldn't remember going to the police station on the night of his accident put the concussion at 'intermediate level'. Most people recovered from a concussion of this kind, he discovered, but some didn't, moving instead into 'post-concussion syndrome', where the symptoms that Will was experiencing could last for the rest of your life.

Lovely.

He saw Dr Lucas twice that week. The second time, on Friday morning, Will was down to eighteen hours sleep per day. His headache had finally subsided that morning, so there was some improvement, but Dr Lucas was still bemused.

'It's not unusual to need a lot of sleep when you are recovering from a concussion. But it *is* unusual to be sleeping this much a week after your accident, considering that you have no other major symptoms. But there we go . . . brains are very unusual and surprising organs.'

'There's one question I have . . .'

'Look, Will . . . I don't know how long it will last. Concussion has to take its time. I'm afraid you'll need to carry on resting up for as long as it takes.'

'That's not what I was going to ask,' Will told him, 'I was going to ask you about *me*.'

'You?'

'Yes, my sense of self. Where does it reside? There's this feeling that I've lost my sense of self, but I'm not even sure what I mean by that. I experience everything differently at the moment, of course I do, but surely that's not the only thing that makes me feel like me? I can't put my finger on it, that's what's so confusing and so preoccupying. I keep on getting this spooky feeling of not knowing who I am.'

'Will,' said Dr Lucas, 'if you want me to sign you off work, say so. I'll happily sign you off for a week. Two weeks. Look, I'd happily sign you off for a month, the way you're talking.'

'Okay, okay . . . it doesn't matter. I work freelance, anyway, so I'll not be needing a sick note, but thanks.'

'You're a therapist. You probably know more about this kind of thing than me. Consult Freud. Or maybe . . .' Dr Lucas stared at him disconcertingly. ' . . . a priest.'

On Saturday morning, Will woke up feeling fine. No, not fine. Fantastic. He was experiencing a kind of attention that was delightful, characterised in part by the absence of woolly-headedness that had been present while he was cognitively subdued.

'Oh my God!' he said to the ceiling.

'What?' asked Lara, anxiously, stirring at his side and opening a bleary eye.

'I feel . . . great! I mean, I feel *really* great. I feel like *me*!'

'Good,' mumbled Lara, 'perhaps *me* can go and get us a cup of tea.'

'Coming up!' Will laughed. He swung his legs out of bed and felt the vigour in the movement.

He went into the kitchen and put the kettle on and felt like himself. He poured water onto the tea bags and felt like himself. He suddenly had all that familiar background *ness*: the way he registered the birdsong outside; the way he noticed the residual scent of roasted vegetables from the night before; the small red circle where a wine bottle had left a new stain on the worktop. He noticed that the floor needed sweeping and that the bin under the sink was almost full. Wow! He was noticing so much! It was fantastic, and so sudden after a week of such muffled interaction with his surroundings.

He could smell the delicate scent of the Darjeeling as he poured water into his mug, and thought, *Hey, I've taken all this for granted, that my brain can do this!*

He'd never realised that cognitive experience could be so rich, and full and beautiful. He laughed and popped out to get some fresh flowers from the newsagent, who always had a bucket outside with a few bunches in it. Daffodils today. And the road was a doddle. He laughed as he crossed and waved at a motorist for no other reason than general ebullience.

Back at the flat, he took tea and flowers to Lara. She was curled asleep in bed with the duvet pulled to her chest, and he looked at her for a moment before leaning down and kissing her awake.

'Let's get out somewhere,' he said. 'I need fresh air. I need *exercise*.'

'When I talked to them last week, Jamie told me that he and Joel were planning to go for a walk on Box Hill today,' Lara said.

'Right. Let's see if it's not too late to join them.'

Jamie was two years younger than Will, who admired his brother's physical grace – had been rather jealous of it in fact. His own lack of co-ordination was legendary in the family. 'You great, lumbering lug,' was a description that had often been used by Kitty, his older sister, when he was a child, and as he thought of it now, Will realised that he'd never forgiven her.

Now that he had a word for it, *dyspraxia*, he was able to shrug off this kind of remark more easily but looking at Jamie's easy loping walk now caused Will a small chirrup of envy. This was something that he could never achieve. Will had made up for his lack of grace with athleticism, by becoming the fastest runner in his school and, later, a valuable member of the cross-country team at university. It was recompense of a sort. Running, running, always running . . .

Lara was a runner too, and she didn't mind his dyspraxia. She sometimes became frustrated by his forgetfulness and lack of organisation, but she had never blamed him for these traits, as if they were some sort of character flaw or deliberate laziness. 'If only you could pay more attention,' his father had sometimes said, 'you wouldn't knock things over.'

He felt grateful that, since the accident, she hadn't mentioned his dyspraxia with regard to his cycling. How generous it was, he realised, that she'd never said, 'I told you so.' It had, after all, been quite a contentious issue for a while.

'You haven't even properly mastered the art of being on your feet,' she'd said to him once, reminding him of his promise not to do any cross-country running after he'd fallen so many times attempting to negotiate gates and styles at speed. Now, he realised, his life as a cyclist was probably over. You could hardly help it if a car slewed across a pavement and knocked you over, but he guessed that if it had happened to Jamie, he might have been able to use his dexterity and that extra moment of attention to swerve and avoid a collision.

He remembered saying to Lara, when he'd bought the bicycle the previous year, 'I can take care of myself. Now, we can give up the car.'

'I like your independent spirit, but you take too many risks,' she told him. 'And they're usually of the wrong kind.'

It was true that he tended to wobble if he slowed down too much, and he would never admit this to Lara, but he'd narrowly missed being hit more than once as he negotiated lanes around Clapham Common. It was time to give up this particular form of risk-taking. He'd explored both excessive risk-taking, and excessive risk-aversion with clients, but, oh, how difficult it was to apply these sophisticated powers of psychological observation to oneself!

Jamie and Will were walking together, while Lara lagged behind, as usual, talking quietly and intensely with Joel.

'How's it going with Joel?' Will asked his brother.

'Better, and worse,' said Jamie. 'I mean, it's better by virtue of the fact that we both know and have acknowledged that our relationship is over, and so we've stopped arguing about what we should or shouldn't be doing with our lives. And, of course, it's worse because we both know and have acknowledged that it's over, and that makes us feel like shit.'

They walked on. Will glanced over at the view down across the undulating Surrey countryside, struck as ever by how wooded the county was. He shrugged himself into his coat. The tufts of grass by the path had small patches of frost where the sun hadn't managed to reach. Looking out over the rolling Surrey countryside, with its delicate mist and the dark smudges of woods and copses, Will had a sense of wistful stillness and of slumber. Spring was underway, but winter still clung on at this elevation.

'I wish we hadn't both become rescuers,' said Jamie. 'At least you've become a therapist and so you have an outlet for your neuroses, but I guess I'm still a little stuck in the ideal of it. It seems so stupid at this point to think that I might heal someone just by trying to love them more – as if that were even possible. But there we are. At the start of my relationship with Joel, my reason for falling in love with him seemed very different.'

Will smiled sadly. 'Joel's lovely.'

'Joel's lovely,' Jamie agreed, 'and his mother committed suicide last year. And he's right to go back to Australia to sort things out with his father.' He glanced across as a couple of magpies took to the air in a squall of noise. 'How's Lara?' he asked.

'Great,' said Will. 'Faultless. She's really taken care of me.' He felt his chest constricting with a tremor of gratitude for these people in his life who cared for him. 'You're the only person who's ever seen that I am a rescuer. A therapist should never rescue his clients.'

Jamie laughed. 'Every client that comes to you and leaves saying that they've been helped, heals another tiny little piece of your heart, Will.'

'Wanting that is neurotic?'

'No, it's beautiful.'

'If only that was the way it worked. Of course, it does sometimes. But I'm hated by some of my clients too.'

Jamie didn't say anything. His Adam's apple moved for a moment as he swallowed some emotion.

Will thought of Joel and Jamie's sadness and wondered what to say. 'My clients have all been left in the lurch this week,' he said, eventually.

'A shame that they haven't had a chance to see you like this,' said Jamie. 'Those parallel cuts look almost ritualistic, and your black eye would have been a thing to ponder. You look so vulnerable, despite your build. They might have started trying to rescue you!'

They went to an Indian restaurant for an early dinner on their return, and there was a touching sadness between Jamie and Joel, which made Will feel pensive. Sad for Jamie and Joel, but sad for himself, too, somehow. An impersonal sadness, a sadness at the knowledge that sadness is an inevitable and inescapable part of life and that there was nothing he could do to lift this from his brother.

As he started on his main course, a fine Rogan Josh, he noticed a man sitting with his family a couple of tables away. He wasn't sure what had attracted his attention to this man, but he noticed that he was starting to tremble. The woman that he was with was studiously avoiding looking at him, and the two teenagers also at the table were intent on their food.

The man, in his late-forties Will guessed, glanced across at him and looked distressed about what was happening. Will looked at Lara to see if she'd noticed, but the four of them were in an alcove so that Will was the only one who could see across the room. He started to watch, amazed that the man's family were ignoring him. The man looked more and more startled and anxious as his trembling started to become shaking and his expression turned to that of panic. As Will watched, he wondered if this was the beginning of an epileptic seizure, and he was about to get up to go and ask the man if he was alright, but the man got up and came over to Will, looking furious.

'What are you doing to me?' he demanded.

'I'm sorry?' said Will.

'You were making me shake. I don't know how you did it, but every time you looked at me, I started shaking.'

Will opened his mouth to speak but didn't have a chance to say anything.

The man gritted his teeth. 'Kindly stop whatever weird trick you're playing on me or I will get very, very annoyed.'

He turned away and went back to his table. Will turned to his companions, who all looked at him with surprise.

'I thought I saw you staring at something,' said Jamie. 'What happened?'

'I thought that guy was going to have a fit,' said Will. 'I nearly went over to see if I could help.'

'Nutter,' murmured Joel.

Lara smiled. 'My husband does have a bizarre effect on people, sometimes.'

'Don't joke,' said Will. 'That's made me feel weird.'

'It made him feel weird, too, by the look of it,' laughed Joel.

'I wonder what it says about me that I find it's cheered me up?' said Jamie.

'Poor Joel,' Lara said later, when they were back home, 'he was saying goodbye to me, really, when we were talking together on the hill and it made me realise how much I'm going to miss him.'

Will nodded. He knew.

Three

Even as he dreamed the dream, he was aware that he was dreaming. He was reliving the moment of the accident. Not the accident itself and the physical impact – but the experience of being airborne. In his dream, this became perpetual, somehow. He was always in the air, moving forward through the cool evening breeze, the moisture of the drizzle against his cheek, but he never arrived at the lamppost. It was a strange sensation, because he felt that he was progressing forwards – he could see the bonnet of the car below him and the changing perspective as he passed over it – but every time he noticed it again, he was back at around the middle of his trajectory over that aubergine bonnet. The unhurried movement was like the earth's slow rotation as viewed from space. He was never going to arrive at his destination.

He woke on Monday morning, and still felt physically great. He had no symptoms of concussion whatsoever and his aches had subsided. There were still signs of his accident – his diminishing black eye and the parallel lines on his forehead where the dark scabs from his cuts were beginning to peel away.

Lara was cheerful, had been glowingly cheerful all weekend, which was lovely, and had raised his spirits considerably. Now, he was ready to face his clients. He'd texted all thirteen of them the day before to confirm the coming week's sessions. He hadn't thought of them at all during his week off, and that had been a kind of rest, too – a holiday from the perpetual subliminal consideration of the psychological jigsaw puzzle that each client presented.

The bike was still obstructing the hall, its mashed wheel a reminder of human vulnerability. He picked it up, took it outside and D-locked it to a railing by the tiny grass triangle that the council referred to as a 'recreation ground' but was in fact a spectacularly unhygienic dog toilet.

Walking was restful, though, and the twenty-five minutes that it took to get to the Claygate Centre gave him space to clear his head and prepare for the day ahead.

On arrival he smiled at Becky, the receptionist, who was taking a phone call. She waved at him and, taking out a new-referral sheet, handed it to him as he came past.

'One moment,' she said to her caller, 'I'm going to put you on hold for a second.'

She looked at Will, examining his face.

'You're looking a bit better today,' she said.

Will was about to say something but Becky had already resumed her call and so he went down the short corridor to his room, feeling a tingle of confusion. Was it just a misperception on his part? She'd made it sound as if she'd seen him since his accident.

His room was small with a bay window that let in plenty of light. It had clearly once been part of a much larger room. It had neutral oatmeal-coloured carpet and two paintings: one of an empty rowing boat tied to a wooden jetty, the other depicting an open rural landscape dotted with trees. Both were used by Will in sessions to discuss aspects of freedom and openness, though sometimes clients would have more unsettling associations of drowning, agoraphobia or more obscure associations with personal trauma. The two large therapy chairs were mid-blue, chunky and comfortable. Behind one of them was a wooden foldaway chair for use in couple therapy or for Two-Chair work.

Once in the room, he dropped the referral sheet into his in-tray and unlocked the filing cabinet. He took out the file for his first client: Irena, a fifty-four-year-old Hungarian. He flipped through his session sheets for her, looking as ever for the notes of their previous meeting so that he could remind himself of where they'd got to. He noticed immediately that there was a sheet for the previous week – 19th March. Last week! While he was concussed. While he was *asleep* . . .

He tried to minimise the oddness of it. Usually, this kind of thing had a mundane explanation, if you could step back from it for a moment. But this time, no explanation occurred to him. The notes were rather bizarre, too, as he'd written only a single line, in a hurried scrawl:

Same old, same old. Did my thing. We'll see . . .

Well, it was definitely his handwriting, but what did it mean? Particularly, what did *Did my thing* mean? He looked at his watch. It was 9.25 and so he had no real time to ponder any of this. Irena was one of his most punctual clients and she would be here in five minutes. Meanwhile, he had to contend with the overwhelming and confusing information that he'd seen her the previous week *and yet had no memory of it whatsoever.*

What should he do? Own up to it immediately, of course. He would have to. But what might he say? *Hello Irena, I seem to have seen you last week, but I have no recollection of what happened.* He looked down at his notes. At least he'd written *Same old, same old,* so perhaps he could trust in that, although, once again, he wondered what *Did my thing* meant.

He went out into the reception area where Steffi, the centre manager, was talking to Becky.

'Hi, Will,' Steffi said. 'You're looking a bit less damaged today.'

'Thanks, Steffi,' he said, then turned to Becky and said, 'can I have a quick look at the diary?'

Becky turned her screen towards him and he scrolled back to his bookings for the previous week. They were all there as usual, except for one client who'd cancelled her Thursday appointment. The cancellation had a small asterisk beside it to show that she'd left with less than twenty-four hours' notice and so needed to pay for the session. Not unusual for this particular client.

Missed sessions? he thought. Well, hadn't each of his clients had a 'missed session' of a kind, if he couldn't remember anything of the content of those sessions?

There was a new appointment in the diary for 10.45 that morning – an initial assessment with someone called Guy. That must have been the referral sheet that Becky had handed to him. He went back to his room, sat down and realised there was nothing else to be done. He would have to steel himself to be honest. He had no more time to think, anyway, as Becky buzzed him on the intercom to say that Irena was in the waiting room.

After he told her about his memory loss, he'd play it by ear. But there was a background sense of anxiety there, too. He remembered, during his training as a therapist, his course leader saying, 'Every session with a client should be a clean slate. Be in the moment with what's going on right now. Don't get too stuck in assumptions about what happened previously. Try and take a fresh eye.' Well, here was his chance to put that advice into practice.

On the second page of notes, after Irena's basic biography, Will had written:

<u>Presenting issue:</u>   I hate myself.
<u>Secondary:</u>   I was always second-best to my talented sister.
<u>Primary statement:</u>   I should never have been born.

Will was nervous as he sat waiting. It was 9.28 and so he'd go and get her in two minutes. This was their eighth session – or ninth if you included the previous week – and Will had never felt so self-conscious about having to say something to a client. On one level, he could say to himself that it was simply the result of unusual circumstances, something to be acknowledged and worked with. On another level, it felt diminishing of his client, that the content of their session had been lost.

When Will went to get Irena from the waiting room, she was her usual elegant self but looked pensive and rather drawn. They went into his room and he sat down opposite her. He took a deep breath and said, 'Welcome.'

Irena smiled. 'Good morning, Will. I wonder if that's going to scar? Your forehead, I mean.'

'Apparently not,' Will told her. 'But I'm pleased you've made a reference to my injury, as I need to say something to you about my accident.'

Irena looked attentive, and Will found that he didn't know quite how to start.

'I suppose it's obvious,' he began, 'that I struck my head quite hard when I came off my bicycle. However, it seems that, as a result of it, I suffered quite badly from a concussion in the first few days. I don't know if you know anything about head injuries, but they can have some quite significant side-effects.'

Irena nodded. 'My grandfather fell and hit his head when he was cutting logs. He forgot who we all were for a day or two . . . In fact, he was never the same again after that. Confused. Irritable. A little mad, actually.'

'My concussion was nowhere near as serious as that,' Will

said, 'and I have now recovered. However, without knowing that this was the case, I saw you last week when I was still concussed. I'm afraid I have no recollection of the session we had together.'

Irena looked confused for a moment. 'Nothing at all?'

'No,' said Will. 'Nothing, I'm afraid.'

'But, Will, you seemed fine. I mean you had that padded sticking plaster on your forehead and you had your black eye, but you seemed fine. I mean, *more* than fine. You seemed to be completely alert and not confused at all. When my grandfather hit his head, he was dazed, and couldn't think of words. You were not like that at all. The opposite, in fact.'

'And yet . . . that's what has happened. I can't remember anything of our session.'

Irena laughed mirthlessly. 'Oh, I see! This is some clever trick. You can say all those incredible things to me while you have a bandage on your head because if you regret it later, you can say, "Oh Irena, please forget what I said, I had a bump on my head and didn't mean it".'

'No, no,' Will said, 'I'm not regretting what I said. I don't *know* what I said. That's my point. I had a concussion and can no longer remember anything of our session. I didn't even know that we'd met last week until I came in this morning.'

Irena looked indignant. 'Do you realise how insulting this is to me? Last week I said things I have never said to anyone – to *anyone!* I have cried every day, all day, and when I say every day, all day, I mean *every* day, *all* day. I have come here to finish this thing that we started last week . . . and you don't even remember it! My God, all those things you said about being witnessed, and being *seen* . . .'

'I can witness you today,' said Will. 'I'll not charge you for last week's session – or this week's. We can spend part of this session recapping what happened last week and then take it from there.'

'But will you remember it for the next session?'

'Yes, of course. I am no longer concussed.'

Irena shrugged. 'I have a bad feeling about this.'

Will did not respond but he agreed with her completely.

'I think you are regretting what you said last week,' she told him, 'and so now you're pretending you can't remember. You're worried that you said something unprofessional and that I will now complain and have you barred from your profession. I could probably do that, you know, now that I think of it. I will admit that I was shocked by what you said, and wondered whether it was professionally acceptable. But it opened me up. It gave me an opportunity to really face my pain. And now you have ruined it, Will. Completely. You are different this week, too. You have no spark, no life in you. In fact, I realise now that you never did. Perhaps your head injury is still affecting you and you will not be able to ever work with me in a professional manner again.'

'I think you may be contradicting yourself,' said Will. 'I'm not sure whether you think I haven't had concussion and am pretending or if you think I do have concussion and am unable to work with you in a professional way.'

'I don't care, Will. Both of those explanations ruin our

work. It wasn't going very well anyway, until last week, was it? Not really.'

She looked at him with a certain anguish, and then briefly out of the window. There was a small lawn outside with a laburnum tree in the middle that was just coming into leaf. Behind it was a low ivy-clad wall over which a 1960's brick church could be seen, looking rather the worse for wear, though it had a fine abstract stained-glass window with vibrant blues and reds.

'No,' she said, 'I cannot do this.' She got up and walked purposefully out of the room.

Will glanced at his watch. It was only ten minutes into the session. He took a deep breath and then got up and followed her out, but she was already in the lobby opening the front door and then closing it briskly behind her.

Becky looked across at Will from the reception desk. 'Was that a slam?'

'Aye,' said Will, 'that was a slam.'

At least the following appointment was an assessment and so more straightforward. There was no 'last week' to consider.

The potential client was called Guy, a twenty-five-year-old accountant living in a small flat in Clapham. He looked confident and smart-fashionable, with slim trousers and a brashly patterned shirt. His hair was curly, quite long and fashionably unkempt. Will took down the basic biographical details before he got to the *Why now?* question.

'The flat is haunted,' Guy said.

'The flat where you're staying?'

'Yes.'

'Oh,' said Will. 'Haunted in what way?'

'It sounds a bit less insane if I say it's haunted. I could also say, "I keep seeing my dead sister", but that sounds mad, doesn't it?'

'No, not mad. Unusual, perhaps. What was your sister's name?'

'"Sister" will do. That's what I called her, or "sis", which she didn't like as much and so I called her that when I was annoyed with her.'

'When did your sister die?'

'Five years ago last month. In fact, it was on the fifth anniversary of her death that she first visited me in my flat.'

'Grief is a powerful process,' Will told him. 'It can give rise to some intense experiences.'

'Yes,' said Guy, 'this was intense.'

There was a short silence as Will scribbled a note. 'Is she visible to you at all?' he asked. 'Or is she just a presence?'

'She stands in the corner of the room and comments on everything that I do. I mean *everything*. Even going to the toilet. I haven't been able to bring a woman home with me since she came to visit . . . she sits on the edge of the bed and criticises me and criticises the person I'm in bed with. She has a way of talking that sounds nice but is actually full of subtext. That was why I chose last year to pay the price and to live alone, to have privacy, which seems a bit of a joke now. And, no, before you ask, the other person can't see or hear her.'

Will glanced down at his notes and then back at Guy. 'Was your sister like that when she was alive? Nice, but saying things that were full of subtext?'

'Sometimes,' Guy said. 'Not often, but it's something I recognise in her personality.'

'And what does she look like when she stands in the corner of the room?'

'Like she did when I last saw her. Red sweater . . . white jeans. And she's wearing my cowboy boots with her jeans tucked into them. She's doing that to annoy me because I thought I'd lost those boots – and there she was wearing them and laughing at me for being indignant that she'd stolen them. It's unusual that we had the same size feet, but mine are small for a man. She used to borrow my shoes sometimes. We were twins so we used to share quite a lot of things.'

There was some more conversation, and more note taking, and Will concluded the assessment by saying: 'I have to be clear with you. I'd be happy to work with you on this, if you feel that it's appropriate, and that I am a therapist that you feel you could work with. But don't decide today. Think it over. In the meantime, I want you to go to your GP and explain what has happened. When people start seeing people or things that aren't there, it could be that the most appropriate person to deal with them is a psychiatrist, not a therapist. You seem to be unsettled by this but not in crisis, which is why it may be my territory, as it were. But I am not a doctor and I can't prescribe medication should it *become* a crisis. Your doctor needs to know about this before I start to work with you, in case medication or onward referral becomes appropriate.'

After Guy left, Will wondered about risk. Seeing your dead twin sister was clearly psychosis, and dealing with psychosis was potentially dangerous territory for a therapist. What was it that Lara had said? *You take too many risks and they're usually of the wrong kind.* Well, perhaps he'd phone his supervisor to check in about this one. He needed to contact him anyway to talk about the larger issue of the unremembered sessions. Unremembered sessions! He'd been due a supervision the previous week and it was alarming to think that he might have actually met with Colin during this time.

He didn't have time to think about the supervision. His next client, Rachel, was due in a few minutes. He took out his notes to check them over. The previous week's notes were exactly the same as for Irena: *Same old, same old. Did my thing. We'll see . . .*

A thrill of unease caught Will as he looked at the words, then he flicked to the front of the file, and Rachel's assessment sheet:

<u>Presenting issue:</u> Commitment to partner. 'I will never be good enough for him'.

<u>Secondary:</u> Commitment to job (or anything?) – 'I am not good enough for anything'.

<u>Primary statement:</u> I am worthless.

Will felt a stab of anxiety. Telling Irena that he had no recollection of their session had not gone well, to say the least. This time, perhaps, he needed to be a little more cautious about what he disclosed to Rachel regarding his concussion and then generally feel his way forward as the session progressed. He was pondering this when he was startled by the buzz of his phone. It was Becky letting him know that Rachel had arrived.

Rachel was thirty-seven. As far as looks went, she had described herself to Will as 'plain'.

'Although my mother described me less flatteringly than that, I can tell you,' she'd told him.

As usual, she was immaculately turned out, well-groomed, and wearing make-up. The underlying message that had been explicitly voiced early on was, *please notice me and find me attractive*, although beneath that was a secondary fear of being seen, but being seen as unattractive – hence the mask of make-up: 'The only way I can face the world.'

Today was their thirty-second session – thirty-third if you included the one from the previous week.

'Hello, Will,' she said. 'Your face is looking better today. How are you feeling?'

'I'm feeling fine, Rachel,' he said, 'thank you for asking. How are you?'

She sat down, and turned to him, placing her small hands in her lap. Instead of looking out of the window, as she usually did when wondering what to say at the start of a session, she looked straight at him, giving direct eye contact, and took a long, deep breath.

'Okay,' she said. 'I wanted to start off by saying something about last week's session.'

Will tried to look neutral but didn't know whether he managed it. 'Alright.'

'As you know, it was a difficult session for me. It's the first time I've left in tears and I was very angry with you for being so direct. It seemed so . . . well . . . so *brutal*, really. I've never seen you as being capable of that kind of assertiveness. You're usually so calm and gentle. If I didn't trust you absolutely – trust your motives, I mean – I'd have worried that you hated me or something, or were deliberately trying to hurt me.'

She laughed, amazed at herself.

'You see! All sorts of things went through my mind, which I couldn't admit to you during the session. But I found that when I got home I really wanted to kill you. I mean literally! I had a fantasy of getting the bread knife out and striding round to your house – except I don't know where you live – and stabbing you to death while you slept.' She laughed heartily.

My God, what had he *said* to her?

'In all the therapy I've had, with you and other therapists, that's never happened to me before,' she said. 'Mind you, no therapist has ever spoken to me like that. And all I can say is, more of the same please! Enough of the kid gloves, let's get into the ring!'

'Oh!' said Will.

They sat for a while in silence, as Will gathered his thoughts. At least silence was a possibility in this context.

'So,' he asked eventually, 'what was it *specifically* about last week's session that you want more of?'

'Well, everything. Although, it's interesting, now you mention it . . . Of course, what you said went straight to the heart of the work that we've been doing, but it was also the way that you said it.'

'Can you be more specific about the way you experienced what I said?'

'It's hard to put a finger on. And I only really had a sense of it in retrospect, when it became clear that you weren't deliberately goading me. Or, that you *were* goading me, but with a specific constructive and kind-hearted intention.'

Will was completely at a loss. What did she mean by *goading*? And especially by her reference to 'getting into the ring'? It was as if she was referring to another kind of therapy altogether, and to another kind of therapeutic intervention, one that Will was neither trained in nor inclined to use.

'I'm interested,' he said, 'in what makes you think that "getting into the ring" with me might be helpful.'

'For a start, it would be different from what you're doing now – querying and questioning my processes without actually *saying* anything. Yes, I know, I know . . . I'm the one who's supposed to be doing the exploration of my own experience. But I did that last week, too. After you'd made your . . . observation.'

She welled up with tears at this and cleared her throat.

'I even talked to my husband about it later, which is a first. I've never been able to talk about my therapy with him before because it's always seemed so private. My space, my time, my secrets . . . And, of course, some of what we talk about here is to do with him, which I would never mention. But even my childhood stuff, I kept to myself. I suppose I never wanted to be seen by him as damaged goods. Pretending to have had a happy childhood meant that I never had to look at that. But, how can you commit yourself to someone – *really* commit yourself, I mean – when they don't really know who you are?'

At last . . . here was a bit of familiar territory.

'We talked a little about comparisons a couple of weeks ago, didn't we?' he said. 'Being compared favourably or unfavourably to others. So, it may seem safer not to be seen, or to make sure that only your mask is seen. Perhaps your husband's first marriage is significant here? The fact that you may be wondering whether he compares you to his first wife.'

Rachel's open expression suddenly closed off, and her eyes narrowed. 'What are you talking about? I'm my husband's first wife! He was never married before!' She stared at Will.

'This isn't some new kind of technique for making me angry, is it? Deliberately getting major details of my life wrong?'

'No, no,' Will assured her. 'I'm sorry if I got that wrong. I can't think where it came from.'

Rachel laughed harshly. 'Last week really instilled some trust between us. Now, you seem to be ruining everything. Don't do this to me, Will, please!'

The session got no better. Everything that Will said after that seemed to be taken the wrong way, and Rachel ended up being aggressive about his 'refusal' to continue in the same vein as the previous week. By the time she left, she was in tears again, and he felt helpless and completely out of his depth. It was his professional duty to know what the content of the previous session had been, and he'd found it impossible, once he'd embarked on the subterfuge, to even consider confessing his ignorance. On one hand, it had been tempting to say the same as he'd said to Irena but, on the other, it seemed such a breach of professionalism that it was difficult to imagine a client being able to easily accept such a statement. He was, after all, there to listen and to remember what was said. That was what the notes were there for, of course, to aid memory, but his notes for Rachel from last week had been woefully inadequate.

He got her notes out again and turned to the initial assessment sheet. He had her down as: *Married, 2 years. Husband, Ben, 41, seems devoted to her but: 'I can't quite believe that he loves me'*. There was no mention of previous marriages. Well, it happened from time to time, information getting muddled up. How could it not when dealing with so many clients in a week, all of whom had complicated biographies?

He remembered being told over and over again, 'You are not expected to be perfect, which is just as well, given that you're not perfect. Mistakes become part of the work. Renegotiating trust can often be the work itself.'

Yes, but thinking of this gaffe about Rachel's husband having been married before made him realise that there are mistakes and *mistakes*. This one was particularly embarrassing, and he realised that it was, yet again, something to take to – now urgent – supervision. It would be useful to unpick with his supervisor what was going on for him and consider how he should proceed. He also wanted to find out from Colin whether he'd been to his last supervision and, if so, how he had appeared.

Was there something unrecognised and unconsidered that was making Will collude with the puncturing of Rachel's rapture about the previous week? As he pondered supervision, he came face to face with the problem of explanation. What could he say? *I seem to have conducted a session with a client, and possibly with you, that I have no recollection of, and yet I went ahead with the next session without admitting anything*? He'd certainly had moments in supervision of wanting to excise his gaffes, but he was particularly proud of the fact that he always tried to be completely honest, warts and all. But this? It would have been one thing if the unremembered session had been another ordinary session but, as it transpired, it hadn't been an ordinary session at all.

'Becky,' he asked when he came back out into reception, 'how would you say I was behaving last week? Did I seem to be concussed in any way.'

'Concussed? No, not at all. You were more cheerful than usual, that's all. That's what happened to my mother when she narrowly missed being killed in a car crash. For a few days it made her more aware of being alive. She was delightful. Full of gratitude and appreciation. Then she had the hassle of dealing with her car being written off, and so she came back to earth with a bump. But it was lovely to see her being so alive like that for a while. You were like that, too. What a shame we can't live like that all the time.'

Will agreed and went back to his room to consider what to do next. He'd upset Rachel and, most probably, lost Irena altogether . . . Clearly, admitting to his clients that he'd suffered memory loss was not going to be as straightforward as he'd hoped.

He had no more clients now until Stuart, an early evening client and the last of the day, and he needed to sit and have a think about what to do . . .

He ended up calling his brother. When he got Jamie's voicemail, he realised he didn't know what he might say.

'Hi, Jamie,' he said, 'I'm having a bit of a weird day at work and was going to have a chat about it. Not to worry, though. Don't bother to call back. Talk soon.'

Now Will felt a bloom of vulnerability rising in him, of being out of his depth and of questionable competence. This was in sharp contrast to his usual sense of capacity and skill, where his acknowledgement of fallibility and willingness to work with it was part of what gave him his confidence. This sense of fallibility was different, however, because it didn't reward scrutiny via logic.

His turning to Jamie for support, rather than to Lara, caused an echo of pain from long ago. He knew from experience that he couldn't push it away when it arose like this or it would overwhelm him. He had to let it pass through him. At least, with several hours to spare, he had the time to allow this to happen, and so he took his coat and gloves and walked from the Centre up to the riverside, by way of Kennington and the Oval.

Four

He dreamed again of those moments after the accident, of being weightless and timeless. Although he seemed to be moving forward through space, it was also clear that he was getting no closer to his destination. And everything was fine. There were no worries. It was as though being weightless, unencumbered – untethered – was an end in itself. He would never reach his destination. At least not via the passage of time.

Will's family had lived in Annan, in Dumfriesshire, when he was a child. The house was on the edge of farmland, idyllic in many ways for bringing up children. When Will was five, he was given a blue plastic dumper pedal-truck with fat tractor-type wheels. By seven, he was far too big for it, but he could squeeze himself onto it and pedal around the back yard every now and then. But he was rather bored by it. To make it into something fun, he would challenge himself to see how fast he could go. It had a red dumper on the back that you could put stuff in and there was a little handle at the front that you could turn to tip the contents out. Latterly, the dumper part had broken away so that it came off completely from time to time. If you slipped through the gate at the bottom of the garden, then crossed the meadow and went down to the stream and Lower Pool, you could play boats with it.

Jamie, who was five, also used the truck and often pedalled about in it when he could get his hands on it.

On occasions when they were playing together, they would take the truck down to Lower Pool with the two big teddies and push the red 'boat' out into the water. Jamie would sometimes put a couple of apples in with the teddies, so that they could be having a picnic. If they took the garden rake down with them, they could push it out with that and, using the tines to hook the edge of the boat, could reach it anywhere in the pool and bring it back to shore. The pool itself was only about a dozen feet across and the stream hardly more than a trickle most of the time. But there were reeds at one end and they would occasionally see ducks there, so it seemed 'proper', and sometimes Will would refer to it rather grandly as 'the lake'.

During the spring, just before Will's eighth birthday, the cherry blossom came out. There was a line of fine cherry trees, laden with flowers, growing by the fence. When the light breeze gusted, petals swirled down like pink snow and Will played with Jamie, taking up handfuls of the pale petals, throwing them up in the air and running through them. It was cold and they wore thick tracksuit tops, but the sun was warm on their cheeks.

It was Will's idea to make a bed of petals in the back of the dumper truck and take them down to the pool with the teddies. It was Jamie's idea to take Charlotte with them. She was in her pram on the patio, sleeping. Kitty, who was nearly eleven, was in the sitting room supposedly reading a book and keeping an eye on Charlotte while their mother was next door helping a neighbour with a burst pipe. Kitty loved looking after Charlotte and had fed her many times. It was easy. She had been told to phone at any time or even call over the fence if Charlotte was unhappy and her mother could be back in moments. Their father was out playing golf.

Will considered whether to take Charlotte along with them. After thinking for a while, he decided that she probably shouldn't be left alone on the patio and he didn't want to go in to tell Kitty that they were going down to the pool in case she wanted to come along. She'd been bad tempered all morning and probably wasn't reading at all.

They filled the back of the dumper with petals and then Jamie pedalled it down the path by the meadow while Will followed with the pram and the teddies. There was some late dew on the grass and the air was fresh. When they got to the waterside, Will took the red dumper box off and put it on the grass by the water, then Jamie said, 'Let's put Charlotte in with the petals. She'll love it.'

Charlotte hardly stirred as Will lifted her from the pram. The petals weren't quite as soft and downy as they'd looked earlier on when he gently laid her amongst them, but there was something compellingly beautiful about it and he wished he'd thought to bring his father's camera with him so he could capture the moment. He'd been shown how to use it only a couple of weeks before and they'd come down here to see if they could take pictures of the ducks.

'It's like magic,' said Will. 'A little princess. We should find her in the reeds and rescue her and take her home.'

They carefully edged the boat into the water, where it sat a little lower than it did with the teddies in it, but it was still fine. Will laughed with delight.

'You wait here, I'm going to get Dad's camera.'

He ran back up to the house, in through the French windows, past Kitty, who studiously ignored him, and up to his parents' bedroom, where his dad kept his camera in a drawer in his bedside table. Then it was out and back down to the pool again. Jamie had pushed the boat with Charlotte in it out a few feet, and it was in exactly the right position, 'in the reeds' where she could be found – a lost princess.

'You go and get the rake,' he told Jamie, 'while I sort out the camera.'

It took Will a minute or two to figure out how to operate the camera but, once he did so, the scene was rather idyllic and he took several pictures. Charlotte opened her eyes at one point, saw Will and smiled, reaching out a little towards him and yawning. Jamie, who had returned with the rake, laughed with delight when he saw this and insisted on taking a couple himself. Then, Will reached out with the tines of the rake and hooked the edge of the boat to pull Charlotte back to the edge. Almost in slow motion, the red container rolled over and Charlotte dropped into the water with hardly a splash and went under.

The next three or four minutes were blurry and confused. Will remembered leaping into the water, the mud sucking at his feet so that he fell, in his haste, lengthwise, going under himself as he reached out for his sister. The water can't have been more than a metre deep, and Charlotte was quite close to the bank, but it was muddy and difficult to stand, to hold her up and get her back to the grass, and once Will had managed it, he found that she was limp.

He had no idea what to do. He knew that adults did something at times like these to save people and he'd heard of 'resuscitation' but he didn't know how to go about it. He held the sides of her tiny chest and squeezed her like he might squeeze a giant tube of toothpaste.

'Get mum!' he shouted to Jamie. 'Get Dad! Get Kitty!'

Jamie, who had been standing there in a kind of paralysis, raced off.

Will must have only been there for a minute or so before Kitty arrived. She had more of a grasp of what resuscitation was, having seen a film in which it had been administered and understood that it entailed trying to blow air into the unconscious person's lungs. This is what she did to Charlotte, who remained unresponsive.

That is how their mother found the three of them. Distraught. In tears. Terrified.

The accident was only the beginning of the awfulness. No one in the family, it turned out, could be seen as blameless. Of course, Will's mother blamed herself in the most visceral way for leaving them without adult supervision. Kitty took some blame because, as the oldest child, she'd been explicitly put in charge of Charlotte. Jamie had pushed the boat out into the reeds. This was something Will would never have done, because he was a little older and because Charlotte had looked just as much like a floating princess at the water's edge as she had done out in the reeds.

Will's father had been criticised for not spending enough time with his family.

Will, though . . . it was Will who'd tipped the boat over. It was Will who, in a literal way, could say, *I killed my baby sister*, although every member of the family could indirectly say the same. Will's father got the vitriol of Will's maternal grandmother: 'If only you'd spent less time playing golf, the tragedy would ne'er have happened.'

After the accident, blame was never explicitly apportioned, but although Will's mother told him in words that she didn't blame him for what happened, she never touched him with affection again, something that Jamie in particular noticed. Much later, when they were old enough to do so without self-consciousness, Jamie hugged Will on a regular basis, and although Will appreciated this – came to depend on it, in fact – it was no substitute for a mother's love. Their mother hugged Jamie almost obsessively, and in just as unhelpful a way, because Jamie said later how he'd felt that his mother was doing the cuddling for herself and not for him.

School became difficult. Everyone knew. Everyone knew that Will had 'killed his baby sister'. Although the teachers clearly had sympathy for him, he was marked indelibly by tragedy and people avoided him. The school therapist was helpful up to a point, but only up to a point. There were aspects of this that Will was too young to process and the therapist was too distant and too reassuring to really make much difference. Jamie and Kitty, too, suffered and, after a term or so, the family moved away from Annan to Carlisle, from Scotland to England, and Will's father took another job. Will stopped seeing the school therapist when he left and didn't start seeing another one in his new school as sufficient time was deemed to have passed for him to no longer need it.

Jamie and Kitty got on well in the new school, but somehow news got out about Will – via Kitty, Will suspected – and people treated him as though he was infectious, avoiding him or even jumping away from him if they came across him in the corridor. He was teased because of his hair colour and his pale skin, though he clung to these proudly as Scottish characteristics and was able to give as good as he got. But it didn't make for a peaceful life and he was disciplined several times for getting into fights, which made him seethe. Saying, 'I didn't start it' didn't go down well or was simply ignored.

Eventually, it was decided that he should be sent away to private school, and a small place, Dalmacallan Preparatory School, was found near Castle Douglas in Dumfriesshire where the fees were just about manageable. It was a 120-mile round trip to the school, and so he became a 'three weekly' boarder, coming home three times a term, two weekends plus the half-term break. He was delivered and collected by his father for the beginning and end of term and for half-term. For his weekends home, the school minibus took him and six or seven other pupils to Dumfries station where he was dropped off to make the forty-minute journey to Carlisle. His father would meet him at the station.

Will knew that his mother was frightened of him. Frightened and resentful. For nearly a year after the accident, she had been virtually incapable of anything practical. She was paralysed by a grief that Will understood instinctively, but which he also found scary. It was impossible to say, 'What about me?' Their father was amazing and kept everything going, cooking and cleaning and putting them to bed.

The thing that spurred Will's mother into action was that, with him being sent to private school, she had to get a job to help pay for the fees. She took work as a receptionist in the County Hotel in the city centre, but soon realised that she was wasted there, and the following year started a teacher-training course to teach geography, which was what she'd studied at university.

In that first summer home from school, Will, at his own request, was enrolled in Scottish country dancing classes in Gretna, which were paid for by his grandparents as a late birthday present. Jamie joined him and they wore kilts with vests sewn into them so that they could be slipped on over their heads and worn easily and comfortably. Somewhere there was a photo of them like this, unbearably cute, with the caption: *The wee lads!* These classes became a longed-for respite for Will, and although his coordination issues meant that he was slow to pick up the steps, once he'd got them, he could relish their energy and dynamism: the Sword Dance, in which crossed batons were placed on the floor as markers for the steps; the Dashing White Sergeant; the Eightsome Reel ... It was all way outside anything to do with home or school or problems with integrating with other people, of being feared or disliked. Will was never as good a dancer as Jamie but it didn't seem to matter. He could jump and twirl enthusiastically and his dance teacher always praised him, even when he got it wrong.

One time, when he was collected from the station after travelling back from Dalmacallan, Will looked at his father and asked, 'Why does Mum never come to collect me?'

'She's busy with dinner,' his father said.

'No,' said Will. 'It's because she hates me. I know she does.'

'Will!' his father exclaimed. 'You know that's not true.'

'She does, Dad, she hates me. That's why she made sure you sent me away to school.'

His father stared out at the road ahead and sighed. 'Will, we all decided that it was best that you moved on to another school. You were part of that decision too. You were having a terrible time here in Carlisle – you said so yourself.'

'I know you can't afford it, Dad. That's what Kitty says.'

'Well, Kitty's wrong,' said his father.

That night, when he was in bed in the room that he shared with Jamie, both his parents came upstairs. Usually it was his father that read them a bedtime story. But this time, there was no story. His father sat on one side of the bed and his mother on the other. She patted his hand and said, 'Will, you know that your father and I love you very much. If we could keep you in school locally, we would. Don't you like Dalmacallan?'

'It's fine,' he said.

'That's good. It's not a big thing still, is it? The . . . accident?'

'No,' Will lied.

'Well, that's an enormous improvement, isn't it? Don't you think it's a good thing that you go there?'

He remained silent for a moment. At nine, he didn't have the sophistication to say, *Whether I like the school or not is not the point*. Instead, he said, 'I suppose so.'

'Good,' said his father. 'Because it's nonsense that we would want to send you away. What we are doing is trying to make your life better for you.'

Will thought about that. 'Okay,' he said.

They both got up to leave.

'I'll be back in a moment,' his father said. 'We'll read the next chapter of the Moira Miller.'

'Mum?' said Will.

'Yes?'

'Why is it that you read Jamie's bedtime story to him when I'm away, but Dad reads to us when I'm back?'

His mother paused, at a loss for a reply.

'Your mother is busier when you're home, Will,' said his father. 'We're a full house!'

But it was a lame answer, and everyone knew it.

There were a couple of boys at Dalmacallan, the sons of farmers, who had good, broad lowland Scots accents, and Will deliberately befriended them, picking up something of their accent 'accidentally on purpose'. Kitty made fun of the yons, kens and aulds that crept into his vocabulary and he retaliated by calling her a Sassenach. In his prefect year at school, when he was just shy of thirteen, he requested that he be allowed to go and stay for half-term with one of them, Allan – or Allie – McAndrew, whose family lived in Kirkcudbright. His wish was granted and this provided further escape from Carlisle. He became a bit of a fixture round at the McAndrews' that year. They were devoutly Scottish and hired a cottage near Melrose each year for a couple of weeks in the summer and Will joined them in the summer of that year. Mrs McAndrew was the perfect mother substitute – affectionate, interested, complimentary – and Will blossomed as he bathed in her attention. He liked that all the McAndrews received this attention but, as a guest, there was always particular focus on him. He wondered occasionally whether it was simply pity for the tragedy that had disrupted his life but, for the first time, it didn't seem to matter – and this was a revelation.

At the end of the next academic year, Will left Dalmacallan and there was some question about whether he might come back to school in Carlisle. Jamie, however, was clear that Will was still 'talked about', although Kitty said that was rubbish. Eventually, it was agreed that Will should go to public school in Edinburgh. Will's parents accepted a sizeable subsidy from Will's grandparents on both sides of the family and Kitty, who was sixteen, exploded.

'Why should Will get everything? He gets all the privilege in this family, and I get nothing.'

'Nothing?' asked their mother.

'Can you define nothing for us?' their father asked. 'Would you call weekly horse riding nothing?' This led to her striding out of the room and out of the house, slamming the front door behind her.

Will's friendship with Allie lasted for a couple of years after they went off to different schools, Will to go to Edinburgh and Allie to Sedbergh in Cumbria, Will going north as Allie went south. Will stayed with the McAndrews several times in that period. Allie never came to Carlisle. This worked perfectly until Will was fifteen and lost his virginity to Allie's sister, Morven, which was not a brilliant success and which made it rather embarrassing to go and stay there again. It was probably just as well, as he and Allie were drifting apart by then and didn't have a school in common in which to form a bond. They'd smoked their first cigarette together and drunk their first illicit quarter bottle of whisky – which had made them both gag at first, but they got it down and it initiated some mildly tipsy hilarity between them. Afterwards, Allie had declared, 'We were reekin'!' which was a bit of an exaggeration.

By the time Will was sixteen, he'd adopted Hugh MacDiarmid, poet and one of the founding members of the National Party of Scotland, as his 'patron saint'. MacDiarmid had had the sort of bombastic and opinionated bad temper that appealed to an adolescent like Will, who needed something assertive and controversial to give him an identity. This was also the year of the opening of the first Scottish parliament for nearly three hundred years – a triumphant moment, and one that made Will feel alive with a sense of purpose and importance.

He had grown to hate Carlisle with a passion, for no other reason than that he'd been unhappy there. His newfound Scottishness made him a stranger in his own family, which pleased him even as it made him more unhappy when he was at home. In that year, he had a confirmation of his dyspraxia, which made him feel more settled in himself and more forgiving of the fact that, in spite of his sturdy frame, he would never make a good rugby player. He took up middle-distance running instead and embraced it enthusiastically as a solitary sport, ending up as the fastest and most dedicated runner on the school team.

Five

Will pondered his current situation and the week of what he now thought of as his 'lost' sessions. There was so much that was unknown and unspoken. For as long as the sessions remained unremembered there would always be the discomfort of not knowing. In principle, he knew, it was alright to allow some things to remain unsaid and unreferred to. But this was different, and he knew it. There was no clear way forward. As far as he could see, he'd tried both obvious strategies – to tell, or not to tell, his client that he had no recollection of the previous session – and on balance it seemed that telling, although ethically more straightforward, was essentially worse for the client.

His next thought was to call Colin, his supervisor, to arrange a session. He had no clear idea of what he might say, but he'd been in that situation many times before, albeit in circumstances that were rather easier to explain. He recalled sitting with Colin and saying, 'I have no idea where to start,' and Colin saying, 'That's fine, Will, start anywhere you want and we'll fit it together as we go along.'

His monthly supervision was still nearly two weeks away and so he phoned to request an additional, urgent meeting. He steeled himself for a potentially difficult – or downright weird – conversation but got Colin's voicemail message saying that he was away for a week. There was a beat of disappointment that went with this, but some relief, too. Relief. That had happened before, especially in the early days when he was in training. There might be a moment of confusion with a client, especially if things seemed to be 'going badly' and a sudden feeling of need for support and exploration, but with a reticence to admit to a 'mistake'. Staying with the work often led to resolution or, if not resolution, then to a contentment with the not-knowing.

Some things had to unfurl, Will knew. They had a journey. At all times the main thing was to serve the client and to be prepared to take the responsibility, if not the blame, if something didn't work out. But he also knew that unconscious agendas abounded in the therapeutic arena. He might decide to keep quiet and think he was doing it to serve his clients, while deep down it might actually be to avoid the shame of admitting to his own fault or frailty. That was the tension that every therapist held – it was impossible to know everything that was going on . . . Hence the need for supervision.

By the time he was getting ready for his next appointment, he'd decided what to do with the session. He would play it by ear again. He would keep quiet about his memory loss but would reveal it immediately if that became appropriate.

THE LOST SESSIONS

Stuart was a gay man who'd come into therapy because his fortieth birthday seemed insurmountable and impossible to accommodate into his self-image.

'I'm not shallow,' he'd told Will, 'but obviously I am over-invested in being youthful.'

Will turned to his notes. There was his comment from last week:

Same old, same old. Did my thing. We'll see . . .

He checked the front page, and the summary from his assessment.

> *Presenting issue:* I have done something that can never be forgiven.
> *Secondary:* I can't forgive myself for being me.
> *Primary statement:* I am bad (?).

This would be their fifth session – sixth with last week's. It felt like very early days in their work together. Stuart still hadn't told Will what the 'unforgivable thing' was that he'd done and there was a definite flavour of, *Don't push me, I'll tell you when I'm ready.* Will wasn't a pushy therapist, so allowing clients to take their time was one of his things. At least, that *had* been one of his things; what he might actually have done the previous week . . . Well, that was an alarming thought, given what his last two clients had told him.

When he came in, Stuart looked bright and energised and Will's spirits lifted.

'I don't really know what to say about how I feel,' said

Stuart. 'It seems as if there's this possibility ahead, like a new direction I can take. But I can't quite see how to take it. Maybe that's the story of my life, always knowing that there's a way out of this but never seeing it clearly. But maybe I've begun to see . . . something . . .' He paused for a moment and looked out of the window, at the patio and small lawn there, and the ivy-covered wall. 'When you shouted at me last week–'

'Shouted?' Will was surprised. Perhaps he shouldn't have been, but he was.

'No, you're right . . . not shouted . . . *screamed.*' Stuart laughed. 'I've screamed at people, and I've been screamed at, but not recently. It really is the most disconcerting and alarming thing. I would guess that you have to be *so* confident of what you're doing as a therapist to be able to use those kinds of shock tactics. I really respect it, Will. It came out of the blue, and I was terrified. Really. I thought for a moment you might beat me to a pulp with your bare fists. I mean, you're physically impressive and I sat there shaking like a leaf. But then when you burst into tears, I could see that you'd really touched into my pain in a way that no one else has ever done. I've spent years trying to side-step it myself, so to see someone go there *for* me . . . Amazing! I now feel – *know* – that you can go there with me when I'm ready.'

'Um . . .'

'This is beyond words, isn't it?' said Stuart. 'But I'm ready. Ready to tell you anything, all the things that I've kept back because I didn't feel safe and ready. Please, ask away.'

Will smiled slightly. 'I think it's your telling. If you're ready to start, start wherever you feel able.'

Stuart sat pensively for a while and there was a calm and settled silence. Will watched him and began to calm down himself. So, he'd screamed and burst into tears during a client session. Wow! But, it seemed that it had been the right thing to do. In this moment, things were okay . . . better than okay. Will couldn't help admiring the 'Will' who had behaved so ambitiously the previous week. He wondered how he could possibly take something like that to supervision, but put the thought hastily to one side so that he could concentrate on his client.

'I suppose that all this stuff about forgiveness has been around forever,' Stuart said. 'It's not just about my relationship with Gregg. I mean, I thought he was the love of my life. I thought I was the love of his life . . . But I was wrong. I have to accept that he never felt that way, don't I? Isn't that your impression from what I've told you so far?'

Will looked questioningly at Stuart. 'And what about the letter that Gregg wrote to you? The one proposing that you get married? How does that fit into this?'

'What?' Stuart looked confused.

'The one Gregg left for you on your birthday, the year before last. You described it very movingly. It was on blue paper and the envelope was scented with Fahrenheit perfume.'

'No . . .' said Stuart. 'Don't do this to me two weeks in a row. Enough, Will. If you're going to start goading me, I really will explode. I'm fragile, right now. Really fragile.'

'I'm just saying what I remember,' said Will.

'Gregg never left me a letter. He didn't ask me to marry him. That's the point. That's the whole *point*, Will. He didn't love me. He never loved me, because he could never forgive me for what I'd done. He's an honest person. Why would he have asked me to marry him if he didn't love me?'

Stuart started crying in earnest at this point and Will watched, helpless. How could he have got it so wrong? As with Rachel earlier, now with Stuart! He simply didn't make mistakes of this kind. Little errors, yes – about names and ages or not noticing a particular emphasis . . .

'If only he *had* given me a letter,' sobbed Stuart. 'That was my heart's desire. But he didn't. How cruel of you to have preyed on my dreams like that.'

Again, the session did not recover.

'There is no consistency to this,' Stuart told him. 'The person you were last week and the person you are now seem to have no connection. How can you be the same person? You have *really* confused me, Will, and I hope you know what you're doing, because I can't take much more of this.'

Even though the session was due to run for a further ten minutes, Stuart got up and left the room without a backward glance, closing the door quietly, almost timidly, behind him.

Will sat in silence for a while. He couldn't quite take in what had happened. In order to do something, he crossed to his filing cabinet and systematically took out each of his current client files and checked the most recent notes page. They all said the same thing: *Same old, same old. Did my thing. We'll see . . .*

It was 8.00 pm and walking home was even more confusing than when he'd been helped home immediately after his accident. At least, then, he was clear what had happened to him, even though his senses were dulled. Now, his mental processes seemed clear. There was no dullness or slowness there. And yet, after 'missing' a week of client work, he had started misremembering things in dramatic ways. Perhaps memory could be scrambled after a head injury, like throwing leaves up in the air to settle in different patterns? But a letter on blue paper scented with Fahrenheit? This didn't apply to another client. It was new information. It was completely imagined.

On his way home, he remembered that Dr Lucas's practice had an evening surgery that was still in progress. He took the short detour on the off-chance of being seen and managed to speak to one of the other doctors from the practice. Dr Gersten was charming and friendly. Will explained to her about his concussion and his worries about his memory.

'No, that's not really how memory works,' she said. 'After a concussion, you may have some confused memories of the period before or after the accident and *sometimes* – usually temporary – amnesia. But you're not going to suddenly start mixing up the names of your siblings or remember that you live in a block of flats when in fact you live in a bungalow.'

'So, what does it mean, if I find I've got things quite dramatically wrong with clients twice today?'

'It probably means you need to take another week off work,' Dr Gersten told him. 'You may need more brain rest, that's all. Anxiety's going to make this worse, too. So, try to relax.'

He got home and phoned his clients to tell them he was taking the rest of the week off work. He almost said *another* week off but, to them of course, that wasn't the case. After he'd made his calls, he looked up and noticed that Lara had hung a painting on the wall by the bay window. It was an abstract with a pale-yellow background and a great curving splash of green and red moving from left to right, brash and confident. It was great. It was typical of Lara to quietly put it on display without mentioning it. Fortunately, their taste almost always coincided and he made a note to compliment her and to ask where she'd got it. Lara wasn't extravagant by nature, but this looked like it might have been expensive.

Monday was currently one of Will's cooking evenings. Lara was working later than he was at the moment, on a commission for a show, and dinner was scheduled for 9.00 pm. There wasn't much in the flat, so he went out to the deli on the corner and picked up some Arborio rice and chestnut mushrooms then went back to make a risotto. There was half a bottle of Chardonnay in the fridge and, after pouring himself a glass, he used the rest to make a flavoursome stock. After his strange day, it was a comfort that he had another week off work coming up. Well, strange was an impossibly understated word to describe the utterly baffling sessions that he'd had. It was simply beyond him that he could have made such fundamental mistakes regarding the details of what Rachel and Stuart had told him. And to have all three clients walk out on him was more than troubling, especially as supervision was not currently available.

He remembered, in the early days of his practice, coming home after difficult days, doing an exaggerated grimace for Lara and moaning, 'I ne-ee-eed supervision!', and she would laugh and comfort him. He smiled now at the thought of it and made a mental note to phone Colin as soon as he was back. He wanted to throw his hands in the air and say, 'What a mess! But at least it was all done in good faith.'

Underneath this, though, there was a beat of disquiet at the fact that the clients he'd seen had all referred to such incendiary interventions on his part. There was Stuart's assertion that he'd screamed and then burst into tears. How was he going to refer to that! He felt a flush of embarrassment at the thought. Not only that, he currently had thirteen regular clients. He'd seen three of them today, all problematically. But that left ten that he'd seen last week and still had no recollection of their sessions. Plus, he had no meaningful session notes to refer to. And having written *did my thing* was not at all comforting when it appeared that, in at least one case, this had included screaming and bursting into tears . . .

His phone rang and he was pleased to be distracted for a moment. It was Jamie, and they talked while he idly stirred the rice and added more stock.

'Are you sure you're okay?' Jamie asked. 'There was something – I don't know . . . a bit *scared* about your voice in your message today. It took me right back. I haven't heard you sounding scared for a long time. I know you can't break confidentiality, but I'm guessing that something happened with one of your clients today that freaked you out.'

'It's disconcerting that you know me so well,' he laughed. 'And you're right . . . my concussion seems to have tampered with my memory, and so I made a gaffe or two today that has left me smarting. I'm taking another week off work to settle down.'

'Good idea,' said Jamie. 'I hope you're going to take as much time off as you need. I know you and Lara are a bit broke at the moment, so if you want to take some extra time off and can't afford it, let me know.'

'You can't afford it either,' Will laughed. 'But thank you. I do have enough money to go out and get drunk if you fancy it and don't mind staying out a bit late.'

'Great idea,' Jamie laughed, 'but not on a Monday. Another time, though.'

'And what about you?' Will asked. 'You sound like you could do with a glass of good malt.'

'Well,' sighed Jamie, 'Joel's gone. He was going to go next week but managed to get a cheap last-minute flight and so he's gone off early.'

'I'm sorry.'

'No, no, it's best this way. I hate lingering goodbyes, and the "next step" can start a little earlier now. I feel weirdly empty and weirdly free, as if one door has closed and another has opened onto a landscape that I don't recognise.'

They spoke for a while longer, then Lara arrived and the risotto was ready.

'Come over,' Will told Jamie, 'there's enough for three if we have bread with it.'

'No, no, I'm fine. I'll see you soon.'

Will ended the call and kissed Lara as she came into the kitchen.

'How's things?' she asked.

Will grimaced. 'I ne-ee-ed supervision!'

She laughed. 'It's a long time since I heard you say that. What happened?'

'It looks like I'm still not back to normal after my bump. I dropped in to see the doctor on my way home, and I've been told to take another week off work.'

'What does that mean . . . not back to normal?'

Will told her what he'd told Jamie. He considered telling her that he'd conducted sessions the previous week, but realised it sounded a bit mad.

Later, after they'd eaten and were relaxing in the sitting room, Will sipped his tea and looked at the new painting on the far wall. 'That painting looks great there.'

'It does, doesn't it?'

'We should have more pictures like that.'

'I agree.'

They lapsed into silence again.

'Last week was lovely,' Lara said after a while. 'Having you all to myself. When you leave work, you're good at putting it down. But your clients are still with you in a way, just as my work is still with me. Especially when I'm working on something new. Last week was Will Thomas, pure and simple. Undiminished.'

'It didn't feel like that to me!' said Will.

'It's counterintuitive. You felt that you were compromised, but you didn't have the energy to be anything other than yourself. You weren't a therapist. You weren't preoccupied with the usual things that we're all preoccupied with these days. I loved looking after you and I loved that I could really see that you love me. Sometimes we're just too busy or too tired to see that, or to show it. I can hardly believe we've been together for nearly six years. I don't want to start taking anything for granted.'

'Perhaps we need to spend more time together,' said Will. 'Working evenings was never great for that, and I didn't really acknowledge that it would make such a difference.'

'I need to work evenings too,' said Lara, 'although not so regularly. Maybe I'm getting to the point where I don't need to do it so often and so I notice it more.'

'Maybe I need to trust that I'll have enough clients who are happy to come during the day. We could think about this more once I'm properly back at work,' he said. 'I'm not going to make any money at all this week and so it feels a bit odd to be discussing changing my work pattern.'

The following morning felt both luxurious and wayward. Again, Will felt bright and energised and full of life. It seemed absurd that he was not going to be seeing clients that day, but he could see the sense in taking a few more days off.

After saying goodbye to Lara at 8.15, he made himself a pot of tea and took it through to the sitting room to relax quietly for a while with his laptop and catch up on his email. There was also a small pile of unread copies of *Therapy Today* that he thought he might have a look at, although ironically Lara was the one who tended to read them.

Among the usual petitions and professional 'stuff', there was an email from Colin, his supervisor:

Dear Will,

I feel the need to respond to you after our last session, to acknowledge the discussion that we had.

I have always thought of you as being an honest supervisee, and I certainly admire your integrity. I had also always thought of you, if I'm honest, as being rather over-cautious, both as a supervisee and as a therapist (no bad thing, the reverse is far more likely to be problematic). So, I am glad that you decided to throw caution to the wind last week and really speak your mind.

I have never been so directly — nor so kindly — criticised by one of my supervisees. I take on board absolutely what you said. It can't have been easy for you to have said what you did. I went to my own supervision the following day and had a rather uncomfortable but extremely helpful session.

I have thought really hard about this, and although I absolutely support you in what you have said to me, I do feel that this would inevitably change the dynamic of our work together, and perhaps there are some trust issues that would always be in the background for you if we carried on together?

With this in mind, I am emailing to say that I feel it may be better for you to find another supervisor with whom you might perhaps work in a more useful way.

I have wondered whether emailing you in this way is cowardly and am happy to acknowledge that there is something of that in what I am doing. I think you will acknowledge, however, that the session we had last Thursday definitely had the 'feel' of a final session?

Do also get back to me if you want some suggestions as to who might be a suitable supervisor for you.

Kind regards and best wishes for the future.
Colin

Will read the email twice. So there it was. He *had* seen Colin the previous week. What had he said? The feeling of loss was huge and tinged with fear. What would he do without a supervisor that he knew and trusted? And how could he start with another supervisor in the circumstances that he found himself?

Six

Will did a lot of walking that week. He kept himself to himself and tried to do as little thinking as possible. This was difficult. No, it was impossible. He seemed to be continually assaulted by cyclic thoughts that caught him up and took him nowhere. He had to figure out how to approach his client work, after all, and had no recourse to his supervisor. Left to his own devices, his thoughts about his clients went around in maddening circles that never moved forward in terms of understanding or decision-making. In Colin's absence, Will realised that his supervisor's presence in the background had provided him with a real strength and stability as a therapist, and although he recognised in himself a certain maturity borne of experience, he also recognised that therapy was a hugely subjective profession and that external perspective was essential. He decided that he would make supervision a top priority and ask around amongst his colleagues so that he could start with someone new as soon as possible.

In the meantime, he realised that he could think of no other approach than to start again with his clients the following week with an open mind and hope that he could cope with whatever came up. He'd had quite a lot thrown at him already and he'd survived. He wasn't sure what might be yet to come, but he experienced a flutter of excitement at the prospect, like a skier, perhaps, on a major mountain who finds that they are unexpectedly off-piste.

Walking was an antidote for this busy-ness of mind. It didn't stop the thinking but it made it more bearable and it was comforting to walk along the South Bank and see the people there. He wandered along by the river, watching them walking purposefully to their destinations, meeting with friends or stopping to watch the London Eye, moving so slowly that at a glance it seemed stationary.

As he approached the eye, with its queue of people waiting to embark even on a midweek morning, he stopped to look up at the passenger pods. From this perspective, he could see the movement of the great wheel and paused to take it in. There was something almost meditatively slow about the pods as they moved off and up into elevation. It was only by pausing that one could notice their movement. They gave him a feeling of weightless momentum, like his recent dreams of being airborne and in slow motion. An all-powerful, unstoppable movement that was utterly unconcerned about Will Thomas and his problems. How refreshing that was! As he gazed up at the pod that was just clearing the departure platform, he saw someone who, through that odd combination of distance, perspective and the curving of the glass, seemed to be looking directly at him. She was tall and slim, of indeterminate age though probably somewhere in her twenties, with shoulder length brown hair that framed her face. She wore a red sweater and white jeans, and – although he couldn't quite see them – he knew with a small thrill that she was wearing cowboy boots. As he had this thought, she raised her hand to him in salute. She had a camera by her side, a big, black, professional-looking model with a telephoto lens. She raised it and pointed it towards him, taking several pictures. Then she turned away to look out at the cityscape downstream. Will looked around to see if there was anyone beside him that the woman might have waved at and photographed. There were several contenders in terms of physical placement, but none of them were looking up at the pods.

Of course, it was coincidence. It had seemed strange because his new client, Guy, had described his dead twin in this way, as wearing a red sweater and white jeans. Lots of women in London had to be wearing a red sweater and white jeans at that moment. That wasn't odd in itself, was it? The woman, now too far away for him to see her clearly, was leaning forward against the handrail in the pod, and – could he see the top of them? – wearing pale brown boots of some kind. With the jeans tucked in.

As he walked away, he decided that this spooky feeling was not because something spooky had happened but because it was an odd coincidence and he wasn't completely recovered from his head injury. In this recuperative state, his mind was making strange connections that seemed significant when they weren't. How disappointing! He kept on feeling so sure that he was back to normal, but for as long as weird things were happening, or at least *seemed* to be happening, then he knew he wasn't ready to go back to work.

As the week wore on, he continued to feel well and settled in a physical sense, though there was an undercurrent of anxiety – but curiosity, too. He was anxious because there was no way to find out if he was ready to go back to client work unless he actually did it. And he was curious because he realised that he had a nascent confidence, or even trust that, however bizarre, outrageous and technically unprofessional his behaviour had been during the lost sessions, somehow all of it had been completely appropriate.

He pondered his inability to tell anyone the full details of what had happened – even Lara or Jamie. But what could he say? He didn't regard himself as a secretive person these days, so remaining silent like this felt unusual and constricting.

He managed to catch up with some of his friends on social media during the week and he put a couple of short but amusing anecdotes out there about mixing up the biographical information of his clients, and he got some ribald comments from his fellow therapists, who voiced a familiar chagrin and who admitted to gaffes of their own. This was one of the things that he really appreciated about social media: that people were so accessible and available. But he couldn't bring himself to even allude to the more disturbing aspects of what had happened. And that was his responsibility. He knew that if he'd posted that he was having a nervous breakdown it would elicit a genuine response and sincere offers of help.

He was particularly pleased to be able to meet up with someone from his course in person: Isobel. He didn't see her very often, and it was a pleasure to meet for coffee and cake in a patisserie in Islington. He spoke briefly about why he was off work.

'Will,' she said, 'you look great. You look swashbuckling with the residue of your black eye and your cuts, as though you should be wearing a kilt and plaid and be brandishing a claymore.'

Will shrugged in embarrassment. 'I don't feel very Scottish at the moment.'

'You are archetypally Scottish,' she laughed. 'Look at your complexion! Your wild hair! Those parallel stripes are mysterious, too. Maybe they could be a kind of clan scarification. But you're, well . . . you're glowing!'

'I do actually feel like I'm glowing. In a slightly fragile but positive way.'

'Yes, you really are. Though how fragile it is, I don't know. What I do know is that accidents sometimes have this strange effect. They make us feel vulnerable, but they can also make us feel that we're alive in a way that is hard to tap into in normal circumstances. You could so easily have died.'

'True,' he said. 'I could easily have died.'

Sitting with Isobel, he remembered being at college with her. There had been a few people on his course who really 'got' each other, and he and Isobel were two of them. She was the one who'd first started calling him 'the baby' – appropriately, because he had always felt like the younger brother of his peers. He was twenty-eight when he'd started the course and had been the second youngest, though he could easily have passed for twenty-two or twenty-three at the time. Most people were in their thirties, forties or beyond, so he really did feel conspicuously young. And conspicuously male, which he hadn't expected to have so highlighted. There were eighteen women and only three men – not unusual on courses of this kind – and so his maleness was something that was actively 'out there', against which certain dramas would inevitably be played.

Isobel was forty-six at the time, married and with two teenaged kids, and it was interesting to Will that he'd fallen into a brother-sister relationship with her, when it might so easily have been maternal. But Isobel mothered her husband, and so needed a male presence in her life that was equal but not sexual, while Will needed a sister who didn't dislike him.

After seeing Isobel, Will returned home feeling a contradictory sense of being both energised and deflated. He realised that he was, once more, carrying something that remained unspoken. It made no difference that it was about his client work and not his past. Particularly disturbing was the fact that he had unaccountably managed to sack his supervisor without any memory of having done so and without any knowledge of what he'd said. When he thought of Colin, Will realised that he had always been hesitant with him. Perhaps he had a distrust of the competence of others? It had taken energy and courage to become more honest about his own processes in supervision, and he had never thought to question whether he was getting the right supervision for his needs. Colin was clinical and definite about factual accuracy and seemed subtly dismissive of Will's intuition, although he recognised it – at least when they spoke of it – as being the lifeblood of therapy. But Will's intuition never quite seemed to satisfy Colin, especially if he referred to it in response to a question such as, 'What was your reasoning there?' It was as though facts held the answers to everything. Occasionally, Will had wondered whether he should change supervisor, more to experience a supervisor with an intuitive and non-scientific perspective rather than because Colin was in any way deficient. But he also felt that one of his issues as a therapist was that he was a bit woolly about the empirical side of therapeutic work. Colin had been able to provide challenge there and Will could keep his intuition to himself.

Now, though, he realised he would miss Colin's helpful insistence.

'But what did you *actually* say, Will?' was a common Colin-ism.

Will had a tendency in supervision to talk in general terms.

'We had a discussion about her inability to speak her mind to her husband and she got angry when I questioned her about it.'

'But what did she *actually* say, Will.'

Of course, in the trying to remember exactly what was

said, Will would often remember other things that he'd omitted for one reason or another. Omission! Well, he'd managed to 'omit' a whole week of therapy this time, which was impressive by any standards.

Later that day, the police came around. The man who'd helped him home after the accident had given a good eye witness account, although he hadn't seen the driver. The car, however, had been stolen, and it now looked likely that the driver would never be found. They'd found no sign of fingerprints when they discovered the car abandoned in Walthamstow. So, that was that as far as the police were concerned. As it stood, the case could go no further.

Will noticed that week that Lara had acquired three more paintings by the same brash artist and had hung two of them in the sitting room to make a triptych with the bold green and red splash that was already there. The last one was in the hall, a welcoming burst of orange to brighten that dim space. There was something assertive and mysterious about Lara acquiring and hanging these pictures without consulting him and he happily accepted this without wanting to question her. She had occasionally brought back objects, such as props from shows that had finished, and so it wasn't unheard of. When she was ready to say something about it, she would.

One evening when Will was seventeen and Jamie fifteen, they were watching a film together and Jamie blurted out quite suddenly that he was gay. Will was shocked into stillness. Not because Jamie was gay, but because he'd been around his 'wee brother' all this time and didn't know this about him.

He could think of nothing to say, and so he smiled in mild embarrassment. But it started a process of . . . something. Jamie's trust was very moving and the following day Will hugged his brother and said not to worry about 'it'. In a family of non-huggers, they had established something very different, but he also realised that he might have said, 'That's okay' or something equally neutral but acceptant to Jamie. But did he find it okay? Would he be able to mention casually at school *my gay brother*. Would people tease him if they found out that he'd once shared a bedroom with his gay brother? Of course they would. But would they do it nastily, and would he care? *My gay brother* . . . Why did those words sound so strange?

That year, Will acquired an elderly 50cc scooter, a reluctant hand-me-down from Kitty, who was off travelling in her gap year. The Lake District was about twenty miles from their house and Will puttered south into the hills a couple of times, but Jamie felt left out, and so they managed to get a few days' casual work on a neighbouring farm to pay for a month's bus pass each and then they went and 'did' all the peaks: Skiddaw, which was the closest, though perhaps the least interesting; Helvellyn; Scafell and Scafell Pike; Bow Fell – a particular favourite. The best thing about these walks was neither the exercise, which was great, nor the scenery, which was spectacular, but the company and the getting-to-know-each-other, which was a revelation. How could they have lived in the same house for so many years and not really known each other?

One afternoon they'd paused for a rest on Striding Edge on the approach to the summit of Helvellyn, enjoying a moment of sunshine in an otherwise cloudy day, and Jamie had said, quite suddenly, 'Don't you love Mum?'

Will paused for a moment before replying.

'I don't think I've ever loved anyone. I think I'm not capable of it, for some reason. Perhaps it was to do with the accident, or something else, but when I see people who are in love or who love each other in different kinds of ways, I don't recognise what I see in them. Not at all. The couple of girls I've done it with, well, that didn't go particularly well.'

Jamie thought for a while but didn't say anything.

'And you?' Will asked.

'I love Mum, but I can see that she's been hard on you. I feel like I've had all my share, plus all of yours as well, which has been a bit suffocating at times.'

'And what about love in general? And boys?'

'Well . . . I haven't done anything about that yet. And I don't think I'd survive at school if I came out.'

'How do you know you're gay, then?'

'How did you know you weren't, when you were my age?'

Will thought for a moment. 'Point taken.'

It started to rain and Jamie pulled his coat around himself. 'Shall we go up or down?'

Will suddenly felt responsible for Jamie. As well as a phone in his pocket, he had a compass in his rucksack, a whistle, one of those emergency blankets made of some shiny metallic-looking material and an Ordnance Survey map in a waterproof holder. He wasn't foolish enough to imagine that going up into cloud on Striding Edge was without danger. But, looking back the way they had come, he reckoned that it would be straightforward to retrace their steps in all but the thickest of cloud. He looked ahead and upward. Although visibility was poor, the cloud was ragged with patches of brightness.

'The path's good, so let's go on. We'll turn back if it gets worse.'

On the summit, the clouds parted and they could see right down past Red Tarn to Ullswater, the air astonishingly clear and cool after the rain. Jamie laughed with amazement at the view and put his arm over Will's shoulder, and for a moment Will felt completely peaceful.

When Will went to university, he chose Edinburgh, quite naturally, where he studied English and Scottish Literature. He felt that *Scottish* should have come first: Scottish and English Literature. At this time his paternal grandfather, a rather dour man, gave him a beautiful eighteenth-century wine glass, with a double twist bubble in the stem and two engraved roses on the bowl, one open and one closed. It had a large chip on the base and was scratched at the rim, so was not anything like as valuable as it might have been, but it was a Jacobite glass nevertheless.

'I want you to have it,' he told Will. 'You are studying Scottish literature and so you have a sense of our culture. I wanted to give it to someone who'd appreciate it, someone for whom its history has meaning. Someone who could respect it and keep it as an heirloom.'

Will knew the story of Bonnie Prince Charlie but hadn't paid much attention to it at school. The monarchy wasn't something he cared about and the fights between Catholic and Protestant kings and queens seemed like an impossible distinction – one kind of Christianity for another . . . who cared? The mild Scottish Presbyterianism of Dalmacallan had seemed like a quaint backdrop to his life, like ridiculously old-fashioned wallpaper. But the romantic story of these glasses was captivating. Once Charles had returned to exile after the rebellion of 1745 in which he and a largely Scottish army had attempted – and failed – to reclaim the British throne for Catholicism, anyone supporting him would be guilty of treason. He was regarded by his supporters as the true king by divine right and so, when toasts were made to the king, these glasses were used, the roses symbolising the Stuart dynasty. Held over a bowl of water, the toast 'To the king!' could be understood as 'To the King over the water', namely Charles Edward Stuart in exile in Europe.

Will had never seen his grandfather so animated and accepted the gift, although he entrusted the glass back to his Grandfather's care when he left as he was terrified of breaking it, given his lack of fine motor coordination. This act of generosity led to regular visits to his grandparents over the three years of his undergraduate life, and to long conversations about Scottish history and the nation's various betrayals at the hands of the English. It was only after his graduation that Will took the glass away and he only handled it occasionally after that, having learned to appreciate and value its significance. He looked online a few times to see what it might be worth. Unchipped and unscratched versions might be worth many thousands of pounds, although his glass was not a particularly rare or fine specimen. So, he stopped looking – there was no point. He would never sell it.

In the first year of his course, Will stayed in Pollock Halls and ran compulsively around Arthur's Seat as often as he could, doing the circuit of Dunsapie Loch in a little over half an hour. He joined the university's cycling club and eventually the team, where he became a stalwart member. His main assets were stamina and dependability. He was good at helping to keep up morale under punishing conditions and, although his dyspraxia meant that he had some difficulty with finer spatial judgement, he was the workhorse for the team and that was highly valued. The cheerful camaraderie of his team mates was refreshing and uncomplicated and made him feel relaxed and at ease when he was with them.

Similarly, his voluntary work for, and commitment to, the Scottish National Party was a great pleasure to him. Joining the party was one of the first things he did on arrival at university, and during his three years he did a lot of canvassing, leafletting and standing on people's doorsteps discussing Scotland's future. He thoroughly enjoyed this work, and at the end of a period of canvassing he always had a pleasantly tired glow of accomplishment. Again, he was dependable, and he certainly had stamina for the mundane tasks that were asked of everyone during busy periods.

He realised immediately that he had no interest in taking up a career in politics. It had no pull for him whatsoever. He saw that, in order to make it happen, he would have to dedicate himself to the party 24/7. But he was an undergraduate with other things on his plate and an instinct that he didn't have the right personality for politics. He just wasn't interested in the cut and thrust of 'rising through the ranks', the spikey aggression disguised as debate. It was interesting to him that he was competitive as a cyclist as well as in the seminar room where the heat of critical argument could get pretty dramatic. However, there was an aspect to getting on in politics that had a hard edge to it that he sensed as being about individuals rather than community and he could feel at times the unkindness of this sort of personal ambition.

When he was in a group of six or seven friends out leafleting and door-knocking, there was the same simple camaraderie as his cycling group. He felt that he was making a significant contribution to society in his own way; something that would help to make the world a better place, something that wasn't centred around him. He was happy to stand up on a platform and speak for the party from time to time, but mostly he would just laugh when asked to do so and recommend fellow youthful party members who were hungry to get these things onto their CVs.

As far as academia went, having dyspraxia meant that essays were a bit of a nightmare. Sometimes he could experience dreadful moments of mental paralysis when faced with his larger pieces of work, but if he took them bit by bit, he found that he could do well enough eventually. He was assigned one-to-one dyspraxia tuition which was helpful, too, but it was still hard, especially given that he was working sixteen hours a week in a hotel just off the Royal Mile.

It was during this time that he had a whole string of confusing experiences with women. He discovered almost immediately that he was attractive to them, not just physically, but also because of his woundedness. Retrospectively, it became clear to him, especially during his later period of therapy, that what he was looking for in women was to be held by them in the way that his mother never had. These women could be many things, but they could never be his mother. They could mother him, but because Will was no longer a child this was never going to work.

It was the fact that all of this was unconscious that made everything so painful. Will thought he was giving himself up to his relationships. He embarked on them with enthusiasm and hope. He was attentive, amusing, generous. He delighted in making his girlfriends smile and feel important. He expressed his gratitude to them in humble and personal ways – giving them small gifts that showed he'd really paid attention to them. But – and there was a *but* – there was an all-important part of him that was unavailable. He was unavailable in a quite literal way, of course, with his cycling, his part-time job and work for the SNP. But he was unavailable in another way, too. He was half aware of this missing part because of the misery that would sometimes arise in him out of nowhere, like morning mist, to engulf him. He knew he should be falling in love, but he wasn't. He knew he was doing all the right things, except for this – this giving up of the withdrawn part of himself. And without that, nothing would ever be enough.

And, of course, the upshot of this was that he felt more and more loveless and more and more sure that he was incapable of feeling love. This had the effect of making him feel tragic about himself, which showed and thereby increased his attractiveness to a certain kind of woman . . . a vicious circle of pain that left all concerned wounded and angry.

His girlfriends would all, at some point, experience and express Will's own reticence. It was inevitable really.

'Why are you so kind and thoughtful but then pull back just as you're about to give yourself up to this?' they might say. 'Is it something to do with a fear of commitment?'

'Not as far as I know,' he told them truthfully.

His answers were never satisfying. Saying, 'I want to commit myself but don't seem to be able to' wasn't helpful.

'Perhaps,' he said once, remembering his grandmother, 'Perhaps I was dropped on my head as a child.'

In the act of saying this, he realised how ridiculous it sounded, and indeed was. He never mentioned it again and dropped it after that, even as a concept.

For Will, it was like looking over the edge of a cliff. The vertigo was so intense, he sometimes felt physically sick. How could he be honest and not cause pain? Some of the young men on his course would say anything, tell any lie, to get a woman into bed. Will couldn't bring himself to go down that route but telling the truth didn't seem to be a successful strategy either. He began to feel that he'd rather be single than cause any more pain. This was fine as far as it went as he had a good circle of friends and an active and sustaining social life, but it wasn't quite enough.

During those years, and before he put a lid on it, Will experienced occasional, intense irruptions of rage. At the time, he didn't understand the connection between them and his apparent lovelessness. They would sometimes arise, apparently out of nowhere, and spill over into acts of drunken brawling. He wouldn't have described them as brawls at the time, but that is what they were. They only happened in very specific circumstances, usually at the end of an evening when he'd said goodbye to his friends and was leaving or had just left a bar or a club. He justified them by only fighting when he perceived others to need his help, wading in to 'rescue' people who were being threatened or standing up for people who were being challenged in the street. Somewhere in his head there was a concept of 'justice', though he understood, at least in principle, that justice should be meted out reasonably rather than punitively.

This led to a number of injuries and hospital visits, but nothing that left him permanently damaged. The lasting damage that he carried was of a different kind.

There was something disconcerting about his self-esteem around this time – he was admired for this fierceness by exactly the kind of people he did not want to impress. His genuine friends were bemused and concerned by what he was doing. Not that they ever witnessed it, but they saw the results in the bruises that were sometimes visible on his face or arms. He knew that there was something childish in what he was doing and that this 'vigilante' concept used to justify his anger was a painfully thin veneer over an urge to self-harm. It was as important for him to be punched as it was to punch, a realisation that was particularly unsettling. One day, he saw a bunch of aggressive young men on North Bridge, above the Grassmarket. He could see quite clearly that the urge he felt to challenge them was virtually suicidal, but it didn't stop him from standing idly against the sandstone balustrade and looking at them insolently as they passed. They beat him unconscious very swiftly and without him having laid a finger on any of them, as far as he could recollect. After he'd been discharged from hospital the following morning, one of his female flatmates said to him, 'You're punishing yourself, Will. I wonder why? You punish yourself with exercise. You punish yourself with these longs shifts with the SNP. You punish yourself by getting into fights. What's going on? Particularly with the fighting. Why do you want people to hit you?'

He'd felt a sudden urge to say, *Because I deserve it*. But that sounded too weird, so he said, 'I don't know', which was also true in its own way. She was right that he was punishing himself, though, and they both knew it. Dimly, at the edge of consciousness, he sensed that he needed to be punished because he'd 'killed his sister', though he could never have said that in words; it was just an inchoate feeling.

He went into the bathroom that morning and looked at his face in the mirror. It was grotesque. He stood for some time looking at it and could see the madness in what he'd been doing. And that was it. Quite suddenly, something subsided in him and he never hit another person in anger again.

This event heralded a period of strange and rarefied celibacy. Will felt an almost prescient sense that he was destined to become a priest. After all, if love and relationships were not really on the cards for him, for reasons that he couldn't grasp, why not go the whole hog and sign up to a life of celibacy? This dream lasted about three months – in fact until the end of his course module on the '45 rebellion that concluded with Will writing a rather poetic essay about Scotland's loss, for which he got his best mark to date. At the time, he had been rather taken by the concept of Bonnie Prince Charlie having been brought up in Rome in the early eighteenth century under the protection and patronage of the

Pope who, quite naturally, had a vested interest in Britain becoming Catholic again. Maybe a career in the Catholic church would be a possibility. Even if he could not quite manage the lifestyle of a prince in exile, it all sounded rather grand. But inevitably the whole romantic edifice, constructed on the foundation of his own sadness, had collapsed under the weight of his intransigent atheism and intrinsic moderate Scottish liberalism. Bonnie Prince Charlie's dissolute later life in exile was less than inspiring, too.

At the end of Will's final year, Jamie came up to stay. He'd just finished the first year of a degree in maths and statistics at Newcastle and arrived in an old Ford Fiesta he'd bought with his previous summer's earnings. He arrived on a Friday night and, on the Saturday, they got up at 4.30 am and drove up to Glencoe to climb the Aonach Eagach. It was a ridge that they'd been promising to climb for a couple of years now, ever since they'd climbed Bidean Nam Bian, on the south side, and looked across at the famous and inviting ridge.

It was on this climb that Will first experienced full-blown vertigo – visceral, physical vertigo this time, not just a psychological reaction to the disappointment of his girlfriends. Part way along the ridge was a short exposed downward scramble to which climbers had to commit themselves. They knew that after a certain point on this short descent it was almost impossible to reverse the scramble unless you had proper rock-climbing experience. They'd seen something about it online.

Jamie went first. 'It's not too bad at all!' he called to Will as he went down.

To begin with Will was fine. There were some good handholds. But when he got part way down, facing inward towards the rock, he failed to properly grasp a small outcrop. As he stretched out his arm, somehow his hand missed the rock for a moment before he took hold of it. And then he glanced below him. He wasn't quite sure what it was, perhaps the way he moved his head so that the surface he was on seemed to tip slightly or the way the drop below him came so suddenly into focus as he glanced down from his hands. Whatever it was, he suddenly froze with terror, gripping his handholds and closing his eyes. Jamie, who was ahead of him, jumped onto a flat expanse of rock below and turned to look up.

'Are you okay, Will?'

Will couldn't make a sound. He was stuck. It took Jamie a few moments to realise that there was something wrong.

'It's alright, Will,' he said, 'it's not difficult to get down from there. Are you okay for a few moments where you are?'

Will nodded with his eyes closed. They waited like that for perhaps thirty seconds and then Jamie said, 'Right, there's a foothold below your right foot, about eighteen inches down and a little to your right. You don't have to look down, I'll tell you where it is. You need to lower yourself gently.'

'I can't move,' Will whispered. The paralysis that he was experiencing went beyond anything that he'd experienced before. It was completely beyond his control. Jamie didn't say anything for a while, but eventually spoke.

'How are you doing now? Still stuck?'

Will nodded. At this point, some climbers arrived above them. Will could hear them, but he still couldn't open his eyes.

'My brother's a bit stuck!' Jamie called up.

'I can see that,' said a voice.

There was a pause.

'Listen . . .' the voice said after a few moments. 'We have a rope. You can hold on to it to steady yourself.'

There was a moment of absolute terror as the rope was dropped down and knocked against Will's elbow.

'Right,' the voice said to him, 'you have a good handhold with your right hand, so I've dropped the rope down by your left. Can you feel it?'

Will nodded.

'Can you take the rope and wrap it round your waist?

Will shook his head.

'Right. Well, maybe you can grab hold of it tightly, then?'

It took almost a minute, which seemed like an age, before Will could open his eyes a fraction, so that he could see the rope beside him and then grab it. He clutched it and swayed with a dizzying movement that caused a wave of nausea, then righted himself.

'Now your brother can direct you down.'

'There's that foothold I told you about,' Jamie said, with surprising calm. 'About eighteen inches down and a little to your right. You'll be fine now you've got the rope to steady you.'

Will tugged gently at the rope to make sure that it was secure. It didn't budge. He let himself down an inch or two, then another inch. Then another couple of inches. It was agony. Before he found the foothold, his left leg, which was taking his weight, had started to shake with a staccato judder.

'Nearly there!' said Jamie.

And then he was down. The foothold was quite deep and Will could put his weight on it completely. This sudden feeling of stability and the fact that he was holding a rope made the vertigo recede so that he could open his eyes again and look down. Suddenly, it was nothing. It was easy, only a couple more steps. He laughed, with embarrassment as well as pleasure and stepped quickly down onto the flat with Jamie. There was a short burst of applause from above.

He looked up. Four men of indeterminate age, somewhere between thirty and forty, were looking down. They all came down, quickly and nimbly. The first man was the one who had spoken.

'Hello lads,' he said, and then turned to Will. 'Not perhaps the best climb to do if you have trouble with heights.'

'I didn't know that I did have trouble with heights,' said Will. 'It's never happened before.'

The man smiled. 'Perhaps not as insane as it looked, then. Where are you boys staying?'

'Red Squirrel campsite,' said Jamie.

'Perhaps you'll be coming to the Clachaig Inn for a beer later?'

'We could do,' said Jamie.

'Here,' said the man, 'take this rope. I brought it in case we wanted to try one of the outlying buttresses, but you can borrow it for the day. You're over the worst part now, though there are one or two exposed stretches to come.' He gave them some brief instructions about how to use the rope safely, then patted Will on the shoulder. 'If any of it seems scary, ask for help. There'll be a good few experienced climbers coming along here today. You can return the rope to me in the Clachaig tonight, where I'll let you have the pleasure of buying me a pint.'

And with that they were gone. As soon as things opened up, Will lay down on a stretch of coarse grass that was back from the ridge, a short way from the path, arms outstretched, looking up at the sky. He needed to feel the solid, safe earth beneath him. His body felt unsteady and slightly nauseous. He lay like that with Jamie beside him for perhaps forty-five minutes.

'We started ridiculously early,' said Jamie, 'we can stay here for hours if you need to.'

Will looked up at the sky. It was palest, arctic blue with high mare's tail plumes. There was hardly any sound except perhaps for the subliminal mournful moan of wind from the far side of the ridge. The air was warm.

'I don't know when I'm going to stop feeling wobbly,' said Will. 'I feel like I've been injected with some sort of drug.'

'You have,' said Jamie. 'Massive amounts of adrenaline for a start, but probably a few other goodies too. Don't expect to calm down for a while.'

After twenty minutes or so, they broke out their lunch and ate where they were, the Mamore ridge and the back of Ben Nevis to the north and the grand buttresses of the Three Sisters and Bidean Nam Bian to the south. It was utterly beautiful. Why was it that his brush with terror made all this seem so much more beautiful to Will? He sat and ate his sandwich, flushing it down with sips of water as he still hadn't got his saliva back.

'We're on top of the world,' he said. 'It looks so different from up here to how it looks from the valley floor.'

Jamie agreed and they looked out at the vista of peaks disappearing into the haze.

'You really gave me a turn back there,' said Jamie. 'When you swayed, grabbing the rope, I thought you were going to fall off. I think the chances of you surviving a drop like that are probably zero. It was quite a moment. I'm glad of the chance to recover, myself.'

Will sighed and looked up at the infinite sky.

Jamie patted Will's foot. 'Don't do that to me again, Will. I love you.'

'I love you, too,' said Will.

There was a short moment while each of them noticed what Will had said. Jamie cracked a broad grin.

'Ha!' he shouted, pointing at Will. 'Ha!'

Later, in the Clachaig Inn, they gave the rope back to the climbers they'd met and Will got happily drunk. *I love my brother*, he thought. *I love my brother!*

'You know, it's obvious, when you think of it . . .' said Jamie. 'If you have dyspraxia, even mild dyspraxia, you're not going to be completely sure of subtle body movements. If we'd thought, even for a moment, to put your dyspraxia in the picture, then we could have predicted something like this.'

Thereafter, they got a book that graded ascents by difficulty. On a scale of one to five, where one was easy and five difficult, Will could manage a four. If a particular ascent was graded five, he knew to avoid it, and so he never had another moment of major vertigo again. Even on a four, though, he sometimes wobbled a little, but they always took a short rope with them and Will didn't mind getting down on his hands and knees to crawl across an exposed stretch.

That weekend changed everything. Will had spoken those words to someone: 'I love you.' He had either to retract them or accept what they meant for him: that he had been wrong. He *could* love someone. Love was an emotion that he was capable of feeling. It was a peculiar triumph because it wasn't one that he could share with anyone, except Jamie. He could hardly go up to a friend and say, *I am able to love another person!* because they would say, *Well, of course you are, what are you talking about?* And he couldn't go back to his old girlfriends because it was too late.

After that, things started to change. He didn't have another girlfriend for quite a while, but when he did it was different. It opened him up to the possibility, later, of training as a therapist, which would otherwise have been impossible. And when he met Lara, he was able to recognise and acknowledge that he was falling in love with her as it was happening.

That day also cemented a bond between Will and Jamie, a bond that was profoundly moving to Will. They topped the weekend off by going clubbing together and taking ecstasy, something they'd done together a handful of times before but which seemed particularly poignant on this occasion. It was an irregular habit that they fell into and which would later include Lara, and which they all enjoyed. But it stopped when Jamie started going out with Joel and then, somehow, it became 'something that we used to do'.

It was with a sense of irony that Will moved away from Scotland and down to London for his first career job in a company that specialised in renovating semi-historic buildings. His degree in English and Scottish literature was of no practical use whatsoever, although it had got him his interview. The work was dull, although the salary reasonable. The girl he'd followed down south turned out not to be interested in him.

His Scottishness was not remarked upon, and it was this bland acceptance that made him realise how much of an 'identity' it had become for him, and how much he had adopted it to feel separate from his family, who were, ironically, Scottish themselves, though not in the same ardent way. Now it became, quite suddenly, a pointless gesture for him to emphasise this part of himself, though he did keep up his annual subscription to the SNP.

At the end of his first year in London, he met and had an

intensely physical relationship with an ambitious young accountant, and it was a great joy to him to experience giving himself up to it without wondering overly about what it was or where it was going. They were very different from each other. She was absolutely sure of what she wanted to achieve and what she wanted to be, which is to say, successful and able to be assertively self-determining without losing her femininity. For Will, life seemed to be a palette of opportunities, none of which had managed to present themselves to him in such a way that he felt inclined to follow them. He knew he would need to move on from his current job at some point but it was sufficient for the moment as he explored making a life for himself in London. And so he found himself to be pleasantly adrift in a sea of possibility.

He was determined that with this relationship he wouldn't fall into his old pattern of behaviour and, in his efforts to be seen, he told her as much about himself as he was able. He had never explicitly told the story of the death of his sister or his part in it to a lover before. Previously, he had allowed people to infer that someone in his family had died tragically and it was left at that – always unspoken, always there, and because unspoken, never diminished. Even on this occasion he only said, 'My sister drowned in an accident when we were playing. It was partly my fault.'

She was suitably sympathetic and was wise when she said, 'It's not the accident itself that makes me feel sad, but the endless repercussions that it has clearly had for you.'

But problems in their relationship were inevitable. She

wanted to be 'doing' things all the time and was unable to relax. She could see no value in anything that wasn't constructively helpful in building her successful life. She was scathing about his friends, who tended to enjoy watching films and having eclectic and rather philosophical conversations.

'You have no ambition,' she said to him one day. 'You're twenty-three and one day you've got to make a decision about what to do with your life.'

'I spent most of my life at university punishing myself with busy-ness and I realised I was just using that to push down something that was dark and unhelpful,' he told her. 'I knew a few people who were motivated to do well in politics, and they weren't a good advertisement for ambition. What you are trying to achieve seems to have no *value*.'

When she left, even though he knew it was inevitable, Will felt empty and deflated. He'd thought that by bringing all of himself to a relationship, he'd managed to triumphantly clear the final hurdle, rather than only just managing, haltingly, to get over the first. But then, what could he expect if he went out with someone who held such a differing world view to his own?

A few years later, when he started his training as a therapist, he thought of her and what she would think of his chosen profession. He could see from her online profile that she was 'doing well' and suspected that she wouldn't be impressed.

He started seeing a therapist. The reason he decided to try this was because he'd been in a pub near the Barbican one day waiting for a friend and someone at the next table had been talking about her therapist. It wasn't that she was saying that the experience was marvellous or even helpful but there was something in the way that she described it that made Will feel that it might be a possibility for him. He yearned for the presence of someone who would listen to him and see the unseen parts of him without judgement, and perhaps help him to make sense of what was happening – that he was clearly playing out something that he couldn't quite pinpoint. When the person on the next table said that she'd found herself a therapist by browsing online, he did the same on his return home.

When he chose a therapist, he didn't explicitly decide to see a woman, but he'd found himself skipping the male names in the listings in his area. Her name was Victoria and she was an integrative psychotherapeutic counsellor who specialised in Gestalt, and particularly in Two Chair work. Will had no idea what this was, but there was something in her listing where she said she dealt with 'life changes' and 'identity', and the fact that she'd put these side by side made him call her.

She sat with him in that first session, a clip board in her lap, and said, 'So, why are you here?'

'I killed my sister,' he said.

She knotted her eyebrows at this and leaned forward a little, before leaning back and writing something briefly. Will was aware that he was trying shock tactics. Could she take what he had to say? Would she judge him? She looked kind, interested and concerned.

'Can you tell me a little more about how you came to kill your sister?'

He told her what had happened, about the blossom, the dumper truck, the pond, the drowning. It took about three minutes, and he realised when he finished that he'd spoken very fast and that he'd probably been rehearsing this speech for years and years.

'That was rather swift,' she told him, 'and a little emotionless.'

'It was the only way I could get it out.'

'And is that how you see it? "I killed my sister".'

'Yes and no. I said it like that for dramatic effect.'

'But on some level, that's how you see it?'

'Yes.'

She nodded.

'Also, I seem to find it impossible to communicate effectively with the women I have relationships with. I thought I'd learned how to do that. But clearly I haven't, given how my last relationship ended. I can't say I have ever really had a relationship with a woman. They always get fed up with me before . . .' He paused. They always got fed up with him before what?

'Before?' Victoria prompted.

'I don't know. They get fed up with me . . . because . . . because I don't give them what they want, or need.'

'And what is that?'

'I thought it was because I don't give them love, but I think I did pretty well with my last girlfriend and she still left me.'

When Will left the assessment session, he felt odd. On one hand he was relieved to have spoken in the way he had. But he also felt that he'd opened a door – at least a tiny bit, a chink of light – and what lay beyond it seemed so impossibly complicated that he experienced a rush of fear as he thought about what might lie ahead. How much easier it would be to close the door and never go back to Victoria or to therapy again. That thought was followed by a recollection of his most recent girlfriend telling him that if he didn't do something about his relationship to his past, he would remain forever in its shadow. And didn't that describe him perfectly? A man in his own shadow? He'd been sent away to a different school from his siblings so that he could be out of the acetylene glare of his misfortune. He'd given shadowy impressions of himself and his sadness to the girls he'd fancied and they'd responded by falling in love with him. Now, he wondered about what he was doing. Wasn't this his prime asset? His damagedness? What would he be without it? He imagined himself simply ceasing to exist.

In his seventh session, he was asked to speak to an empty chair.

'Imagine your mother is in this chair,' Victoria told him. 'What do you need to say to her?'

Even though he had been told, in principle, something of

what he was going to be asked to do, he was still rendered speechless. Not by the fact that he was trying to imagine that his mother was sitting in the chair, but that he had an audience for what he might, or might not, say to her.

'I can't think of anything.'

'There's no time limit to this, Will,' Victoria told him. 'Take your time. This can stretch over more than one session if you need it to.'

Will looked at the chair. What did he need to say? Quite suddenly a depth charge seemed to explode in his gut, not towards his mother but towards Victoria.

'I'm too embarrassed!' he gasped. 'Don't push me!'

Victoria smiled. 'Stay with it.'

Will sat with it for an uncomfortable length of time. It felt like ages but was probably less than five minutes. At last, he spoke.

'Part of me wants to say, "I hate you", but part of me knows I don't hate her. Part of me wants to say, "Why did you go cold on me? Why did you turn away from me?"'

'Say these things to your mother,' said Victoria.

Will looked at Victoria and realised that he was blushing. He could feel the prickle of it in his cheeks. He looked across at the chair and took a breath.

'Why did you go cold on me, Mum?' he asked. 'Why did you turn away from me? Why didn't you read me bedtime stories, like you did with Jamie?'

He felt a prickle of embarrassment and nakedness. He wanted to say *Why didn't you hold me?* but found that he couldn't in front of his therapist. 'I think I'm going to be sick,' he said.

'Do you think you're going to actually be sick, or do you just feel sick?'

'I feel sick.'

'Stay with it. In any case, you can be sick into the bin by your chair.'

Will laughed. 'I hope it's watertight.'

'Don't distract yourself. What's happening? What do you feel?'

'It's gone,' said Will. 'The nausea has gone. I feel fine.'

'You deflected into humour,' said Victoria.

He felt her disappointment and a quiet pulse of shame rose up in him.

'Now, get up. Go and sit in the chair that you imagined your mother sitting in.'

Will did so and looked expectantly at Victoria.

'Right . . . now, you are your mother. Imagine you are your mother and you have just listened to your son, Will, ask the following questions . . . "Why did you go cold on me? Why did you turn away from me? Why didn't you read bedtime stories to me like you did with Jamie?"'

Will felt trapped. He hadn't thought, even for a moment, that he would be asked to do this.

'I can't,' he said.

'Don't worry. Stay with the "can't". What does that mean, "can't"?'

'I can't tell you what my mother would say. I'm not my mother. How would I know what she would say?'

'This is an act of imagination. I think you probably know your mother well enough to imagine what she might say in response to your questions.'

Will shook his head. He needed to feel the way he did. 'I don't want to change.'

Victoria shrugged. 'I wonder why you're here, then.'

He suddenly felt a stab of hatred for Victoria. He glared at her but fell silent.

She remained silent, too.

When Will left the session, he felt confused. What had happened? He felt hatred towards his therapist. He felt hatred towards his mother. What was going on? Was he turning his therapist into his mother?

In the next session, he said to her, 'I feel that I need to hate you or be hugged by you. I presume this is what I feel about my mother. And that this is why I chose a female therapist.'

'I can't hug you,' said Victoria. 'It would be against my professional ethics. Does that mean you have to hate me?'

'I don't want to hate you.'

'Try reframing that. Try saying, "I don't want to hate myself."'

Bang! There he was, up against it!

'That makes me feel so angry,' he told her. 'I don't hate myself.'

'Then what is this rage you hold? Rage against your

mother for being distant? Or rage against yourself for "killing" your sister?'

She held up her hand. 'Hold up your hand. Like this.'

He held up his hand.

'I've decided to risk it,' she said. 'I'm not sure what'll happen, but let's have a go.'

She leaned towards Will and reached her hand towards him. 'Reach out to me,' she said.

Will hesitated, then leaned in towards her. As he did so, she moved her middle finger forward. He did the same. There was a moment of hesitation before the tips of their fingers met.

'This is contact,' she said. 'It is possible for you to have contact.'

They remained like that for perhaps ten seconds and then Will broke the contact and sat back. 'It makes me feel like a failure,' he said. 'It feels like you're telling me that I should come into contact with my mother, that she's reaching out to me, and that it's my fault we haven't met.'

'Oh, Will,' Victoria said, sadly.

'You have no idea what it feels like to be me, in relation to my mother. You have no idea!'

'No. No one will ever feel what it's like to be you. Other people may get an inkling, but no one else can ever be in your head.'

Will looked out of the window and away from Victoria.

'I am not your mother. You can still hate me – that's fine.

That's information that we can work with. But I am not your mother, Will. I can never be your mother. I can't take you to my breast and hug you and let you cry the tears that the seven-year-old Will needed to cry but was denied the chance to shed.'

'Then I don't really see any point in being here.'

So, this was the impasse. Will 'needed' something from his therapist that she was unable to give him, just as he had needed the same thing from the girls he'd dated. Was this a demand that he was going to make forever, to people who were unable to comply?

In many ways, that session of the touching fingers was the end of his work with Victoria. He could see, quite clearly, that he was facing a movement that he was not able to make – to come into contact with his mother, even in his head. At least seeing this clearly was something, positive in the sense that knowledge might be considered better than ignorance. But Will felt stuck. He realised that working through his stuckness wouldn't happen overnight and that he felt unable to be stuck with Victoria. Those first sessions with her had been sessions in which he'd uncovered new information each time. He could leave her with a 'Wow!' feeling of understanding what was going on a little better. But he didn't want to be seen to be stuck. The idea that he might sit with Victoria for many sessions, simply being stuck, had a caste of humiliation to it. If he was going to be stuck, he might as well be stuck on his own and save himself the money.

He'd been given information, and now it was up to him to do something with it. With this, came gusts of ill will towards his mother as well as towards himself. He realised that his fantasy demand was for his mother to apologise to him, abjectly and completely, for her coldness; an apology that he would refuse to accept at first before magnanimously giving in. And his inability to immediately accept her imagined apology somehow put him in the wrong. He also felt gusts of ill will towards Victoria. He'd imagined that therapy would make change happen without effort. This gave rise to a wry smile, even while he blamed her for his stuckness.

How ironic, then, that three years later he made the decision to train as a therapist! The three siblings had been left a few thousand pounds each by their grandfather, the one who had given Will the Jacobite glass. It was a sad few months for Will. His grandfather was the first adult he'd known closely who had died, and he remembered vividly the friendly conversations they'd had. It seemed fitting to spend the money on something beneficial and to do with getting a further qualification – something of which his grandfather would most definitely have approved. So, from his full-time job, he went down to three days a week, which just about covered his living expenses. His legacy covered the costs of his course and the two years of therapy he had to take as part of his personal development.

When asked at interview why he wanted to become a therapist, he said, 'I don't know.'

This answer seemed to be satisfactory up to a point, but Geraldine, the woman who would become his course tutor, wanted him to explore what he meant by 'I don't know.'

'Well,' said Will, 'part of me wonders whether I am wanting to train to become a therapist so that I can have two years of therapy.'

'You could have two years of therapy without training,' said Geraldine.

'Yes, but I wouldn't allow myself to do that. If it's a course requirement, then I'll do it.

He paused to consider. 'Also, I've been reading up about the training, and so I'm familiar with the concept of the wounded healer. I suppose I have a worry that I'd be trying to heal others in order to heal myself.'

Geraldine smiled. 'So, these are the fears, the bad reasons for training to be a therapist. Do you have any good reasons?'

'My job is meaningless,' said Will. 'I'm not even sure what I mean by meaningless. But it seems to give me no meaning. I want to have a chance to connect with people and to find meaning with them.'

So, he was accepted on the course – a training in psychotherapeutic counselling that was heavy on Gestalt. Precisely the training that Victoria, his therapist, had undertaken.

Many months later, when Will referred to his conversation with her, Geraldine said to him, 'We're always most wary of people who say, "Because I want to help people". When they say that, I say to them, "There are many ways of being helpful in the world, why choose this one?"'

It didn't take long in his training for Will to see that he had mixed reasons for wanting to be a therapist. He'd felt, vaguely, that with his psychotherapeutic knowledge he'd be able to dress himself up as worldly and possibly even wise. Words like *projection* and *introjection* and *transference* were all tools that he could use. He also realised that he wanted to become an expert in the field of emotion, so that he could continue to judge his mother with authority, to refuse her imagined apology even whilst understanding that this was damaging him and was the result of childish, misplaced rage.

Will got on well with his fellow trainees and it was a delight to him at first to be surrounded by women who were, in general, either friendly in an uncomplicated way or uninterested. As time passed, that dynamic changed, but in those early days it was something of a revelation. He was cheerful, affable, but inauthentic, superficial. Not because he wanted to be inauthentic and superficial but because he hadn't yet learned not to be. This put him quite firmly outside the inner circle. Not that the inner circle was one of selective friendships or of coteries or cliques; it was an inner circle characterised by a kind of honesty that he hadn't yet mastered. Neither had most of them at that stage, to be fair, but it seemed that people were up for having a go and it was this willingness that put them in the inner circle.

Everyone knew, almost straightaway, that something terrible had happened to him. Not because he spoke about it – it wasn't at all straightforward to tell his story. It was something about the cheerful cover-up that convinced no one. He found, in fact, that it was almost impossible to tell his story, especially as time passed. He explored this in his own therapy – with a man this time – the fact that he yearned to be seen, but feared drawing attention to himself in an explicit way. He could cope with people seeing him but it was impossible for him to say out loud, *Look at me*.

In February of that first year, he became aware that his silence was going against him. In his mind, he imagined that his tutors had a metaphorical clip board with everyone's names on it, and a series of boxes to be ticked. Have they done their studies? Participated in discussions? Acquitted themselves in the exercises? Cried? As each person cried for the first time, Will imagined a tick going in the box for that student. There was no doubt that it was more difficult for the men to cry than for most of the women, but the other two did it fairly early on. One about a love affair that had been particularly painful and the other about an act of betrayal by a male friend. But for Will, it became more and more difficult. It was as if he felt the weight of expectation on him and the 'secret' that he held about his sister's drowning became more and more problematic.

'If I hold something so huge,' he told his therapist, 'why don't I reveal it?'

'Are you ready to?' Felix asked him.

There he was. Back at stage one. He didn't really want to do anything for himself, he wanted other people to be the ones to do his process for him. Once he'd put himself in a psychologically acceptant environment, he'd expected everything to open for him like a flower, in spite of anything that he might do to resist it. But, as with the business about contact with his mother – and his sister, Kitty, as well, if he thought about it – in the end it came down to him; down to his own effort and his own resistance. He felt distanced from them both, he could admit that now, but he wasn't ready to take responsibility for the animosity in that, as though the feelings of anger had been put in him by his mother and his sister and that he'd had no part in creating them.

Right now, his resistance to change was more powerful than his desire for it, and so he remained in stasis. And it was movement that he was after. Stuckness was not the best state to be in when it came to being open about one's past, and everyone on his course noticed it.

'Why don't you trust us?' one of the women in his personal development group said to him angrily.

'That part of him is too young,' another one said. 'Still a baby, with all that infant vulnerability. If he showed himself to us, we might not accept him and then he would die. The death of a baby is the most tragic thing in the world.'

And then Will cried. He was taken completely by surprise that his tears should arrive without warning, as though he might have rehearsed the moment and know in advance exactly when he would shed them. The death of a baby! He told his story and he moved quite suddenly from being outside the circle to inside, which felt nourishing and healing. This change was helpful, but also disappointing. He had hoped that being heard and fulsomely accepted would somehow cancel out what had happened. But it didn't. The pain remained. Perhaps he got bigger, so that the pain became less of the whole, as it were. But the pain itself remained undiminished.

It was only much later that his tutor said to him, 'We are much more worried about people who blurt huge things out before the space has been made safe, than people who take their time. So long as they get there in the end.'

Ha ha! So, there *had* been a tick box!

At the end of his first year, before he took up his training placement at the Claygate Centre, he travelled up to Carlisle to talk to his mother, and to Kitty. He tried not to have an agenda, except to try to see them as human beings and not as hate objects. He was glad that his father would be there. At least there was that. His affection for his father. Love, even – that difficult word!

He was also wary of falling into the trap of asking them to apologise. He didn't know what it took to come into contact with an estranged family member, but he remembered touching fingers with Victoria and how that had been too much for him to manage at the time. Perhaps all one could do was be seen to be available, and not hostile. As with sowing a seed, he might have to leave it to germinate.

He'd talked to Jamie about his intended visit and Jamie, who was now also working in London, had volunteered to come along too. Will accepted Jamie's invitation with gratitude. It had been over a year since he'd been home and so he hadn't spent time with his family since starting his training as a therapist. Felix had said to him, 'Don't forget that your parents may well feel nervous about the possibility of being under the scrutiny of a fledgling therapist.'

'They will be under scrutiny,' said Will.

'That's what I mean,' said Felix. 'They will know this, perhaps unconsciously, and so they may be defensive. Everyone knows that parents get the blame when their children go into therapy. I'm reminded of your experiences as a student, when you used to get into fights and mete out "justice" in a rather brutal way.'

'I was just a kid then,' said Will. 'I've grown out of that sort of thing.'

'Have you?'

He paused to think for a while. 'Well, my dad has nothing to worry about – he's always been great. And Mum and Kitty have nothing to worry about either, really. It's not as though I'm going home to wreak revenge or pass judgement.'

'Aren't you?'

It was summer, so he and Jamie went for a week, leaving London at dawn on the Saturday morning and arriving for a late lunch. Their mother was cheerful but a little distracted as she served it. Will's father chatted congenially and hardly seemed to notice when they dashed off afterwards to get a short hill walk in before dinner.

They took the opportunity that week to do a couple of their favourite climbs – the twin peaks of Scafell and Scafell Pike via the Corridor Route and Pillar, with its vertiginous 'High Level

Route' via Robinson's cairn. This was a top-end walk for Will and one that always gave him a pleasantly manageable tingle of exposure. But this wasn't the purpose of his visit and he realised on his third day that he still hadn't seen or requested to see Kitty. He knew that unless he did something soon, his visit would pass without anything having happened.

So, on the Wednesday, at his invitation, Kitty came over with her husband, Mike. Will realised as soon as she arrived that she wouldn't have come unless Jamie was there. She kissed Jamie affectionately then absent-mindedly half-kissed Will as she turned to ask Mike whether he'd remembered to put the rubbish out.

Jamie sorted the pre-dinner drinks. Kitty and his mother had a gin and tonic. Will had a whisky with ice and Mike joined him.

'I'll just have the one,' he said. 'I'm driving.'

Will's father came in from the garage where he'd been giving his thirty-year-old Peugeot convertible an oil change. There was something comforting to Will in his scent of engine oil and soap. It embodied trustworthiness, somehow. Dependability. His father looked older, having managed to go from dark to grey in a couple of years. He was fifty-six but looked older, though the extra years suited him. He and Kitty were very close, Will noticed. He'd always known this, of course, but it was very obvious this evening. Mike was polite and friendly. Will realised he hardly knew him. He did conveyancing in Carlisle for the same firm where Kitty was a solicitor, and he seemed to be making her happy.

'How is the car?' asked Mike.

'More trouble than it's worth,' said Will's father.

'You always say that when it's going badly,' said Kitty, 'but you love it when it's running well.'

'That is true,' he agreed. 'It's also true of life!' he added and laughed.

'Now that Will's a budding therapist,' Jamie said, looking over at his brother encouragingly, 'he's becoming an expert on life and relationships.'

Mike, who was sitting next to him of the sofa, turned to him and gave a friendly smile. 'There's a practice in the next building to our office. I've got to know one or two of the therapists, at least a little. We get sandwiches and coffee from the same deli across the road. What sort of therapy are you studying?'

'Gestalt, mainly,' said Will, 'but with elements of person-centred and psychosynthesis.'

'Oh,' said Mike, 'that doesn't mean anything to me, I'm afraid.'

'Jamie tells me that you have to be in therapy yourself,' said his father, 'as part of your training.'

'Yes,' said Will. He took a sip of his whisky and looked at his dad. 'As a matter of fact, I've learned a few important things . . .'

There was an electric moment, as everyone in the room realised that Will was about to say something. Jamie smiled. Will took a breath.

Kitty stood up. 'No. No, Will, I don't want to be a part of

your therapy. What right have you got to come up here and unburden yourself on us, just because it's the next step for you? What about us? Did you think to ask us whether it was okay for you to come up here and say your piece, feel better about it, and then go back down south leaving us holding whatever it is that you're about to dump?'

'That's not what I was going to do at all.'

'What did you want to do?'

'I wanted to say that there seems to have been an air of blame at times over the years. But blame of any kind, and towards anyone, now seems . . . inappropriate. Redundant.'

Kitty stared at Will. 'That's great,' she hissed. 'You're the one who got all the privilege in this family. You're the one who got everything and we got nothing, and now you waltz in, all magnanimous, and forgive us all? Well, how generous! How noble!'

'Kitty . . . I–'

'Kitty, it's fine,' said their mother. 'If Will wants to talk about this, it's fine. I think it's probably a good idea for us all to talk about this.'

'Mum!'

'No, Kitty. Will wasn't talking about forgiveness. He was talking about blame. And he's right. I've thought about this and I think that there has been a lot of blame about, and I think maybe we should talk about it.'

'No,' said Kitty. 'No.' She looked around the room. 'Come on, Mike, I think we'd better go.'

'Wouldn't you rather be part of this, than be outside it?' Mike asked.

'No, I wouldn't.'

Mike got up with an apologetic shrug. Kitty walked out of the room without saying anything to anyone. Mike followed, closing the door gently behind him. They could hear the murmur of voices from the hall and then the closing of the front door.

'This had better be worthwhile,' said Will's mother, 'given the fallout your father and I are going to suffer as a result of that departure.'

'I'm sorry,' said Will.

'That's okay,' she said. 'Now say what you have to say.'

'I don't really have anything specific to say,' he said.

'Well,' she said, 'that scene was unnecessary, wasn't it?'

'It wasn't that I wanted to say anything specific,' Will told her, 'but that I wanted this not to be off limits, something that we don't talk about.'

'That's what I mean. Let's talk about it. You start.'

'I feel you're being hostile.'

She laughed a quick brittle laugh. 'No, Will, I'm being accommodating. I want you to say whatever it is you have to say, and then I can respond to it. I suppose you feel that I blamed you for how things were after the accident?'

'I'm not sure blame is the right word. But you distanced yourself from me after that.'

His mother threw her hands up. 'I knew it would come back to me like this. I knew it!'

She closed her eyes for a moment, took a deep breath before opening them, then looked intensely at Will, as though she wasn't sure that what she wanted to say could be communicated in words alone.

'After the accident,' she said, 'you took all the blame on yourself, Will. I told you that you weren't to blame. I was very specific about it. Perhaps you remember that and perhaps you don't. But you withdrew into yourself, into a cocoon of blame. I tried being close to you. I tried to cuddle and hug you, or simply to touch you, but you froze and drew back whenever I did that. And so I left you alone. That's about the hardest thing a mother can do to a son – a much-loved son, I might say – but there was no choice in the end. You hid yourself and became untouchable, unreachable, and then you pulled away from us as a family by going all Scottish on us.'

Will felt a frisson of embarrassment and could feel his cheeks flush red.

'And the ridiculous thing is that you're all Scottish except me,' he said. 'What an irony!'

'Of course you're Scottish,' said his father. 'Your mother and I were both born in Scotland and two of your grandparents are Scottish. So in my book that makes *you* Scottish.'

'But I was born in England,' said Will. 'I was born in Carlisle. I'm English! Mum was born in Scotland to English parents and she sees herself as Scottish, so what's the difference?'

'You were only born in England because that was the nearest maternity hospital with a bed,' said his mother. 'You can look at it either way, I suppose. I think of all of us as Scottish, we're a Scottish family.'

'I never bought a kilt when I went to university,' Will said suddenly. 'I could be all Scots to everyone, but I knew it would be a step too far to wear a kilt if I was born in England.'

'We can argue about kilts another time,' said his mother. 'Even without a kilt you became more Scottish than the rest of us. You used it to be different from us, to distance yourself from us.'

Will shrugged, and then nodded. 'You're right. I did.'

'Do you have any idea what it was like for a mother to have a daughter drown, and then for a son to withdraw from her? It was like a double bereavement.'

'It felt like I was just trying to survive.'

'We were *all* trying to survive,' said his father. 'And, in general, I'd say we did quite well.'

'I wasn't cold towards you,' Will's mother told him. 'Precisely the opposite. But you were so distant. It was frightening, once it became so rigid and unchanging. I was frightened of what might come up in me, too, if you ever tried to get closer – frightened of the pain and loss and grief, especially if you ever withdrew again. I have wondered for many years whether we could ever get closer, and I've been preparing myself for a conversation like this. I don't think I would ever have made the first move, but . . .'

'You had to become a teacher to help pay for my school fees. You must have resented me for that.'

'Teaching was the making of me,' his mother said, simply. 'I resented it at the time, but it gave me something tangible to do that wasn't just the kind of part-time work I'd had before. It had some career logic to it that was in addition to bringing up a family. I have now helped hundreds of children. My own family may have been a bit of a disaster area in some ways, but nevertheless I do feel that I am of some use in the world.'

Will felt blindsided by the flooding sense of love he felt for his mother and found himself unsure what to say. He'd presupposed she'd put herself at a great distance from him, and that to start to bridge the gap he would have to call to her from afar. And now, here she was right beside him. It was immediately clear that his assumption of the necessity of an apology from her was selfish nonsense.

'The problem as I see it,' said his father, 'is that you held it all in, Will. You could never share it. You never saw the tragedy of Charlotte's death as being something that we were all in together. Every one of us. It nearly broke us apart as a family – your mother and I nearly didn't survive together. Our relationship nearly came apart, and that was because we held it all in, our grief. It was only when she and I realised that we were in the same boat together that we began to talk to each other again. You mentioned blame earlier. Well, it's true what you say about it being inappropriate. I think we all have reason to blame ourselves for what happened, me no less than anyone else. And every one of us could come up with reasons to blame others, if they wanted to. But blaming just keeps a wound from healing.'

He paused to consider what to say next, finished his drink in a single gulp, and then continued.

'When you went to Dalmacallan, it seemed to you that you were being "sent away", but what were we to do? Keep you in Carlisle, where your school life had become impossible? We even considered home educating you, which might have been a good option considering the expense of school fees. But you were too uncomfortable in this house, and in this family. We could see that we were losing you, but what other option was there? We could see that Kitty aimed all her anger and guilt at you – she still does, of course. And you took all that blame and put it on yourself. But there was something else as well, something hard to put into words . . .'

'I think I blamed "the family" both as a set of relationships and as a concept,' said Will.

'At least you had Jamie,' said his mother. 'We were glad about that.'

'I think I was too young to really understand what was going on,' said Jamie.

'No,' said his father, 'you took it in alright. I'm sure Will can corroborate that. A five-year-old is incredibly aware of what's going on.'

Will nodded. 'It's true, Jamie.'

'Children may not be able to express themselves well in words,' said their mother, 'but that doesn't mean they don't understand.'

'Well, perhaps if I felt anything,' said Jamie, 'maybe I felt that it was my responsibility to keep us all together.'

'Yes,' said his father, 'you were the one who did that. I remember you doing it, even when you were five, coming round each one of us in turn and making sure that we were okay.'

'Perhaps it's because I'm gay.'

'It's because you have always been sweet natured,' said his mother.

'Burdened by responsibility,' Jamie said, and laughed.

'That's true,' said his father. 'It must be true. Why would you have taken that on yourself, unless you had a sense of responsibility?'

Jamie nodded. 'I'm a rescuer. Will and I have talked about this before, not just since he's started training as a therapist. I'm a rescuer. I always have been. This is where it came from. I see that now.' He looked across at Will. 'Perhaps one day I'll manage to stop falling in love with men who need to be rescued.'

So, something had happened, something positive had shifted. What a revelation that was! Will had been so clear about what the situation was with his parents and what he believed about it, and he'd been so wrong. It was going to take time to assimilate what had happened, but it was a real first step. The rest of the week had been positive, too. Quiet, almost deferential to this burgeoning new dynamic. It was as if he had discovered that his parents were benevolent strangers, that he did not know them at all. And they, likewise, needed to feel their way forward with Will. There was something both beautiful and fragile about this, like a delicate flower opening. At the end of the week as he and Jamie left, it felt new and straightforward to say, 'See you soon.'

When Will returned to London, he felt both pleased and surprised. The conversation hadn't happened at all as he'd imagined. Not that he'd had any particular idea of content, but he'd imagined that he would have to draw his mother into some sort of dialogue, and then other family members might join in. But his parents had been ready to come into contact with him, had been waiting – maybe for years – for him to make that first move. How strange! He suddenly felt an overwhelming sense of love for both of them, and for Jamie, and for Kitty who was still locked into the story of how things were. How ridiculous and narcissistic of him to imagine that they were the ones who needed to apologise!

When he saw Felix again, he gave him a blow-by-blow account of what had happened and said, 'My mother was never cold towards me! She was cautious. She was giving me a respectful distance. Why did I see it the way I did?'

'A child will interpret things using a child's logic. It was completely logical to interpret what was happening to you in the way you did. Your mother kept a distance from you because it was too painful for her to keep trying – and failing – to come into contact. It was logical for you to imagine that she had become cold towards you. You went to school away from home, and it was logical to feel that you were being sent away. Your logic was faultless. It was incorrect, that's all.'

'And I became locked into my own loveless world.'

'From which you eventually emerged.'

'That is true, up to a point, but there's something that hasn't yet emerged. I can feel it but can't put my finger on it.'

Felix pondered this for a few moments. 'You need to own this, I think. That there remains something in you, a residue from the accident that you still haven't addressed.'

'It's clear that my parents don't blame me for what happened. And that has made me stop blaming them. Quite suddenly, that's gone! But the person I have always blamed more than anyone else is myself. How can I stop doing that?'

Seven

Will went to the Claygate Centre on Monday feeling as rested and ready as he would ever be. He was pleased that his first client was Guy, the man haunted by his dead sister, now booked for weekly therapy in the 'quiet slot': 9.00 am on Monday mornings. It was their first proper session after the initial assessment.

Will started by checking that Guy had been to his GP to discuss his state of mind, which he had, so that was good. In the session, though, Guy avoided the subject of his dead sister and spoke about his travels abroad over the past few years, backpacking around Asia and Australasia. He was suffering the young professional's dilemma of finally earning enough money to travel but having no time to do so. Will couldn't help smiling to himself during the session. Guy reminded Will of his younger self. He had that same tragic air of carrying a secret, of being unable to express the apparently unspeakable.

Quite often, Will found, prospective clients would blurt out the reason why they wanted therapy in their assessment only to shy away from the subject once they'd started the work.

And this, it seemed, was true of Guy. He didn't mention his sister at all, but her 'ghost' was in the room nevertheless, unacknowledged. And that was fine. She could remain there until Guy felt able to acknowledge her and then they could ask her to step into the space in an appropriate way. As he thought this, Will shivered, remembering the woman in the red sweater and white jeans apparently looking down at him from the London Eye.

The session concluded and Guy left. How pleasant to be at the beginning of building a relationship and not to have any conflict! He'd had his fill of that during previous client sessions and, whatever might lie ahead, it was great to have got one unproblematic session under his belt.

His next client was supposed to be Irene, the Hungarian client to whom he'd admitted being unable to remember their session. He sat in his room waiting to see if she would turn up and was unsurprised when she didn't. There was a certain slamming of a door that was decidedly final. Of course, he would contact her to offer her a last session, but in this case he was sure that it would be a mere formality. He spent the rest of the hour writing up his notes for Guy's file.

Rachel was next, and he found that he had a nervous flutter in his stomach at the thought of seeing her. She had left in such a rage the previous time, after his assertion that her husband had been married once before. Perhaps, like Irene, she wouldn't turn up, which would be both a worry and a relief.

He sat expectantly, trying to clear his mind for what was

coming and glanced through his notes from the previous session, which made disquieting reading. It wasn't unusual for a client to leave in tears at the end of a session, but it *was* unusual for the therapist to be as out of his depth as he had felt and, he reminded himself, for that therapist not to have had supervision in the meantime. He tried to calm himself but found there was an agitation that would not subside, an agitation coloured by a risky sense of anticipation that was all the more disconcerting because it contained an undeniable tinge of pleasure. He went out into reception to chat with Becky for a few minutes until, bang on time at 10.30, Rachel rang the bell.

She looked rather tense as she followed him into the room.

'Good morning,' he said to her as he sat down. 'How are you today?'

She looked a little wide-eyed for a moment before settling back into a neutral expression. Her hair and make-up were perfect, as usual, and she wore a pale green dress that made her look slimmer than he remembered.

'How did you know!' she demanded, almost belligerently.

'Know what?'

'How did you know that my husband had been married before?'

'I didn't. I don't know where that came from, and I apologise to you unreservedly for my mistake. I sometimes make a howler like that, and all I can say is I'm genuinely sorry for the distress it caused you.'

'But it was true.'

'Oh . . .' Will was lost for words.

'I went home and told Ben what you'd said, and it was the strangest thing . . . he burst into tears.'

He waited while Rachel gathered herself to go on. Sometimes he had to force himself to show interest in what his clients were saying, but this time he had to restrain himself from leaning forward.

'It was a bit weird,' she said, 'because I've only ever seen Ben cry once before, and that was when the side of the conservatory he built on the back of the house collapsed. But I was sitting there with a glass of wine before we had dinner and I told him what you'd said. And he started crying.'

She paused, breathless at the memory.

'And then he blurted it all out. That he'd been married before and hadn't told me straight away when we first met. And then he said that he'd started to realise that I have a habit of making unfavourable comparisons between myself and other people, especially women. Which I do, I know.'

She laughed briefly at that thought, surprised by it.

'Well, it turns out that his first wife was a model. Not a glamour model, but someone who demonstrated luxurious stuff at boat shows at Earls Court and that kind of thing. It was a short, infatuated marriage that lasted for as long as it took him to realise the mistake he'd made, and for her to spend all of his money. Then he left her and he put it behind him. He admitted that he'd always felt uncomfortable about not telling me because he's not a natural liar, which is true.

But he said that as time passed it became more and more difficult. Which I suppose is true. Hard to say those things in a casual way, isn't it? You know, dropping it into the conversation after you're married as though it's insignificant.' She laughed. 'He was so relieved, at the opportunity to confess, bless him!'

Will smiled. 'Well, it's funny how sometimes a mistake like that can happen at the right moment. I'm really pleased. For myself, too, because it seems that this has turned out well.'

She smiled, but there was a hint of incredulity there. 'There's more to this than meets the eye,' she said. 'And I'm not going to question it, because I am beginning to realise that something really important is happening here. I don't know how you're doing what you're doing, Will, but thank you. I mean . . . well, thank you.' Tears welled up and she looked away.

Will smiled but spoke seriously. 'Please, Rachel, don't try to make this all seem supernatural. If there has been some movement, you are the one who has to take the responsibility – and credit – for that.'

Rachel shrugged. 'Have it your way.'

Will spent the rest of the session bathing in reflected glory. He was aware that a therapist needed to refrain as far as possible from taking too much credit for a client's progress, but this was extremely pleasant after their last session and after what he'd been fearing.

At the end of their time, as Rachel was getting up, she

smiled. 'I have to say I'm really looking forward to our next group session. It's a shame we didn't have one last week.'

Will tried not to look surprised, but he froze a little in his chair. Rachel didn't seem to notice. She was leaning down as she picked up her bag.

Group session? What did that mean?

He took out his phone after she'd gone and checked his calendar. There it was. On Thursday evening. *Therapy group. Training room. 7.30pm – 9.30pm.* The previous one had been two weeks before, during his concussion. When had he booked them in? And who was going to be coming along other than Rachel? He went out and checked the computer in reception, looking up the practice room bookings. Yes, there it was. He'd booked the main training room. He smiled at Becky but didn't say anything. He realised, as he'd realised before, that saying anything at all would be to make him sound insane. But then, how did he know that he wasn't?

Suddenly, he found himself back in that vaguely panicky state of wondering what was going to happen next, a shadowy feeling that anything was possible. And not in a good way.

In the evening, he saw Stuart, his about-to-be-forty gay client, and Will was pleased to be seeing someone so genial. Granted, their last session had ended in tears, but at least Stuart was straightforward in his own way. When he turned up, he looked calm and settled, which was helpful. Even though Will was very clear that appearances could often be deceptive, it was still comforting when a client arrived looking cheerful.

'I'm sorry about what I said last week,' Will said. 'About the letter. I know you were distressed by–'

'But Will,' said Stuart, leaning forward. '*How did you know about it?*'

Will was speechless. He'd imagined the letter, hadn't he? Stuart had been emphatic about it. There had never been a letter.

'It was exactly as you described. The letter from Gregg, asking me to marry him. It really was written on blue paper and scented with Fahrenheit perfume. And he left it on my pillow, like you said.'

'Well,' said Will, 'I'm glad you remember it now. That's how I remember it, too.'

'But I didn't know. So I couldn't have told you! How could you remember something that I didn't know?'

'You must have told me and then forgotten about it.'

'No. I saw Gregg last night and told him what you said. And, do you know what? He burst into tears!'

Will's sense of *déjà vu* was increasing by the second. But there it was – again – a little thrill of awe and admiration for what had happened. He didn't say anything and waited for Stuart to continue.

'I related what you'd said to me, and Gregg was amazed because that's *exactly* what happened. He *did* write to me and ask me to marry him. He wrote the letter on blue paper and scented it with Fahrenheit and left it on my pillow for me to find later in the day. He was going away for a fortnight on business, so wouldn't be around for a while. The letter was a spur of the moment thing. He was going to Zoom me from Rome. But then he had a change of heart. He realised that I would never settle down in the way that he wanted me to.'

Stuart began to cry, in a quiet way, calmly, so that tears rolled down his cheeks but without any other sign that he felt this sadness.

'And he was right,' he said. 'I've never been capable of staying in a relationship with anyone. Not that that was a problem in some of the easy-going and relaxed liaisons I had, because it wasn't asked for. But I have, at times, asked it of myself. That's really why I'm here – it's not because I'm going to be forty! Or maybe it is because I'm going to be forty, but not in the way that I presented it to you before. It's more like, *Oh, for God's sake, you're nearly forty, Stuart, and you still haven't sorted this one out!* I realise that I am compulsively unsettled because I feel that I'll never be forgiven for what I have done. I *wanted* Gregg to leave me, to punish me.'

He laughed at himself and wiped the tears away with a brisk swipe of his arm.

'But that's not really the point, right now,' he went on. 'The main thing is, how did you know that Gregg left the letter for me? After he'd done it and had time to think, he went back to the bedroom, took it from my pillow and destroyed it. And told no one. No one, Will, and particularly not me. So how did you know?'

Will raised both hands. 'I don't know.'

Stuart looked at him.

'Gregg left me shortly after that, you know,' he said. 'I think it broke his heart. To love me and to know it wasn't going to work. Well, it is heart breaking. I'm amazed that we're still friends.'

They fell into silence for a few seconds. Seconds that began to stretch. Usually, Will made himself allow his clients to break the silence, but there seemed to be an imperative for him here, rather than for his client.

'Stuart, I have never felt that I have to hold the same worldview as my clients. Otherwise, how would an atheist therapist ever be able to work with someone who was religious, or vice versa? But this . . . well, it sounds like you're making an assumption that I'm psychic.'

Stuart looked as him as if to say, 'Well, aren't you?'

Will took a deep breath. 'Stuart, I am not psychic.'

'So how did you know about the letter?'

'I don't know. Some things are mysterious. Sometimes, when two people are in tune, the intuition that arises can feel a little psychic, when it's not.'

'It's not intuition to know something so specific, so detailed.'

He had a point, and Will was also puzzled by this. He'd had situations before where he'd been spooked by apparently keying into an unspoken secret that his client was holding. But this was rather different.

'Something's happening, isn't it?' said Stuart.

Will looked at him but could think of no rational or reasonable response.

'Ha!' Stuart cried, gleefully. 'You're not denying it! That means it's true!'

'Stuart, the fact that I have no explanation for this is no reason to imagine complicity, or even a conspir–'

'No, no! I'm not accusing you of trying to deceive me. I'm just saying something's happening. I'm not being personal.'

'Something's always happening.'

Stuart grinned. 'No worries, Will. You're a therapist. I understand.'

This time when silence fell, Will made no effort to end it. He made no effort to end it because he didn't have any idea what to make of what was going on. This was not unusual, but there now seemed to be extra layers of not knowing, from a vague puzzlement, to this – which on the surface was about as challenging to his world view as it was possible to get.

'Sometimes,' he said to Stuart eventually, 'it's important to sit with something and let the meaning gradually percolate to the surface. The process of understanding life and relationships is littered with plausible assumptions that turn out to be false. So, let's put that to one side for the moment, if we can. I want to go back and acknowledge what you said in earlier sessions, about having done something unforgiveable. Can we go back to that? You said in our last session that you felt ready to tell me about it, although that was before I mentioned the letter, and before you got upset.'

Stuart smiled with an air of indulgence as though Will was a child. 'I don't want to talk about that right now. It's funny, but I thought telling my secret to someone who could listen and not judge me was the most important thing in the world. But you're right . . . there's something here that needs to be left alone to percolate to the surface. Telling you what I've done might burst that feeling of mystery. Yes, I know . . . you might say that keeping my secret right now, when I feel strong enough to tell you, is resistance of some kind. Well, that may be true, but let's leave it alone for now anyway so that I can sit with this feeling of, well . . . *possibility*, for a while. Please.'

Will smiled. 'It's your session, Stuart.'

Stuart continued to smile for the last few minutes. When they were ending, he said, 'One other thing, Will. Thank you for the group session a couple of weeks ago.'

Will made a non-committal noise.

'I'm looking forward to the next one,' Stuart said.

He took Lara out for a late meal that night, at Belluno's, an Italian restaurant in Clapham. He didn't want to be at home. Somehow, the fact that he felt weird didn't matter so much when he was out in public, surrounded by bustle and anonymity. To be at home and still feel weird would be too much to bear. When Lara asked him if he was okay, he said, 'My clients are freaking me out a little, that's all.'

'Oh? In what way?'

THE LOST SESSIONS

'I seem to know things that I shouldn't – or even couldn't. It's made a couple of them think I'm psychic.'

'Wow! You could play havoc with them if you wanted to be mischievous. Maybe you should tell them that you know, psychically, that they should pay twice as much for their sessions.'

Will laughed with her for a moment before sobering. 'It is a little freaky, though. Without going into detail, I really did seem to "know" one or two quite striking details that I shouldn't have known.'

'Well that happens, doesn't it? It's standard coincidence that happens from time to time.'

Will remembered the expressions of both Rachel and Stuart and felt a beat of strangeness.

Lara, put her hand on his and squeezed gently. 'You've been really unsettled by this, haven't you? Do you remember the time when that guy mistook you for the undertaker who buried his mother? That was weird, but when we looked up their website, you looked so similar to him that you could see why the mistake was made.'

'Point taken. Although perhaps that was a little different. But let's talk about something else. I'd rather hear about your day. Listening to you will also have the side effect of stopping me from over-thinking what's going on with my clients.'

'You haven't done that since your very early days. Are you sure you're okay? Maybe you need to take more time off work? Maybe, if it continues to unsettle you, you could sort out an emergency supervision session.'

'Mmm.' He sipped his beer and looked expectantly at her.

'Alright!' she said. 'Actually, it's been a good day. I think I've been asked to design an eight-week physical movement course for De Beauvoir Studios. They think they might offer a programmatic and structured therapeutic movement course, then see if anyone's interested.'

'What do you mean you *think* you've been asked to do it?'

'No one ever says things directly at De Beauvoir. That's how they are. There's a code to it all, as if it's a little rude to ever talk business. But, yes, next year's brochure was being discussed and they've offered me a slot.'

'That's fantastic. You look both pleased and not pleased. Is there a catch?'

'Well, I have to design the course and work out the content. There's no fee for that. I would only get paid if people sign up for it.'

'Will that take a little time? A lot of time?'

'Lots and lots of time. The idea is to break everything down neatly so that it can be covered in eight sessions. I need to revisit all my theory of movement and tie that into what I have learned as a practitioner. In any case, it's long past time I pulled it all together into something consistent. If it works, it can be offered as a regular slot. And of course you only have to design it once. If it works *well*, I could offer it elsewhere, too.'

'The Thomas Method.' He smiled. 'It worked on me.'

'I wasn't Thomas, then,' she said. 'It's the Armstrong Method. It was you who used the Thomas Method.'

'I love you.' He reached out to take her hand. 'I really need that at the moment.'

'Oh, Will . . . you're trembling.'

The unpleasant thrill that passed through his body as he'd taken her hand subsided and they sat like that for a while. In fact, it was in this romantic tableau that they were disturbed by someone who stopped at their table.

Will looked up. It was a woman in a red sweater and white jeans. He glanced down involuntarily. Yes, her jeans were tucked into cowboy boots. She was looking at him as if undecided about what to say. She was pale, with distinct dark eyebrows and intense green eyes, half closed in a slightly mischievous expression. She opened her mouth to speak and then, quite suddenly, changed her mind and walked away.

Lara watched her go and then turned to Will. 'Who was that?'

'I have no idea.'

'Well, she certainly seemed to know who you are.'

'Yes, she certainly seemed to.'

'She's not your secret mistress?' Lara wore a playful smile, as if trying to lighten the mood.

Will smiled weakly.

She laughed. 'It's okay, I was only joking.'

'I love you,' he said.

Lara welled up and took his hand again.

'It's been a bit of a freaky day,' he told her, 'and with that strange woman, the evening seems to be continuing in a similar vein.'

Lara smiled. 'I could cope with a bit of weirdness right now. My life is too straightforward these days. I wouldn't mind a vibrant and youthful stranger coming up to me as though I really meant something to him. It might make me feel . . . well . . . mysterious and important.'

'No, it wouldn't. It would freak you out. It would make you wonder if he was insane and dangerous.'

'Yes,' she said, thoughtfully. 'I guess you're right. How sad that we can't be simply mystified any more. We're all too suspicious.'

The following day, Will only had two clients, Debbie and Christina. Debbie was a fifty-seven-year-old woman who'd recently had a terminal diagnosis and was struggling to come to terms with it. Christina was a twenty-four-year-old bulimic. Both were trying to cope with a feeling of emptiness. As he waited for Debbie to arrive, Will had the strange sensation that he had entered a new psychological landscape for himself. It was as though he was finally listening to the advice he'd given to Stuart the day before, and to the advice that his course leader had given endlessly over the two years of his training. Take it as it comes. It's fine to not know. Allow things to simply be and something will arise. Don't force the rational mind to interpret and inevitably then to judge.

Still, for both of these clients, it was their first session since the lost sessions and so there was some anxiety. But Will had reached a place that seemed, on the surface at least, to have some of the qualities of acceptance.

When Debbie started to talk of what had happened in their last session, he braced himself. He couldn't change what she'd experienced, but perhaps he could allow himself to be present and hear her account properly, rather than be defensive as he had been with the others.

'I was bemused,' she told him, then stopped for a couple of breaths. 'Yes, *bemused* is the right word. I was bemused when you lay down on the floor at my feet and went to sleep. I sat there and looked down at you, looking so calm and so benign, and so happy as you slept. Of course, I was concerned about you because of your black eye and your bruised face and that huge dressing over your forehead, and I wondered if you were ill and needed attention. But before you lay down, you said – in such a quiet voice that I barely heard it – "Don't worry", and that was helpful. I spent the whole session looking down at you as you were sleeping. It was hard at first because nothing seemed to be happening, but then I started to realise you were giving me permission, though I couldn't be sure what kind of permission. And then, when the time came, I let myself out of the room as quietly as possible, so as not to disturb you. Although I was also a bit worried that you might not wake up in time for your next client.'

'On the face of it, that seems to be quite an unusual thing for a therapist to do,' said Will.

Debbie nodded. 'Yes, I thought so too. But, you know, there was clearly something to be learned from it. I thought I was sitting in this room for the purpose of telling you my woes, but you weren't listening. I mean, it wasn't that I was being ignored, either. It wasn't a case of someone being in a position to pay attention and then choosing not to. Perhaps it was important for me to witness peace in another person and to be allowed to sit and take it in. I would never have chosen to sit in a room with a sleeping person. That was the bemusing bit . . . to sit there and think to myself, "What am I supposed to be doing"?' She laughed at the thought of it. 'But there wasn't any room for my pain and that was actually – and I don't know what this means for me – it was actually alright.'

Later, Christina, the client with bulimia, made no mention of her lost session. It was as if Will had conducted a perfectly ordinary session with her and that, in its own way, made her case as mystifying as the others.

When Will finished at 2.30pm, he had, yet again, a feeling of strangeness and an unwillingness to go home. He still couldn't say why this was the case, but he felt instinctively that he should heed the intuition. He walked to Kennington Park and sat for a while on a bench. It was a cold day for late March, with a keen wind, and he sat huddled into his coat in the thin spring sunshine, looking out at the ducks on the pond. He phoned Jamie at The University of the Arts London, where he worked in the IT department. When Jamie answered, Will said, 'Hello Jamie, I don't really know why I'm calling you. I feel a little strange and I don't feel I can go home right now.'

'Where are you?' Jamie sounded concerned. When Will told him, he said, 'I'm on my way.'

They met in a small, traditional neighbourhood bar. Will felt quite peaceful, but just . . . strange.

'How are you?' Will asked.

'How are *you*?' Jamie countered.

Will shrugged and went to get them a coffee. When he got back, Jamie said, 'I was thinking of you this morning. I was remembering our visits to Caerlaverock Castle when we were kids.'

'That must be an early memory. I don't think we ever visited Caerlaverock after the accident. You must have been, what? Four? Five?'

'No, we went with Sarah Galloway, do you remember? That means I must have been at least ten.'

Will smiled at the memory. 'That must have been the day we went to climb Criffell?'

'Yes, it must have been,' said Jamie. 'The Big Hill.'

They'd been able to see Criffell in the distance from the kitchen window when they were still living in Dumfriesshire. The Big Hill. Their mother often spoke of it. Of course, the Lake District mountains were closer once they'd moved, but the Big Hill was in Scotland, and that made all the difference. Caerlaverock Castle itself represented something of that too, the magnificent ruin. Didn't that fit their family, too? A noble image of the aftermath of tragedy.

'Never mind that, though,' said Jamie. 'What's up?'

Will sat silent for a moment. He pondered Jamie's question but no simple answer arose.

'Will, spit it out. Don't go all older-brother and silent on me or I'll clock you one.'

'I don't know what to say . . .'

'Right,' said Jamie. 'Let's start at the beginning. Why don't you want to go home?'

Will couldn't say.

'Look,' said Jamie, 'I think I've decided to start worrying about you. I'm giving myself permission to do this because you're sitting beside me and you're behaving out of character. I'm not going to let you go until I understand this. It's not the usual melancholy, is it?'

'No. And please, don't worry. I'm not upset or ill or anything. I just feel a little strange.'

'I think I'm going to take you to hospital. It's only a few days since you bashed your head.'

'No, no!' said Will. 'That's stupid.'

'Why? Last time I saw you, which isn't that long ago, you were telling me that odd things were happening in your client work because your memory had been affected by your head injury, and that you were going to take another week off work. Now you're acting in a very other-worldly way. Like someone who's still being affected by concussion if you ask me. I think it's legitimate for me to worry.'

Will laughed. 'Alright, yes. Point taken. I am acting that way, it's true. But, actually, it's for a completely different reason. I'm a bit baffled by my clients at the moment. It's not concussion. I've been trying to "let things arise", and maybe I need to be away from home to let that happen.'

'You'd need to be on your own for that. But you asked to see me. So, tell me what's baffling you. And, I'm sorry, pleading confidentiality is not allowed. You can talk in general terms if you need to.'

Will thought for a moment. 'I don't know. It looks like some of my clients are beginning to ascribe supernatural powers to me.'

'Isn't that standard stuff in therapy? When I saw the child psychologist at school after the accident, I sometimes thought she was looking inside my head and reading my thoughts. Sadly, that wasn't true, or she wouldn't have been such a shit therapist.'

'This seems different,' said Will. 'It's difficult to give a concrete example while talking in general terms.'

'Have a go.'

'You know that I mentioned making gaffes with my clients last time I saw you?'

'Mm-hmm.'

'Well, it looks like some of them at least weren't gaffes.'

'And?'

'I seem to have somehow "known" things that were impossible for me to have known.'

'Well, we've always known that you were intuitive, Will.'

'I also seem to be seeing someone that one of my clients described to me.'

'Unusual, maybe, but surely not impossible?'

'This person is dead.'

Jamie looked concerned. 'I think I should take you to hospital.'

Will sighed. 'I'm not concussed, Jamie, and I don't need to go to hospital. Let me sit here and be a little freaked out, please. That's all I'm asking.'

'Okay, okay. But I reserve the right to take you to hospital later, if I think you need it. Agreed?'

'Agreed. Now, let's talk about you instead. Help me take my mind off this. How's it going, without Joel?'

'Will, it's Tuesday afternoon. I've just walked out of work. This is not nothing. I am going to have to explain myself to my manager tomorrow. And if I say, "I went off to a bar to discuss boyfriend trouble with my brother", do you have any idea what he'll say to me?'

'Yes, but of course you'll find another way to describe it, especially if you say I was acting strangely and you had to decide whether or not to take me to hospital.'

'True. If I really went for it, I could make this scene sound full-on worrying.'

Will didn't say anything. He sipped his coffee pensively.

'If you could see how not-exaggerating I was when I said that, you would perhaps be a little bit more worried about yourself than you are.'

'I'll have a think about that. Let me settle and then I'll be fine. So, come on and tell me how you're feeling now that Joel's gone back to Australia. You're just deflecting.'

'And so are you! Still, maybe if I tell you, then we'll get that out of the way.' Jamie paused, looking suddenly sad. 'It's a bit like giving up smoking. I say that and I've never even smoked! But I've talked to people who have, and they say that it's fine most of the time, but there are certain moments – like when they have a coffee after a meal or when they have an alcoholic drink in a social setting – when it's absolutely hell and the longing for a cigarette is overwhelming. Well, that's what I feel about Joel. And it happens at really odd moments. Like when I'm choosing vegetables in the supermarket – he was so particular about that – or when deciding whether to cook Italian or Indian. And it's not the sex I miss – well, I do miss that – but it's more the comfortableness of it all, you know. I could get sex right now, if I wanted to. Just by clicking an App. But that's not any relief from loneliness, is it?'

'No,' said Will.

'Loneliness is an itch,' said Jamie. 'Well, not exactly an itch. But something. I used to think of it as being boredom, but that doesn't describe it either because there's an agitation in there that stops me being able to settle to anything. I decide to read a book, but then that seems boring. I watch a film and switch off after twenty minutes. I phone a friend and find myself saying goodbye after five minutes, and then I feel . . . well, anxious and unsettled, and lonely. It's strange, I have so many friends and people who support me, and here I am, lonely. Really lonely. Heart-wrenchingly lonely. So lonely, it's an anguish to carry on and pretend that I'm not lonely. And it's not being without Joel. Not really. I feel this every time I'm alone, which is why I grab the next man that needs to be rescued, because I can't bear the emptiness I feel when I'm on my own.'

'Oh, Jamie, I'm sorry,' said Will.

'It's okay,' laughed Jamie. 'Like I say, it's like giving up smoking. It's actually fine most of the time, but then there are these moments when it's hell.'

Somehow, Jamie's words made Will come down a level and into his own skin. He realised that this was why he'd wanted to see his brother. He'd wanted to be with someone who could bring him out of being stuck in his own stuff. Being concerned about Jamie had nothing of Will in it. What a relief!

'Maybe this afternoon has gone past the point of no return?' he said. 'Let me buy you a wee drink.'

'Well, there probably isn't any point going back to work now,' Jamie agreed, 'especially if I need to keep an eye on you.'

'But I suddenly feel okay!' Will laughed. 'Really. Out of nowhere. It's like a shadow lifting. Or suddenly realising that what you'd thought was something dangerous in the bushes is in fact just a trick of the light and not a monster at all.'

'I'll drink to that,' said Jamie.

Eight

The next day, Will was pleased to see a new assessment in his diary for a potential client called Emma, who was booked in for mid-afternoon. He'd had a couple of regular client sessions the evening before that had the by-now familiar pattern of sitting with the unknown, of allowing his clients to talk about their lost sessions. One of them, Matt, a thirty-two-year-old with two broken marriages under his belt, had spoken with wonder about how Will had taken all his clothes off and sat, relaxed and completely naked, for most of their session.

'What a risk to take!' said Matt. 'I could probably have you struck off for doing something like that. But it was the right thing to do, wasn't it? There was nothing sexual in it at all.'

He laughed with an uninhibited brightness, a naked honesty in his eyes, as Will winced inside at the thought of it, and the thought of what a supervisor might say.

'It unlocked something for me,' Matt continued. 'I had never thought before that I have sexualised my body and what I do with it, that I walk through the world primarily as a sexual being and that's what I mean when I refer to myself as a man. But you sat there, fully a man, without any overtone – or undertone – of that being sexual in the context of sitting in a room alone together. Obviously, I wasn't attracted to you, but that was the point, wasn't it? You can be a man without the need for sexual desire. I can be a man without the need for that. I can be a man with women without the need for that. Wow! That's what you've been trying to tell me all along and I didn't get it until you showed me that being naked isn't sexual – it's truthful in a sense that I have yet to grasp.'

He smiled at Will with a tenderness that caught something in him, that somehow mellowed his caution, enabled him to smile back, to be tender, too.

'You risked a lot to show me that, Will,' said Matt. 'I'll never forget it.'

Once again, Will had the eerie sense of stepping into someone else's shoes. It was as if another therapist had been doing his work for him. Like a locum doctor, this person had stepped in, and now Will was taking over from him on his return from whatever mysterious place he had visited. The thing that was unsettling and challenging was that this other – unknown and unmet – therapist had been so radical. He'd disregarded professional ethics, shouted at his clients, gone to sleep at their feet, burst into tears, and now, Will discovered, taken his clothes off. The scary thing was that everyone seemed to have been helped by it. And now they wanted more. Will was willing, in principle, to comply. Therapists needed to take risks after all, within certain parameters. But more of what? He had some facts, some details, of what had happened in Matt's session and he had Matt's interpretation of Will's nakedness. But he didn't have any sense of why the choice had been made to become naked. Why that particular intervention? If he were to take his clothes off with all his clients, he could guarantee that they would have very different interpretations of that, some of which would not be therapeutically helpful. Also, his clients did not all give blow-by-blow accounts of their lost sessions. Why would they? They alluded to the content in vague and unsettling ways.

Will wondered about congruence and authenticity. Unless he could understand the motivation of this 'person' who had held the space in his absence, how could he possibly give anyone more of the same?

The other thing that intimidated – and excited – him, along with the breathtaking risks that this 'other' Will had taken, was how impressive he'd been. From time to time, he felt an awe that prickled his skin.

Later, he had his assessment with Emma. Becky phoned through from reception to say that she'd arrived and Will went to collect her. As he entered the waiting area, he recognised her immediately. Red sweater, white jeans. Cowboy boots. Emma smiled and stood, putting the magazine that she'd been looking at back on the coffee table in front of her. Will stood there, breathless and rather taken aback.

'Um . . .' he said.

Emma smiled, and Will, frozen for a second, jerked back into movement and managed to speak with surprising calm.

'Come this way, please,' he told her, and she followed him down the corridor to his room.

When they entered, sunshine was falling across his chair and he could feel the warmth of it on his hands as he sat down and placed them in his lap. On one arm of his armchair he had a clipboard with the assessment sheets and a pen.

'Of course, you know who I am,' she said as she sat down.

'I don't, I'm afraid,' he said. 'We have never met.'

'No, but you saw me at the London Eye, didn't you, when I waved and took pictures of you? And I considered saying hello to you the other night in Belluno's but decided against it. The woman you were with – who I presume is your wife – looked a little startled by my presence.'

Will picked up the clipboard and looked down at it. 'Perhaps we can start with some of your personal details?'

Emma laughed. 'That's fine, Will, if that's the way you want to play it.'

She remained silent. He remained silent. They sat like this for some time. Will looked at her and after the silence had stretched for a while said, 'Who are you?'

'You know already. I am Guy's dead twin. Guy, your new client? The one who started by telling you that he's been seeing me all the time – that I'm watching him and commenting on everything that he does. I have to tell you, by the way, that he's lying to you about all of that. He doesn't see me around his flat at all. He's made that up so that he can sound more interesting. He *imagines* that I'm watching because he's in such a mess. This get-up that I'm wearing . . . that's what I was wearing when he last saw me. So, when he was inventing his story, that was what he described. He's rather fixated on me, you see. My death weighs quite heavily on him, wouldn't you say? From the assessment you did with him?'

'I never discuss a client's work with third parties,' said Will. She smiled. 'Not even with me?'

'No.' Will felt a grim, surreal humour in this. He'd come across psychosis before, of course he had, but he'd never come across someone who thought they were dead. Metaphorically, yes, of course – that was a primary statement that some of his clients held: 'I feel dead inside'. But Emma seemed to have literalised this. 'You say you are dead, but you look lively enough to me. Why would you want me to think that you are dead?'

Emma laughed. 'I don't expect you to believe me straight away. I'm not sure what evidence to give you at the moment. I'll think of something by the end of the assessment, though.'

'There's no point in doing an assessment. If you are Guy's sister then, for ethical reasons, I can't work with you.'

'Yes, you can,' she said.

'It would be a breach of professional practice. It would compromise my work with Guy, and it would compromise my work with you.'

'What would you say to him? "Your dead sister came to ask me for therapy and I told her to go away".'

'I don't believe you are Guy's dead sister. I think you need to go to your GP and tell him what you've told me. They will be able to support you in an appropriate way.'

Emma laughed again, a bright joyful burst of sound as though she'd figured something out. 'Right! Two things . . . Firstly, when you get home, look on your wife's bedside table. You will see a £1 coin. She keeps it there because she's not quite sure whether she wants to try for a baby. Every now and then she wonders, "Shall I? Shan't I?" She's only tossed the coin twice. Heads is yes, and tails is no. Both times it's been tails. Ask her.'

She got up from her chair. Will stayed where he was.

'And secondly . . .' She crossed to the door. 'Have a look at the paintings that have mysteriously appeared in your flat. Look carefully at the signatures on them.'

Then she left.

Will sat alone for a while, not sure what to make of what had happened. He hadn't written anything on the assessment sheet. He had no address or contact number for her and no biographical details or presenting issue. He sighed and went out into the reception.

'Becky, did Emma make an appointment with you when she was leaving?'

'Yes.' Becky glanced at the screen. 'Same time next week.'

He shrugged.

Becky smiled. 'That was the quickest assessment you've ever done. Just over ten minutes.'

Will sighed. 'Yes, it was quick. There's quite a lot of information I still need. Did she leave a contact number with you when she first phoned to make an appointment?'

'It wasn't me who took the booking. Didn't you put it on your assessment sheet?'

'No. She left in rather a hurry,' Will said, a tinge of defensiveness creeping in as he saw her surprise. 'I'm not even sure I'm going to work with her.'

Becky didn't say anything as Will turned to go back to his room.

When he got home, Will went straight to the bedroom. Yes, there it was: a £1 coin on the bedside table. Now that he saw it, he realised that it had been there for some time. He'd noticed it peripherally on more than one occasion without consciously wondering about it – well, why would he wonder about it?

Then he went into the spare bedroom. This was Lara's 'creative space'. There was no furniture in here, as such. Instead, there were four yoga mats on the floor so that she could experiment with movement, plus a full-length mirror on the wall. It was a smallish room, so there wasn't much further space, although in the corner there was an easel that he hadn't seen before and a small stool with a palette and some acrylic paints on it. He didn't come into this room often – hadn't been in there in months, in fact.

There were three canvases at different stages of completion, one of which was on the easel, nearly finished. They were clearly further paintings in the series, four of which had recently been put up in the flat. He'd had no idea that Lara had started painting. She hadn't mentioned it.

These 'in progress' pictures had a vibrant dark red foundation, almost crimson, that made him think of the word *sanguine*. Layers of brighter colour were being built up on top of it. He leaned down to see if they'd been signed but caught himself and laughed. Of course they weren't signed. They weren't finished.

He went into the front room and over to one of the paintings hanging there. Yes, in the bottom right-hand corner there were some stylised initials. He leaned down and looked. *WRT*. They were *his* initials, not Lara's. William Richard Thomas. Baffled, he looked at the other pictures. They all had the WRT initials on them. It took a few moments for the truth to filter through to him. He'd painted them! They were his paintings!

He went through to the kitchen, opened a bottle of wine and poured himself a large glass. So, he'd painted some pictures. He'd painted some pictures and had no recollection of doing so. He'd also had a session with his supervisor that he couldn't recall. On top of that, he'd conducted thirteen client sessions plus a group session of some kind and couldn't remember having done them, either. Someone had come to see him today who claimed to be dead, and who was aware of these pictures. And who also knew about the coin on the bedside table. Again, he got the sense of discomfort that had beset him the last time he saw Jamie. It was disconcerting to feel it at home in such familiar surroundings, the place that he thought of as a sanctuary.

Lara arrived then and joined him in the kitchen. She knew immediately that something was wrong. 'You look baffled,' she said. 'Or scared. Or both.'

Will tried to smile but failed and hugged her, feeling an immediate sense of relief in doing so. 'I have a client who's pretending to be dead. She left before I had the chance to challenge her properly.'

Lara pondered for a moment. 'That's weird. But not scary. Or did she seem dangerous?'

'Not violent, no. It was as if she wanted me to think she was coming back from the dead to give me a message.'

'She probably needs psychiatry, then, not therapy.'

'Mmm . . . The weirdest thing is . . . she was kind of convincing.'

Lara laughed for a moment and then must have noticed his expression. 'Seriously?'

He turned away from her to pick up an onion. 'I know that that's how psychosis works,' he told her as he started chopping it up. 'We covered that in some detail when I did my trauma training last year. The patient is completely convinced that they are Cleopatra or Boadicea or God, and then they behave from that conviction. It's oddly compelling.'

'I see. Like a good acting performance is convincing?'

'Yes, maybe.'

But it wasn't quite that and he didn't know how else to explain it.

'Oh, good,' said Lara, 'I see you've started on the wine. You can pour me some while you're at it.'

As he passed her a glass, he changed the subject and asked her about her day. It was comforting to listen to her talking about ordinary things as he cooked. Ordinary, straightforward things that were logical and made sense.

When they were sitting at the small table in the kitchen, he decided to take a risk.

'What do you think of the paintings I'm doing?'

'The red ones in the spare room?'

He nodded.

'They're quite a lot darker than the others. Not sinister, but . . . perhaps a little melancholy. No, not melancholy. Dreamy. Dark but warm.'

'I haven't really discussed them with you.'

'Some processes have to remain internal or else they disappear. I never talk to you about my movement stuff, do I, when I'm working on something new? I never invite you into the work room and ask you what you think. I have to work it out myself. And I'm really pleased that you've been using that room, by the way. I always felt uncomfortable about you calling it my space, as if you weren't allowed in there.'

When they went to bed, he said, 'That pound's been there for a while.' He kept his voice as casual as possible.

Lara looked slightly startled as he said this, and said, 'Yes.'

She picked it up and tossed it onto a pair of her jeans that were draped across a chair by the window. It came up heads. What had Emma said about trying for a baby? That heads meant yes? Lara looked at the coin and Will thought he could detect a wistfulness there but couldn't be sure.

They'd talked about the possibility of having children in a Yes-let's-do-that-one-day kind of way, but it was in the ether at the moment. They were waiting for a financial security that still seemed as far away as ever. Neither of them was in a profession with a steady income, let alone a permanent contract. They'd spoken about this a year or so previously and wondered whether they were using a financial barometer simply as an excuse to not consider the matter further. Lara was also frightened of the disruption to her work if she became pregnant.

Will agreed with Lara's parents. If you have kids, you cope with the financial side of it. You just do. He'd done a head-and-heart session with Lara about this. 'What does your head tell you? What does your heart tell you?'

'My head tells me I'm terrified of having children,' she said. 'My heart is strangely silent. It notices the clock ticking, but still it remains silent. If there were words to describe that silence, they would probably be something like . . . *There's plenty of time. You don't need to decide yet.* But I've felt like that for a number of years and that statement becomes less true with each year that passes. What about you?'

'I would love to be a dad. My head tells me I'm still not ready for it. My heart tells me that my head will always say this and that it's ready for the adventure whenever it happens.'

So, what could it mean if Lara was tossing a coin to decide whether or not to try for pregnancy without discussing it with him? And why was he even considering it as a possibility? Because Emma had known something about the paintings? If she was right about them, no matter how impossible that might be, what if she was right about this – something so intimate. He felt a shiver of disgust as though he was being spied on – or stalked.

As he lay there, unable to sleep, he realised he felt violated by his encounter with Emma. Was there no privacy left in his life? Things had become so unfathomable lately that, in his half-asleep state, he could almost believe that she really was dead and that these things that she 'knew' were messages from beyond the grave. He could sense a paradoxical state in which he could both believe it and disbelieve it at the same time. He could believe and disbelieve that he had 'known' things about his clients. He could be excited by it and frightened by it. He could want to continue with an exploration of what was happening more than anything he'd ever been involved with, and he could want to stop it completely. But the only way he could be sure of stopping it would be to give up his work as a therapist. And he couldn't do that, in a practical, financial sense as well as a psychological one.

On waking, he realised that a subtle, but profound shift had taken place while he was asleep. He found that he no longer yearned for supervision. What was happening to him had got so far beyond anything that he could explain to a supervisor that it didn't seem possible to make the attempt, particularly with a supervisor he'd never met before.

It was as if a major question had been posed and answered unconsciously while he slept. Did he carry on with this or try to stop it? And he knew he did not want to stop it. As he shaved, he tried to smile at himself in the mirror. What he saw was a cross between a wolfish grin and a rictus.

He was only slightly nervous about the group session that evening and, as it began to loom, he wondered what it meant that it no longer scared him. In fact, he was looking forward to it.

At six-thirty he popped out to get himself a take-away pizza and then went to sit and eat it in the training room, opening the window to make sure that food smells wouldn't linger. As he ate, he noticed the flip-chart on its easel in the corner and he went to check that there was some unsullied paper and a marker pen or two that worked. When he flicked back the cover of the pad, he saw a diagram titled THE CONTRACTED AND OPEN HEART. He could see at once that it was a diagram that he had drawn himself. It was done in his messy style, and it was his handwriting. He looked at it for a few moments and could see that it was an amalgamation of some of the approaches he'd studied. He then flicked on to the next sheet, which had the word BULLSHIT in large letters across the top and then underneath, as bullet points:

- Notice it
- Own it
- Deal with it

He smiled at this, recognising it as something his course leader had often spoken about, and flipped over to the next sheet. This had two words on it. DREAMS and FLIRTING. But the rest of the page was blank. The following page was completely blank. Will left the pad like that and went back to finish his pizza. Afterwards, he set out a circle of thirteen chairs. One for each of his pre-accident, clients – minus Irena, who had left him in anger – and one for himself. He stood the flip chart easel a couple of metres behind his chair.

I can lead a group, he thought. *I can do this well!*

By 7.30, all of his clients were assembled, with the exception of Guy, who hadn't been a client at the time that he'd set up the group. Emma wasn't there either, but then she hadn't been taken on as a client. As he looked at the assembly, he wondered about the ethics of this. To say that they were potentially dodgy was an understatement. But here he was and he tried to open himself up to . . . whatever was about to happen.

'Hello everyone,' he said.

The previous year, he'd done a stand-alone certificated course over three weekends: *An Introduction to Group Work*, and he'd co-run a six-week art therapy group with someone on his course who was also qualified as an art therapist. He ran through some of the basic principles: don't let one or two individuals monopolise everything . . . invite people in, in a neutral way, if they find it difficult to talk . . . don't shame them if they want to stay silent . . . slow things down, if necessary, to allow people the space they need . . . be aware of what is not being spoken.

This was comforting up to a point, but the more risk-averse side of him was saying, *What are you doing? This is madness!* Yet another part of him was determined to take this opportunity. Whatever had happened in his 'absence' seemed to have a plan to it and a purpose, and maybe he needed to see if he could go with that. Maybe he could learn from it as much as his clients.

'Welcome,' he said. 'This is our second session together.' He took a breath. 'We're going to start the session with a recap of the first.'

He stood, pulled his chair back and went to the flip chart, flipping the large pad back to the Contracted and Open Heart diagram. 'Right . . . perhaps someone is prepared to recap this?'

There was a thoughtful silence in the group. No one spoke for a while, and then Matt, the client with two failed marriages, shifted in his chair.

'I can't really say anything apart from what I have taken from it, personally,' he said, 'but what I can say for myself is that I've lived most of my life from my head rather than my heart. It's so clear. Yes, I had a longing to be loved, but I can see that my love has always been conditional. I gave love, but only on the condition that I got it back. It's odd . . . I can see this, but I can't see how I can change it.'

There was a short silence.

'I sometimes feel that it may never be possible for me to love myself enough,' said another client, 'although, paradoxically, saying that properly to myself seems to help.'

There were a couple of nods at this.

'I think,' said Christina, Will's twenty-four-year-old bulimic client, 'I think I want to die.'

She said it in a quiet and gentle voice.

'Why?' asked Debbie, Will's client who was struggling with her terminal diagnosis. 'Life is so precious, Christina. Why do you want to kill yourself?'

'I didn't say I wanted to kill myself,' said Christina. 'I said I wanted to die, which is different. Maybe I said it wrong. What I mean is, I think a part of me wants to be dead. I look at that diagram, and the part of Will's drawing that represents existential fear seems far too small. The personal neurosis seems far too small, too. In me they are huge. And, as for the dark, unknowable place . . . That seems to fill my whole existence. If I was dead, I wouldn't have to be in so much darkness anymore.'

'That's what the diagram's for,' said Stuart, Will's soon-to-be-forty client. 'As Will said last time, you need to place yourself where you are currently dwelling. It sounds like you are dwelling down here towards the bottom. If you know you are there, then you can turn your attention to starting the process of trying to move up to somewhere more appealing.'

'And you?' Christina asked Stuart, 'where are you dwelling?'

'That's easy. I'm also somewhere in there too – where you are. Though it's not quite as dark.' He pointed to the lower part of the diagram.

'Take a marker pen,' said Will, 'and show us.'

Stuart got up and went over to the diagram. He took a blue marker from the easel and drew a small circle towards the lower part of the diagram. 'I'm afraid it just looks like a circle,' he said, 'but I was thinking of it like a bubble in thick liquid. It's gradually working its way upwards.'

'Do other people feel able to place where they are right now?' asked Will. 'In their heads, at least?'

'It would be useful to have a copy of the diagram,' said Rachel, 'and then we could mark where we are from day to day.'

'I can do a copy for you all.' Will, made a note for himself to that effect. 'Christina . . . I wonder what you can take from the group in terms of support? You're obviously in a dark place.'

Christina didn't say anything.

'Would you like someone to respond to what you've said? Or perhaps it's enough to have said it and to have been heard?'

'It was a confession,' said Christina. 'It wasn't meant to be responded to. I don't really know anyone here, so I don't know who I could trust, who I could turn to.'

'It's odd,' said Rachel. 'You know us all, Will. But we're strangers to each other.'

'You can have a human response towards someone you don't know,' said Will. 'But the point of group work is that trust has to build. And I also take your point. What do you think we all need to make this place safe?'

'Time,' said Stuart.

When Will felt ready to do so, he flipped to the next page on the chart. The word **BULLSHIT!** glared into the room. There was a hint of mirth in the group.

'So,' he said, 'who is going to recap this one?'

'I tried it on my wife at the weekend,' said Laurence, a middle-aged IT consultant. 'I have to tell you it was not a success. I don't think I've quite got the neutral assertiveness that you have, Will.' He pointed at Will and shouted, 'Bullshit!' He sighed. 'You see? It comes out aggressively when I say it. Or at least that's what my wife said.'

'What were you referring to, though, when you shouted at her?' Stuart asked him.

'It was supposed to be funny. She said she was looking forward to her sister coming to visit us the next day. I challenged her. Looking back on it, I can see that it was inappropriate. But I still felt better for having done it. It was true after all.'

'Seeing as it was me you pointed at,' Debbie said to Will, 'I think I'd like to try it again, after having had time to reflect on what happened. When I said to the group that I had come to terms with my terminal diagnosis, I suppose I really did feel that that was true. Your *Bullshit!* was quite a shock, I have to say. But, as it says on your chart, the first thing is to "notice it", which I guess I did after my initial shock at your challenge. "Owning it" is going to be a bit more difficult. And "dealing with it" . . . well, who knows?' She smiled, but there was a quiver of sadness there, and an energy, despite the static way she held herself. 'Perhaps I can have a go this week, at what you told me to try out last time. I couldn't do it then, but maybe . . .'

'Go ahead,' said Will, 'please.'

She got up and sat cross-legged in the middle of the circle, facing Rachel. They looked at each other, tenderly.

'I don't want to die,' said Debbie. 'And I know I am going to, quite soon.'

Rachel leaned forward towards Debbie but didn't say anything. They looked at each other. The other members of the group were attentive, silent, respectful.

'I don't want to die. I'm afraid of dying. I'm really afraid.'

Rachel leaned forward again and reached her hands out to Debbie, who took them, and they sat like that for a while. Quietly, with a connection that was lovely to watch. After a short period of stasis, Debbie seemed to become more relaxed. She released Rachel's hands and dropped her own into her lap.

'Thank you,' she said to Rachel. She put her weight onto her palms and pushed herself up onto her knees. Standing, she went back to her seat and smiled sadly at Will.

'I have a long way to go with this,' she said. 'After the last session, Rachel and I went for a drink at the Camberwell Arms, which was really helpful, and made it possible to do what I have done just now, because I know her a little better.'

As he looked at her, Will thought, *I can take no credit for this.*

When he asked them to recap *dreams* and *flirting* there was some general laughter and a reticence to say anything.

'No description, then, but how about an impression?' asked Will.

Again, there was silence, but perhaps not quite such stubborn silence – it had more of a contemplative quality.

'Well,' said Stuart, 'I think that the most difficult thing for me was to find something to flirt with. I got what you meant when you told us to loosen our focus and see whether anything in the room might become significant. But there wasn't a great deal of potential. It's quite a bare room, after all, and the light fitting, which is what I chose in the end, isn't exactly something that I could see as flirting for my attention. I used it because I couldn't think of anything else. I'm not sure it actually answered my question. I'm not even sure I get what that means.'

'That's rubbish, there were masses of possibilities for flirting,' said Rachel. 'There were all of us for a start, and our clothes, and the cornices in the room, and the slightly flaky paint by the windows, and what we can see outside – the laburnum tree and the back of the church. I was overwhelmed with possibilities.'

'What did you choose?' asked Christina.

'I . . . I think I'd rather not say. It's too personal. I mean, especially as I haven't really faced what I asked and what my dream might have told me.'

'That's the thing,' laughed Stuart. Dreams don't talk to us in words, do they? What they tell us can't always be spoken.'

'And anyway,' Rachel went on, 'I think we need to get to the main business, don't we? Otherwise it'll become the elephant in the room.'

'Elephant in the room?' Will asked.

'The glass,' she said. 'The glass you smashed on the ceiling.'

Will almost smiled. So, he'd smashed a glass on the ceiling.

'What a shame!' said Laurence. 'After the story you told us about it, too. Bonnie Prince Charlie and the '45 rebellion.'

Will's breath caught for a moment. 'And I smashed it on the ceiling?'

'I don't think it was real,' said Rachel. 'It was a £10 reproduction from Ebay.'

'No, it was real, alright,' said Laurence. 'I had a good look at it when Will passed it around. You can't fake the patina of old glass. I have some old glass myself, and that was old glass.'

'Then it was criminal,' said Rachel.

'No,' said Stuart. 'No, it was a metaphor, don't you see? Images, dreams, they don't talk in words and neither do gestures. Will was showing us that we have to let go, let go of everything.'

'You could have given it away,' said Laurence. 'You could have given it to a museum. It deserved to be in a museum.'

Will didn't say anything. He felt as shocked as Laurence sounded. What did it mean? Was this a message meant for his clients or was it meant for him?

'"Sacrifice and surrender",' said Debbie, 'those were the words you used. Who really knows what they mean? Who really knows how to give themselves up to any of this?'

Once more, Will chose to walk for a while rather than take the bus home straight away. The night was cold with a breeze from the north and it was refreshing to be outside, even in the middle of a large city.

There was something about the group session that was both comforting and disturbing. Comforting because most of it had gone well and disturbing because he had no idea how to proceed with it. Clearly the most significant aspect of that first meeting had been him breaking his glass on the ceiling, and he had no idea why he'd done that. No idea at all. Spending a session recapping was fine as far as it went, as the group members seemed keen to discuss their experiences. But then there would have to be something to follow that, something to build on what had already been started. And he was uncertain what the group was set up to be. Open-ended? Or was it for a set number of sessions? Six, or perhaps twelve? The dream workshop he'd done with them was familiar in principle and, he now realised, there was plenty of potential for working on this in his one-to-one sessions. That was where he was going to have to do his research into what had happened, and what needed to happen.

Another thing that was disturbing was the fact that two of his clients had met socially outside the group. Of course, that was understandable, especially under the circumstances. But ethically, it was problematic. He could imagine Colin, his ex-supervisor, saying, 'This is madness, Will! They may talk about you and compare notes and compete for your attention and affection. You're going to have to stop working with one of them, or both.' He could also imagine Colin refusing to allow him to set up a group of this kind in the first place. *Inviting* and *trouble* were two words that sprang to mind.

He was beginning to realise that each thing he did that could be regarded as a boundary issue took him another step beyond what his supervisor – and he, ordinarily – would describe as safety. How many small steps did it take before a person was in full-on danger territory? Being-struck-off territory? And what did it mean when his clients talked of 'something happening'? *Something's happening here, Will, something meaningful.* Well, yes, he could agree with that in principle, but he was as unsure about what that 'something' was as everyone else, which felt uncomfortable, intriguing and curiously inviting.

One of the most eerie things, he realised, was that 'he' hadn't set up this group. Of course, in a court of law, it might be proved that it was him, but even if that happened, even a murderer could plead not guilty on the grounds of diminished responsibility. Perhaps he could make the same plea to his therapy group. Except that, bizarrely, this seemed somehow to be the reverse of diminished responsibility. He had been brilliant.

If 'he' hadn't set up the therapy group, then who had? Who was it that had been seeing his clients for the lost sessions? It wasn't a simple case of dissociated identity. Or was it? In any case he could say, absolutely, that the work that had been done was not recognisable as the work of Will Thomas the careful therapist and certainly did not fall within the parameters of his training. Although, unlike some person-centred approaches, there was room in his approach to be directive, his was not an approach that included screaming at his clients, falling asleep at their feet or taking all his clothes off.

From a certain perspective he could see quite clearly that it *was* him who had behaved in this way, albeit an unconscious part of himself. He had conducted his sessions as a sleep walker might. And the sleep walker – the dreamer – was still the same person as the one who woke up from the dream the following morning. Wasn't he? And if he said, *it wasn't me, but a part of me*, then would that mean that, paradoxically, it had both been him and not him at the same time? A part of him of which he'd previously been unaware? Well, of course, that was clearly true. His training told him so, and his client work proved it. Clients would continue to do things over and over again that were not self-cherishing or were downright harmful without any knowledge of why they were stuck in such self-destructive patterns of behaviour.

So . . . if it was a part of him that was out of consciousness, which part was it? And, more importantly, what was it trying to tell him?

He stayed with the question as he walked, but all he came up with as he pondered it was . . . nothing. A complete but uninformative internal silence.

When he got home, he looked in the kitchen cupboard in which he'd kept his Jacobite glass. Of course, it was gone. But what did that mean? What had he given up? What had he surrendered? His Scottishness? His heritage? His grandfather had bought it at an antique fair as a young man, so it was an element of his family identity . . . wasn't that, at least partly, what made him him?

Nine

There was the dream again! Will could see the bonnet of the car beneath him and watch his slow movement forwards over it. He could sense the endlessness of it, sense the impossibility of ever getting anywhere in terms of space and time. He also noticed, for the first time . . . the silence. The utter silence in which this was happening. Along with this, and not disturbing or reducing the silence in any way, there was noise. A roaring in his ears, of wind and shock. The silence had nothing to do with sound. This was a silence in which sound was happening, stillness in which movement was happening. How strange and how beautiful that was.

One evening, an old university friend of Will's came over for a meal, along with his wife. Dan was a deputy head teacher at a school near Bow, while Aimee worked in the HR department of a bank's head office in the city. They were lively and friendly and much valued as friends by both Will and Lara. In fact, it had become something of a tradition for the four of them to go for a week's walking in late September or early

October, the time of year when weather could still be fine, and a little cooler. Will was pleased to see them and realised that he'd had far too little social contact recently.

As soon as Dan came into the hall, he stopped in front of Will's painting. 'Wow! Where did you get this?'

'Will painted it,' Lara told him.

Dan looked at Will and grinned. 'I didn't know you painted.'

'I don't really,' said Will.

As they went into the sitting room, Dan was even more amazed. 'My goodness, these are fantastic!'

'You're a dark horse, Will,' said Aimee.

'Dead right,' said Dan. 'He didn't show any interest when we were at university. Put an art gallery on one side and a mountain on the other and there's no doubt which one he'd choose.'

'I've always appreciated culture,' said Will. 'I admired Alasdair Gray.'

Dan patted Will's arm. 'For his writing, not his painting.'

Lara laughed. 'There are some interesting ones on the go, too, in our spare room.'

'Can I have a look at them? After I've absorbed these?' Dan sat down on the sofa and contemplated the pictures. 'They've got that touch. They have that alchemy of juxtaposition of shape and contrast that is so rare, and so recognisable when you see it. I've a number of friends in the art business and so I've been around galleries for years. In that time, I suppose I've developed a bit of an eye, and these . . . well, you could sell these. For money. I mean for *money!*' He turned earnestly to Will. 'How long did it take you to do them?'

Will gave a non-committal shrug. He didn't know.

'I love them,' said Aimee. 'I mean, they're so bold and spontaneous, and full of life.'

Dan was as impressed with the work in progress. 'Although they're not quite so obviously commercial as the brighter ones, they've got depth and a haunted quality about them . . . and maybe a sadness that counterpoints the liveliness of the others?'

As the night settled down, Will felt himself relaxing into a sense of normality as he chatted to Dan and Aimee. It was almost as if nothing unusual had been happening in his life. He'd been friends with Dan almost all his adult life and it was helpful to be with someone who knew him so well.

'By the way,' Dan said, 'did you get an email about having a uni cycling club reunion next year in Edinburgh?'

'No,' said Will. 'I haven't been good at checking my emails lately. It sounds like a great idea. I'll have to borrow a bike off someone, though.'

'Won't you be replacing yours?'

'I doubt it. I'm not really cut out for cycling in city traffic, and that's all I've been doing lately.'

'But you could get out into the country. We could go together sometime. I'll lend you one of my bikes. We're about the same height.'

'I'd love that,' said Will.

The paintings weren't mentioned again until the end of the evening. When Dan and Aimee were leaving, Dan said, 'Look,

Will, is it okay if I ask a friend of mine to come in and have a look at these? He runs a gallery in town.'

'Of course,' said Will.

A few days later, Dan came over with Linus Marshall from Marshall and Allen, a gallery in Chelsea, to look at the pictures.

'Well,' he said, 'Dan's right, I could sell these. But I'm not really interested in a handful of paintings. I'm interested in on-going business. Can you produce work of this quality consistently? That's the question. Some artists can. Most can't.'

He left Will with his card, and that was that. Lara was so excited she could hardly sit still. She kept jumping up and dancing across the sitting room with exuberant delight.

The next morning, Will went into the spare room and looked at the three paintings there. The dark reds still reminded him of the warmth of blood. But they weren't his. He had absolutely no idea how they had been painted, nor how to complete them. He looked at the palette and took some of the tubes of acrylics out to see if he could reproduce the colours. He managed this quite well in time, but as soon as he started to apply paint to the canvas, he could see that the whole thing was hopeless. It looked as if a child had smeared paint over a picture painted by someone else. Fortunately, they were acrylic paints and so he could wipe off most of his disastrous attempt with a damp cloth from the kitchen. The residue of what he'd applied was visible as ghostly smudges on the canvas but looked as if they might be deliberate, somehow, neither enhancing nor detracting from the picture.

He stood and stared at the pictures. He had no idea how he could complete them.

'Of course you can see me, Will,' said Emma when they next met. 'Let's forget about the assessment. I'm dead, so I don't have an address. I don't have a telephone number. And please don't start talking about money and how much it all costs. Money is meaningless to me, so you'll have to see me for nothing. Although, when I say nothing, I mean nothing financially. I'm going to give you something of considerable value, but value is diminished by the concept of money, isn't it? We would have to start by considering what is meant by value before we started wondering whether it was being given. Or taken?'

Will hadn't been certain how he would react to Emma when he saw her, but now he was clear.

'You have no choice,' he said. 'I am not going to work with you. You can't force me to do anything.'

'To some extent that is true, but I'm hopeful that I can be quite . . . persuasive. Also, you haven't mentioned anything about what I said last time we met – about looking for a coin on your wife's bedside table and at the signatures on your paintings.'

'So, you've been in my flat. You've been stalking me. Quite apart from my feeling of violation, it certainly makes any kind of client-therapist relationship impossible.'

She laughed. 'It makes no difference whether I've been in your flat or not. As a matter of fact, I haven't. That's not how I know these things. But even if I had been in your flat, how would I have known, just by seeing it there, that your wife has been tossing that coin to decide whether or not to get pregnant.'

'I have no idea whether that's true.'

'Yes you do, you know in here.' She placed her hand gently above her heart.

'So, you're trying to tell me you're psychic?'

'No,' she sighed. 'I'm not psychic. Or at least not psychic in the way you mean.'

'And what is the purpose of doing this to me?'

'To mystify.'

'My profession is to do the reverse.'

'Is it?'

He felt a small prickling of danger.

'I still don't believe you are dead,' he told her. 'I don't know why you are here or why you are doing what you're doing, but you can never be my client. I think you need help, but I have to tell you, clearly and absolutely, that I am not the person to do that for you. The boundaries here are already far too blurred to allow it to work.'

'Boundaries? I wonder that you can mention boundaries with a straight face, given what's currently going on in your practice.'

Will blinked. He wasn't sure whether she'd spoken with hostility or amusement.

'Nevertheless, I have made my decision that I can't work with you. I am hoping that you will now leave.'

She sat and looked at him, unmoving. He sat silently, watching her. The moment was perfectly balanced. Things could go either way, into acquiescence or into conflict. He looked at her, trying to read something from her body language, but she seemed relaxed, poised and neutral. She was giving nothing away.

Will felt anxiety flutter up. What would happen if she didn't go?

He'd had his moments, when clients were bursting with anger at the world, or at him, and these had had their own dangers. There was something about these moments that was never straightforward. When he'd been in training, they'd had sessions about safety, about avoiding lone-working; about 'containing' a session before it spiralled out of control. None of that had ever really helped to stop the prickle of fear that arose when he began to feel that he was no longer fully in control of what was happening. Of course, boundaries and preparation weren't designed to stop a therapist from feeling fear – fear was a useful pointer, after all, and if you never felt fear, who knew what boundaries you might break? It was how you responded to the fear that was important. But this was different.

Emma smiled after a while and raised her eyebrows. Will involuntarily opened his mouth to speak, but then closed it again decisively, which made Emma laugh. Still, they said nothing. Will started to realise that this was becoming therapy. Sitting in silence to see what arose was a therapeutic context.

'Right,' he said, 'I am now asking you to leave.'

'That's fine. I'll leave. All you had to do was ask.'

'I did ask.' Will stood up.

'No. You said you were *hoping* that I would leave. That's different.'

'That's just semantics.'

'I think you'll find that there is a world of difference between hope and certainty. And, by the way, I'll come along now and then. No need for a regular slot. I can fit around your other clients and sort out sessions when I need them.'

And then she left.

That evening, Will sat waiting to see Stuart. What was it about him that was so comforting? There was a straightforwardness about him that meant that, even if a session was difficult, Will still felt he knew what was going on. This was incredibly helpful given that other clients could be confused, or confusing. However, Stuart didn't arrive for his session. Will waited for ten minutes and then switched on his mobile – sometimes there would be a message from a client to say that they were stuck in traffic and would be a few minutes late or unable to attend at the last minute for some other reason. Instead, there was a brief message from Jake someone-or-other, a duty police officer, who left a number for Will to phone.

Will called the number immediately.

'Oh, hello Mr Thomas,' the police officer said when he answered. 'I'm up at St Thomas's Hospital Accident and Emergency department with a client of yours . . . Stuart Morton. I'm afraid he made an attempt on his life earlier today. He's had his stomach pumped and seems to be in a stable condition. He gave your name as a next of kin, but he said that you are his therapist?'

'Yes, that's right,' said Will.

'Are you free to come over and see him?' the officer asked.

'Of course,' said Will, automatically.

'Do you know where we are?'

'Yes. Yes, I can be with you in twenty minutes.'

Will jumped into a taxi at the rank at the end of the block. His first reaction was, 'What do I need to do to be helpful?' But along with that was the question of whether there was a protocol to be followed. It was simply luck that his late slot was free and so he didn't have another client that evening. What if he'd had another suicidal client who'd been just about to arrive for a session?

I'm hiding, he thought, *I'm hiding behind my therapeutic identity. I'm asking myself what a therapist should do in this situation, because I don't know what I should do.*

Clients had become actively suicidal occasionally and he'd sent them to their GP or the Wellbeing Service or up to A&E once or twice, but this was the first time he'd come up against an actual hospitalisation in his practice. He wondered briefly whether Stuart had intended to die or whether it was a non-life-threatening manifestation of his distress. And did it matter? Either way, it showed that he was *in extremis*. Will felt a wave of love for his client, followed swiftly by sadness. What had been missed in their sessions? Will had always looked forward to seeing Stuart, looked forward to the comforting quality of their time together. But comforting to whom? Not, perhaps, to Stuart. Why hadn't he seen this? This thought was followed by a thump of guilt and then a wash of shame. A whole monologue bloomed inside him, already spoken, and accompanied by a malevolent pointing finger:

You're his therapist. You're supposed to help clients, not make them want to kill themselves. There'll be a court case when Stuart accuses you of negligence. They'll seize your client notes and see the session sheets from the lost sessions. They'll see that you've done something terrible to all your clients. Then it'll become known that you were working with clients without supervision. They will all testify against you. Not only will you be struck off, you'll be found guilty of criminal negligence and sent to prison.

Woah! Where had that come from?

The Malevolent Finger. It sounded like something from a nightmarish myth or a bad 1970's horror movie. The Finger of Destiny. *The sinister priest pointed at him with his Malevolent Finger.*

Enough! he told himself. *Who is important here, me or Stuart?*

This enabled him to begin to put his own concerns to one side, and as the taxi pulled up into the empty ambulance drop-off zone, he found that he was calm and ready.

Forget yourself, Will, he thought, *this is not about you.*

Stuart was not immediately apparent. He was in a bed at the far end of the emergency treatment room in a one-bed alcove. When Will came to the bedside, Stuart, who looked impossibly white, with a greasy sheen to his skin, smiled at him and said, 'Hello, Will, how are you?'

There it was, thought Will – the comfortableness. Stuart had always tried to make him feel comfortable, at his own expense. And Will hadn't seen it.

'I'm fine. What about you?'

'Weird,' said Stuart. 'I feel really weird. Not only because I took the pills but because in the moment I took them, it seemed completely sane. The sensible thing to do. Now, that seems just . . . weird.'

Will sat down on the edge of the bed. Stuart reached out and took Will's hand, and Will squeezed it gently.

'I couldn't think of anyone else when they asked me who they should call,' said Stuart, 'so I said to contact you.'

'Good idea,' said Will.

'Have I ruined your schedule?'

'I didn't have to cancel any appointments to come here if that's what you mean.'

Stuart closed his eyes and seemed about to fall asleep, his head listing to one side for a moment. There was a brief shudder in his abdomen as if he was about to retch, but it subsided and then he opened his eyes and looked at Will.

'It seemed for a moment that I couldn't go on,' he said, weakly. 'It was as if I could see the task ahead of me, and there was this one moment when it seemed the easiest thing in the world to let it go. All that anguish about the absolute shit I've been to some of the men I've had relationships with. All the anger and the pretending that I was strong and in control, and that what was happening was everyone else's fault and not mine. And then, the hugeness of how to work with all of that seemed completely overwhelming. As if I was standing in front of a mountain of wreckage with just a small spoon to dig it all away. Even if I had one of those massive diggers, it felt like it would take a lifetime.' He sighed. 'Well, perhaps I have to acknowledge that this is big. I've been pretending that it's not big, but it's huge.'

Will nodded but didn't say anything.

'It was seeing Debbie in the group saying, "I don't want to die." Hearing her say that made me realise that I've never really been alive.'

Will was about to say something when Stuart interrupted him.

'Yes, I know,' he smiled, 'killing myself is a good way of trying to deal with wanting to start to live a little!'

'We're all a bundle of contradictions,' said Will. 'It's part of being human.'

Stuart gestured vaguely. 'I'm sorry to have burdened you with this. I should have got a friend to come over.'

'You always try not to burden me,' said Will. 'I'm pleased to be here.'

He smiled at Stuart who squeezed his hand briefly before closing his eyes. Will sat like that for a while and then laid

Stuart's hand gently on the blanket and went off to get himself a coffee, and to text Lara to say he was going to be late. It was one of her late evenings, too, and he had no idea how long he would be here. *Client emergency. Get a carry out*, he texted her. *I'll do the same. I'll see you when I see you.* When he got back to the ward, the duty doctor was discussing Stuart with a nurse.

'I'm going to be kept in overnight,' Stuart said cheerfully.

'I'm afraid Stuart's blood pressure remains worryingly low,' said the doctor. 'We had hoped that you would be able to take him back to his home this evening but, as he lives alone, we have decided that he should remain here under observation.'

'It'll take an hour or two to get hold of a ward bed,' the nurse said to Stuart. 'I'll be back as soon as I've got one for you.'

They left. Stuart looked serene as he lay there, a little saintly in his paleness as if made of marble.

'I need to make some plans with you,' said Will. 'Do you have anyone who can come and collect you tomorrow? I don't think you should be going anywhere on your own. Depending on when you get discharged, I could come over myself.'

'No, it's okay. I'll get Gregg to take me home. In fact, I'll get him to come over now if I can get hold of him. He wasn't available earlier but he'll be around by now. I think I can face him, too. I couldn't before.'

'I'll call him if you like. Have you got his number?'

Stuart nodded.

'I should have waited for him rather than asking them to call you, shouldn't I?'

Will laughed. 'You're doing it again, Stuart. Apologising for being a burden. I'm happy that you asked this of me.'

He took Stuart's phone and called Gregg. It felt strange talking to Stuart's ex, a man who had figured so prominently in their sessions. Gregg sounded guarded but agreed to come over as soon as he could.

'He'll be here in about an hour,' Will told Stuart, who visibly relaxed.

'Thank you, Will. You don't have to stay, I'll be fine now.'

'No, I'll stay. I'd like to.'

'I've put you out enough already,' said Stuart.

'I am here as someone who likes you and is concerned about you, and I'd like to stay.'

'I suppose this looks bad – at least in terms of my state of mind?'

'I am not here as your therapist,' Will said. 'You haven't paid me, for a start.'

'I'll pay you double next time.'

'I was making a joke.'

'So was I.' Stuart smiled. 'I'm not doing very well in the humour department, I'm sorry.'

'Our relationship is not friend to friend because I am your therapist. But it is a friendly relationship, I hope. Well, it is from my side at least. And, what I have to say is meant in a friendly way, but if you don't stop apologising, I'm going to start getting very, very annoyed.'

'Will!' Stuart laughed. 'That was camp!'

They both laughed. Will took Stuart's hand again and they laughed again and got eye contact.

'Your eyes are so blue!' said Stuart. 'I hope that you have someone who appreciates your eyes.'

'My wife has been very complimentary about my eyes. I am a Scot. Well, sort of a Scot. I have Scottish blood, anyway. Blue eyes, pale skin, light hair and freckles – well they go with the territory . . .'

As he returned home, Will resented having to take public transport. This journey would have been so much quicker by bike. With all the waiting at the bus stop, it took nearly twice the time. However, he had to take responsibility, as he had done on the Aonach Eagaich, for the fact that he was not as competent, physically, as other people. Oh, he was strong, but strength and precision were two different things. And as for competence, that was a concept he preferred not to address right now.

Lara was bright and cheerful and happy when he got home, pleased with what was going on for her and she greeted him with a smile and a kiss. She was considerate and attentive when Will explained why he was late, and they spent the rest of the evening in a tender intimacy that was a balm to Will and helped him to relax.

The following evening, as he let himself into the flat, he heard the familiar, comforting sound of a frying pan sizzling in the kitchen. It was only 6.00 pm and he was surprised that Lara was home already.

'Hello!' he called, 'I didn't think you'd be back so early.'

He came into the kitchen to find Emma there, wearing Lara's dark blue striped apron and frying some onions. The smell of basil filled the small room.

'Hello, Will,' she said. 'I thought I'd rustle something up for you, considering both you and your wife are so busy. I thought it might be helpful. Appreciated.'

Will stared, speechless for a moment.

'What are you doing here?' he demanded. '*What* are you doing here!'

'I'm helping out.'

'What are you doing in my home? You are not invited! You are not welcome!' He held out his hand. 'Give me your keys. I have no idea where you got them from, but give them back to me and then get out. I am being polite at the moment, so please don't push it.'

'Will . . .'

'Do you have any idea how completely out of order this is?'

Emma looked at him with an enigmatic smile. 'Do you think,' she said carefully, 'that you are in a place, psychologically, that has any *order* to it? At all.'

Will stared at her. 'Are you trying to tell me something?'

'Listen. Just listen to yourself.' She looked down at the pan. 'I know that you like basil,' she added conversationally. 'I was thinking of adding some herb salt too, but you're a bit ambivalent about highly seasoned food, aren't you?'

'Get out!' he yelled. 'Get out!'

As he shouted there was the sound of the front door being opened.

'Ah,' said Emma, 'your wife. We haven't met. Perhaps you can introduce us?'

Will glared at her.

'Hello?' Lara called from the hall. 'Will?'

Will didn't say anything. Lara appeared in the doorway with her outdoor jacket on. Will stood there paralysed. Emma, still in Lara's apron, reached her hand past Will and said, 'Hello, you must be Will's wife.'

Lara was visibly surprised and looked at Will, who was clearly not giving out any useful information. 'Who are you?' she asked. Not hostile. Simply confused.

'I'm Emma,' said Emma. 'This is . . . Look, I hope you don't mind me being here.'

'Get out!' Will shouted again. 'Get out of my home!'

'Hang on,' said Lara, 'I recognise you. You're the woman who nearly spoke to Will at Belluno's the other night, aren't you? Who are you? Who is she, Will?'

'She's leaving,' said Will.

'This was an experiment,' said Emma. 'Don't blame Will for it. I'm afraid I don't know your name . . .'

'Lara,' said Lara.

'Lovely to meet you, Lara,' said Emma. 'This was an experiment,' she repeated. 'It may take some time before we know whether or not it has worked.' She undid the apron and handed it to Lara. 'Well, as I say, it was lovely to meet you.

Enjoy your dinner. Someone is going to have to finish preparing it, but what I've prepared so far, I prepared with love.'

With that, Emma patted Will's arm in a friendly way. He flinched. But then she was past, and out in the hall.

'Have a nice evening!' Emma called. 'Don't mind me!'

With that, she let herself out, and was gone. Lara looked at Will, dumbfounded.

'Don't say anything,' said Will. 'I am as confused as you are.'

'No,' said Lara, 'I very much doubt that you are as confused as I am. I think you'd better explain. That woman came up to you in Belluno's the other night. I thought nothing of it at the time, but now I come home early and find her in our kitchen, wearing my apron and cooking dinner. I think that puts it on a different footing.'

Will took a breath. 'She's asked to be taken on as a client.'

Lara paused for a moment. 'Okay. I didn't expect you to say that. But I'm not quite clear as to why you have a prospective client in our home, cooking dinn–'

'Neither am I. Believe me.'

'Believe you that you don't know why she's here?' asked Lara. 'Why should I believe that you don't know why she's here? I didn't invite her, which means that you must have.'

'I can see why it might look that way.'

'So, who is this person? Why was she here?'

'She's the person I told you about . . . the one who claims to be dead. I've refused to take her on. I refused to take her on because her psychosis places her in a psychological arena that is outside my professional area of expertise.'

'A madwoman asks you for therapy and you turn her down. So far, so good. But that doesn't explain why I find her in my home, cooking dinner in our kitchen.'

'Yes. That's where it gets confusing.'

'Please, just explain. I can't stand it when people are evasive.'

'Bear with me,' said Will. 'I'm not trying to be evasive. It's not just confusing, this is where it gets really weird. This person comes to my office, claiming to be dead, but she seems to have access to our flat, and to know things about us that she has no reason to know.'

'Such as?'

'That you have a coin that you keep on your bedside table, that you flick every now and then to decide whether or not to try for a baby.'

Her body, which had been fizzing with energy, suddenly became still. 'Will, you're frightening me.'

'It *is* frightening.'

Lara gave him a hard stare. 'Look, this is the worst excuse I've ever heard. I come home unusually early from work to find an attractive woman cooking dinner in my kitchen. You tell me that you haven't invited her. That she's dead–'

'Claims to be dead.'

'*Claims* to be dead . . . What am I supposed to think?'

Will didn't answer. He couldn't think of anything to say.

'And then my husband screams, "Get out! Get out!" at her and pretends that he didn't invite her in.'

'I didn't invite her in!'

'Then that's even more scary!'

'Yes!' Will shouted. 'It is! It's *even more* scary!'

'Don't shout!' Lara shouted back at him. She raised her hands and took two long breaths. 'Let's stop. Let's be calm and quiet.' She looked at Will. 'From where I'm standing, it looks as if I have a husband who is either being unfaithful or who is completely insane. It's not a very happy distinction to try to make.'

Will shrugged. 'I'm not being unfaithful.'

'I can't deal with this, Will. This is the nightmare I thought would never happen in our relationship – you lying in this ridiculous way.'

'I'm not lying. I'm telling you the truth. I said I always would.'

She glared at him.

'What else can I say?' he said.

'Nothing, really. Unless you want to be honest.'

He shrugged again. 'I've already done that.'

Lara's eyes welled up with tears. 'Will, I have to go. I just have to go. I've been in this place too often before.'

'Don't, Lara . . . Stay, and we can talk this through. Now that I've told you what has happened, I'd really appreciate your take on what's going on.'

'Is there anything you can add to what you've said or are you going to carry on saying that you didn't invite her in?'

'I didn't invite her in,' he said, simply. 'I have no idea where she got the keys to get into the flat. I don't keep a spare set at work.'

'Bad lies sound even worse when you try to stick to them,' said Lara. 'Just stop it. This is so unlike you.'

'Which, if you don't mind me saying so, is circumstantial evidence that I'm telling the truth.'

'No, Will,' she said. 'You're not telling the truth.'

He turned to take the pan off the cooker, where the food was beginning to burn. 'That £1 coin . . . it *was* to decide whether to try to get pregnant, wasn't it?'

She didn't answer.

'That's not very democratic,' he said.

'Don't deflect. This isn't about me. It's about you and the fact that you are lying.'

'How many times can I say I'm not lying.'

'I need to leave,' she said.

Will watched as she turned and went back down the hall. What could he say to bring her back? When the door clicked shut, he felt . . . completely alone.

The following day he spent several hours – and more money than he would ever have guessed possible – on a home visit from a locksmith to have the locks changed on the front door. He was determined that Emma should stay away from him. It was bad enough that she knew where he lived. He didn't want her letting herself into his home again under any circumstances.

Ten

Lara didn't come home the next evening. He'd texted her several times during the day and received nothing back from her until late afternoon, when he received one that said, *Have you changed your story?* He replied, *No, but let's talk it through. I want to tell you everything about my clients and the strange things that have been happening.*

There was an intense period of anticipation as he waited for her response.

She texted back: *No. Let me know when you're ready to tell the truth. And don't text me until then.*

Over the course of that week, his client work went surprisingly well. People grappled with 'stuff' in the way that clients often did. There were more, tantalising references to the content of the lost sessions, and he couldn't help getting a further eerie sense of the stranger who had taken over in his absence – a stranger who was beginning to become familiar. He was a person who acted with certainty. Or perhaps certainty was the wrong word. Authority. Authenticity, perhaps. Someone who acted authentically and then waited to see what might happen? He'd also acted with an absolute confidence that what he was doing was worth a try. Whether it worked or not, there was no sign of doubt, just a preparedness to deal with the consequences of the risks that he took. In a curious way, Will realised, he found himself liking this other Will, perhaps even aspiring to be more like him, despite knowing that his behaviour would be roundly denounced by therapeutic accrediting bodies. But he'd discovered in his own practice that emulating another person could be disastrous. He remembered once making an intervention that he knew his course leader would have made in exactly the situation that he found himself, and his client looking at him with surprise and saying, 'That's a weird thing for you to say!' Will had laughed, embarrassed, and changed tack.

I invite clients into a co-created space, he thought, *which is a perfectly good way of going about it.*

Was that a defensive statement? It had that flavour. The other Will had challenged clients with an assertiveness that was breathtaking, and yet his clients had believed in his sincerity sufficiently such that they had accepted the challenge.

The disconcerting thing about this was that it had made Will start to doubt his own competence as a therapist. Of course, he didn't know a single therapist who wasn't in an active process of questioning themselves and the work that they did. But this was different. Some of his clients wanted him to go back to working as this other Will had done; they preferred his work. But just as he had discovered that he couldn't emulate his course leader's work, neither could he emulate the other Will's work. *The other Will.* What did that mean, anyway? In saying *I am not that other Will*, was he really saying, *I am not myself*?

Still, at the moment, his clients seemed happy to be in the aftermath of challenge, just as they had been happy to spend the last group session recapping the first one. But, inevitably, there would come a time when they would go back to the 'more of that, please' that he'd been confronted with initially.

When he saw Guy, he made a decision that was outside his usual way of working, in that he decided to start with a particular kind of direct question. A question that was specifically for himself, Will Thomas the therapist, and not for his client.

'I'm wondering about your sister's name,' he said. 'It's quite unusual to call your sister "sister". Was it because there was something you didn't like about her real name?'

'No,' said Guy. 'There was nothing wrong with her name. She started this thing off when we were quite young, about my name being generic. Guy. "You know, there's this guy I met at school." She joked about it with my parents, that they hadn't given me a name at all. They might as well have called me "bloke". So, I retaliated by calling her "sister".'

'It does seem that there was a rather combative element to your relationship,' said Will. 'Can you tell me what her real name was?'

'Of course. It was Jo.'

Will tried to hide it, but he couldn't help feeling a wash of exhilaration. He nearly said, *So, it wasn't Emma, then?* but of course that would have sounded mad. He smiled to himself. So, who was this person who had muscled in on his life, if she wasn't Guy's sister? And why had he asked Guy this question anyway, as though Emma's story might have had even a speck of truth in it?

On Wednesday evening the phone rang as he came into the flat.

'Will, what are you doing?' came Lara's voice. 'You've changed the locks on the door. I can't get in.'

'It's not to keep you out. It's to keep that woman out. Emma, the woman I've refused to take on as a client.'

'She's stalking you?'

'I don't know.'

'Have you been to the police?'

'No.'

'You see, Will, this is what's so crazy. If there's a mad woman breaking into the flat, you call the police. Well, any sane person would.'

'I know this seems bizarre, Lara. You're going to have to work out what you think about it yourself. It's clear that any honesty from me is going to make things worse. I can lie if you want. I can say that I'm having an affair with this woman just to get you to meet up and talk to me.'

'Are you having an affair with her?'

'No!'

'Things like this happen, Will. The mature thing is to be honest about it.'

Will sighed again at the impossibility of persuading Lara to believe him.

'I've had some spare keys made for you,' he said, 'but I didn't know how to get them to you because I don't know where you are. I'll put them under the yucca pot and you can collect them whenever you want.'

There was a pause. 'Okay,' she said.

'I love you, Lara.'

'Yes, somewhere in all this, I think you probably do.' She rang off.

All week there loomed the group session on Thursday, which would be preceded in the afternoon by a session with Emma, who had mysteriously booked in the day before. When he'd seen the booking, he'd asked Becky, 'When did this one come in?'

'I thought you'd booked it,' she'd told him.

When Becky called through to say that she was there, Will wondered what would happen if he refused to see her. Perhaps they would have to call the police and have her removed from the premises.

'Hello, Will,' she said as he came into the waiting room to get her. He didn't answer and remained silent as they walked down the short corridor to his room. Once inside, Will didn't even wait until she sat down before he spoke.

'I'm not usually the one who starts a session off with a direct comment or specific question,' he said, 'but seeing as I haven't taken you on as a client, then this isn't a session and I don't feel I have to treat you as a client. I happen to know that you are not my client's dead sister. Her name was not Emma.'

'Oh,' said Emma, 'what was it?'

'That,' said Will, 'is confidential.'

'So, I call myself Emma,' she laughed. 'I'm still Guy's dead sister.'

'No, you're not. You're deluded and you need help. And I'm not qualified to help you. You need to go to your GP to sort out some psychiatric support.'

'You can help me.'

'No, I can't,' said Will.

'I guessed you would say that – after you were so unwelcoming to me the other night. I'd gone to all the trouble of coming over to cook dinner for you, too. However, I have a proposition. If you take me on, I promise I'll restrict my contact with you to this room.'

'What do you mean?'

'I have access to your home.'

'No, you don't. I've changed the locks.'

She smiled in a condescending way. 'I think I'm being reasonable here. I have no desire to make life difficult for you, Will. Really.'

'Not make life difficult for me! I suppose you know, or might guess, that my wife has gone to stay with friends.'

'Stay with friends? You mean she's left you.'

'My wife has gone to stay with friends, for an undisclosed period of time. Because of you. She thinks I am either being unfaithful or have taken leave of my senses.'

'Anything can happen when you take leave of your senses,' she said.

'That's just an easy slogan when you say it like that,' he said. 'Now, I want you to listen to me carefully, and respond in an appropriate way. I don't know why you have turned up or what you are hoping to achieve by coming to see me like this, but I am asking you to please go away and leave me alone. You say you don't want to make life difficult for me. Well, try sticking to that. Maybe there's something that you want or need to say to me, and if that's the case, then I'm happy to listen to it. Please, say what you have to say, and then leave me and my wife alone.'

Emma paused to gather her thoughts.

'Your wife has moved out for an undisclosed period of time because she doesn't believe you, even though you're telling the truth. She's passed judgement already.' Emma looked concerned for a moment and then her expression softened. 'But, in answer to your kind offer to listen to anything that I need or want to say, I have a question.'

Will looked at her expectantly.

'What do you think would happen if everyone – and I mean *everyone* – in London flushed their toilets simultaneously?'

'What?'

'It's a serious question.'

Will looked at her.

'It's a serious question,' she repeated.

'I don't know.'

'It would be disastrous,' she said. 'London has huge centralised sections of its drainage system, so it would all converge. Localised parts of London, especially in low lying areas, would flood with sewage. Can you imagine? It would burst up out of the drainage system, which would be unable to cope. We would have raw sewage flowing in the streets.' She paused and glanced out of the window before looking back at him. 'The point I'm making is that we're hovering on the verge of disaster all the time and it's only a matter of chance that it doesn't happen. But, just as once in every forty-two million games a person wins a lottery jackpot, so, every once in a while, something quite apocalyptic might happen. By chance, if that's what you want to call it.'

'And what has this got to do with me?' asked Will.

'Alright,' said Emma, 'let me tell you a story. You can check this out if you like because it actually happened, I'm not making it up. It was in the *Evening Standard* last December. There was a custody case where a mum and dad had a fight over who was going to have custody of their daughter over Christmas. The suggestion was that the daughter should spend the morning with her father and the afternoon and evening with her mother. This was hotly contested by the father but, in the end, there was nothing he could do and so that was how things were settled. However, because the argument had been so nasty, the social worker checked up with each parent afterwards to see how the day had gone. Each parent – and this is the point – each parent said that their daughter had been with them for the whole day.'

Emma shut her eyes and paused for a moment.

'What did this mean?' She opened her eyes again and looked at Will. 'The social worker, of course, wanted to find out which parent was lying, and to stop the huge, and violent, row that broke out between them after they both claimed to be right. But – and again, this is the point – what if it was true? What if the little girl really had been in both places at once? When questioned, she said that she'd spent the day with both her mum and her dad in their respective homes. Naturally, the social worker didn't believe her. But isn't this what subatomic physics has taught us – that a particle can be in two places at once? Well, why not a little girl?'

Will looked at Emma. 'I still have no idea what this has got to do with what's going on here.'

'Some things are more unusual than they seem on the surface, that's all.'

'That may be true. Now, I am asking you to leave.'

'Your receptionist is going to start wondering why our sessions are so short.'

'That's the least of my worries.'

'Good,' she said and got up. 'By the way, I really am Guy's sister. I was born Emma, but from about the age of nine, he called me Joe, Joe with an E, that is. It was in retaliation for something I said about Guy being a generic name. He started calling me Joe, because Joe is a generic name too, *Just another Joe*, as in *guy*. And it's a generic name that can apply to either gender. A little bit clever, but not very funny, particularly after a while. But it amused us when we were young. Why don't you ask him about it?' She narrowed her eyes a little and almost in a whisper said, 'And remember my promise . . . if you agree to see me here, I will restrict my contact with you to this room.'

And then she was gone. Will looked at the door that she'd left slightly ajar. He could hear a short murmur of conversation from the reception area, a burst of light-hearted laughter, and then the distant closing of the practice door. Nothing had been sorted. No agreement had been made about whether she would come back. Perhaps Lara was right and it was now time for him to involve the police.

In the evening, preparing for the group session, he felt the beginnings of some real confidence. He had a concrete idea of what he was going to do. He'd spent an evening on his own at home, drawing a neat version of the 'constricted heart' diagram. This was at least partly to distract himself from Lara's absence and to stop himself from texting or phoning her, which he had a constant urge to do.

He'd printed copies of the diagram and was going to do a *Where would you place yourself on it now?* exercise with the group. That should be enough to get people talking. He was reminded of the fact that the diagram was something that the other Will had created, but in this case it was easy to see where to go next.

He sat in the training room, a circle of empty chairs in front of him, and suddenly felt a welter of loneliness sweep over him. How was he going to get Lara back? How was he going to convince her that he loved her and that he hadn't done what she believed him to have done? Perhaps if he could explain properly about the lost sessions? But where would he start? And that still didn't explain Emma.

He closed his eyes to calm his thoughts and to still the flutter of unwelcome nerves about what might happen to his marriage. As he did so, the front bell of the practice sounded, and he buzzed Matt in, swiftly followed by Christina. He smiled as they came in, pleased to be doing something.

More clients arrived and there was something settling about everyone's gentle friendliness. This was their third session, and people were beginning to become familiar with each other. Quietly, Will thought how much he would need the extra money that this group afforded him if he was going to have to cover the cost of the flat on his own for a while.

He leaned down and busied himself with getting pens together to hand out with the copies of the heart diagram, then buzzed the last person in. It was Rachel, who came in with Emma. His heart skipped a beat when he saw her. She noticed his shock and smiled, then went to the last remaining seat and sat down.

'How thoughtful of you to put a chair out for me, Will,' she said.

Will felt a flash of annoyance. Of course, he hadn't factored in that Stuart wouldn't be coming this week, and so there was an extra chair. He noticed the room becoming quiet and the group members looking at him expectantly. He cleared his throat.

'Hello everyone,' he said, 'there seems to have been a misunderstanding this evening. Emma, here, has come to the meeting in error. I'm sorry, Emma, this is a closed group that is already established and it would be too disruptive to allow you to join us now.'

'You put a chair out for me,' she said.

'I'm afraid that chair was for one of the other members of the group who is unwell.'

'And yet you still put it out.'

'It can be helpful to have an empty chair when someone can't come to a group, so that their absence can be noted.'

Emma lifted her chin in subtle dismissal then looked around the assembly. 'I'm really sorry if it seems like I've come uninvited. I was under the impression that it would be alright for me to participate in the group. I wonder what other people feel about my presence, now I'm here?'

'It doesn't matter,' said Will. 'I am running the group and I'm quite clear about this. You will have to leave, Emma.'

'And yet all your clients were invited to join your group, so why not me?'

'You are not a client. I have refused to take you on as a client.'

'Why have you refused to take her on?' asked Debbie.

'Let's just say there is an issue of confidentiality,' Will told her. 'And I haven't invited all my clients to this group. I invited all the clients I had when I made my decision to form the group. I have started with a new client since then, who has not been invited here, and so it is also logical and consistent that, if I didn't invite him, I wouldn't have invited Emma. As I said, Emma isn't even a client and is therefore ineligible.'

'Why would you want to join?' Matt asked her.

'Because this is such an important moment,' said Emma. 'Don't you all feel it? Don't you understand, intuitively if not intellectually, that something incredibly special is happening here? Will has hit on . . . something. Something that defies rational explanation. You all know what I'm talking about because you've experienced it yourselves. He knows things that he shouldn't know, doesn't he? He does things in his sessions that, somehow, hit the nail on the head. What is that? What's going on? I have a sense of this something and I want to explore it and share it with other people who are experiencing the same thing.'

There was a pause. Nobody spoke for nearly a minute. A long time in a group situation.

'She's right,' said Rachel eventually. 'Will knew something impossible about my husband. Something that I didn't even know myself, and so he couldn't have got it from me. I think we should let Emma stay, if she's a part of this, and especially if she can name it and get it talked about. This really is important. And I'm beginning to think that it might slip away if we don't talk about it.'

'Good,' said Emma, 'I'm here because I want to talk about it.'

'I think she should stay,' said Matt.

'I'm not sure,' said Debbie. 'We don't know her. Will thinks she shouldn't be here because it would be too disruptive. That's important to consider, too.'

'We didn't know each other three weeks ago,' said Christina. 'I think she should stay.'

'Let's vote on it,' said Emma. 'It's a group after all.'

'No,' said Will. 'My decision is final. I know what I'm talking about when I say that it's not a good idea.'

'Why?' asked Emma.

'Because of what's happening right now,' said Will. 'Because you are too assertive and too domineering. It's not helpful in a group.'

'I'm being reasonable,' she said. 'There are thirteen of us here and we all want to talk about what's going on. Why won't you let me stay to be a part of it?'

'Because you are too disruptive.'

'But we all know that you won't talk about this unless I stay and make it happen.' She looked around the group. 'You know this is true. None of you have the assertive energy that's needed to challenge Will about it and get him to talk about what is going on here. I won't take over, I promise. I'll let people speak. I won't dominate. But I will make sure that we talk about what needs to be talked about.'

'You're already proving that you're too disruptive,' said Will.

'The only disruption is you asking me to leave.'

'And I'm not going to change my mind. We will start our session when you have left.'

There was a silence.

'I'm not going until we've had a vote,' said Emma.

'I'm not allowing a vote,' said Will. 'I'm running this group and I'll decide, using my professional judgement, what is best for it.'

'I think we should go with Will's decision,' said Laurence, 'but I think we need to be clear that it's on the condition that he agrees to talk about the mysterious things that happened in our one-to-one sessions.'

'What about the mysterious things that have been happening in my one-to-one sessions?' demanded Emma.

'You can talk about them in person with Will,' said Debbie.

'Not if he won't take me on as a client,' Emma said.

'Then he must have good reason not to take you on,' said Debbie.

Thank goodness! The group were moving towards a decision that Emma should leave.

'As I say,' said Will, 'this session will start after you have left.' He leaned back in his chair and crossed his arms.

'I thought I could persuade you to let me stay,' said Emma, 'but if you're determined that I should leave, then I'll go. But I have something to say first.' She leaned forward in her chair and looked around the group.

'Will is a fake,' she said. 'He's a fraud. He's a fraud as a person and a fraud as a therapist. He has no idea what he's doing with this group. That's why he spent last week going over what you'd done in the first session. He's completely lost his way. You know this is true.'

'How do you know what happened in previous sessions?' asked Matt.

Emma ignored him.

'There was that week, last month, when he was scintillating, when this *thing* happened. This mysterious thing happened, when he seemed to have almost supernatural powers. And now he's back to his old self, and it's all disappearing, isn't it? This isn't what you want. You want Will to challenge you again, to challenge you in particular and unpredictable ways. But Will himself is a total fraud, because he's asking you to do what he can't do himself.

'He is so stuck in his own story that he can't experience anything else. He feels that he's marked by tragedy. And do you know why? Because his sister died in an accident when he was seven-years-old. He blamed himself for it when it wasn't even his fault. He's carried that blame for years and years and it's a story that has no truth. "It was my fault" – where's the truth in that?' She looked directly at Will. 'You don't even know how to face up to that. How can you demand that others face these things when you can't do so yourself?'

'What have you faced up to, then?' Debbie asked her.

'I was kidnapped by my brother and taken to an isolated house in Norfolk,' said Emma. 'He tied me up and kept me there under his control until I nearly died. Will sits there with his little tragedy, when out there in the world there are people who are experiencing hell. Not some quiet existential anguish. I mean *hell!*' She looked at the faces of those around her. 'Can't you see it? Will has no backbone, because he's crippled. By guilt. How can he be in there with a client, if he can't be in there with himself?'

'I don't know what you're trying to say,' said Will. 'That a therapist – any therapist – has to have been in hell before they can be "in there" with a client?'

'No,' said Emma, 'but they need to have been honest about their own experience.' Her voice suddenly seemed to run out of energy, and she looked back at Will.

'It was inevitable that I would succumb to the desire to take my own life. Ask my brother about it when you next see him, Will, if you dare. Ask him why he told you that I was called Joe, rather than Emma. Ask him why he kidnapped me and tied me up until I was nearly dead. See what he says.'

'Why are you doing this?' asked Will. 'You're making it clear that there is no place for you in this group. I thought you wanted to discuss what was going on?'

'I do. But you've asked me to leave.' She held up her hands. 'Don't worry, I'll go. I've said my piece.' She looked at Will. 'Remember, Will. Remember the promise that I made to you today.'

He blinked and remembered. 'So, you'll disrupt my life until I agree to see you?'

Eleven

Will woke up. There was a moment when he was still groggy, emerging gently from a deep sleep. Then, suddenly, full wakefulness jolted him. What was he doing here? What had happened in the group session? He could remember Emma agreeing to leave, but that was it. Nothing after that, and now he was at home, in bed . . . He looked at the time. It was half past midnight. He threw back the duvet and discovered that he was lying there fully dressed.

Then he realised. The other Will had taken over! *The other Will*. He said it to himself, but what did that mean?

He looked out into the hall, noticed that the sitting room light was on and got up to switch it off. Then he noticed that the kitchen light was on as well. He went in, wondering whether to get himself a drink, then decided against it and turned the light off. He heard a sound in the hall. Looking round quickly, he noticed in the gloom that someone was already halfway out of the door. He couldn't see a face, but he could see the white jeans and cowboy boots.

'Emma!' he exclaimed as the door closed.

THE LOST SESSIONS

He ran to the door and opened it but there was no sign of her. He ran across the communal lobby, out of the main door and onto the street. Again, no sign of her. And yet . . . And yet, he was certain that he'd seen her. As he went back into the flat, he remembered that he'd changed the locks. Emma couldn't have had access to the flat.

Unless the other Will had invited her in?

A now-familiar confusion arose – he'd felt this way when he'd still had vestigial concussion and discovered that the lost sessions had taken place. Something had happened that made no sense.

The following day he went into the practice and checked his calendar for the next week. There she was. Another booking had been made for Emma in an apparently arbitrary slot. Well, he had five days to decide what to do. He thought of Lara and what he might say to her about this, if asked. He didn't understand it himself, so how could he possibly explain it to anyone else?

Debbie was his first client of the day. She was another punctual client and so he was a little disconcerted when she didn't turn up. After ten minutes, he switched his phone from silent. There was no message from her. It wasn't unusual for a client to miss a session, but it was unusual for such a reliable client to do so. He was aware that the last client to miss a session had been Stuart, and that was because he'd been in A&E.

As it happened, the next session after that was with Stuart, who was well enough to come back into therapy, if not to go back to his employment. He'd booked an extra session at a time when he would otherwise have been at work.

'Hello, Will,' he said, as he sat down. 'I've been signed off for another week, but I must say I feel much better.'

'Good,' said Will, aware that the last time they'd met, the circumstances had been very different.

Stuart, he now knew, had a habit of trying to please him, to be 'okay' for him, 'much better' even.

'I'm aware,' said Will after a while, 'that you tried to say that you were fine when I saw you in hospital. I want to check out that you're not holding anything back?'

'Well,' said Stuart, 'I suppose I'd better come clean.' He laughed. 'I've met someone. I can't believe it, really, because I wasn't looking for anyone. And it wasn't in the usual context of a bar or something. At the weekend, when I started feeling well again, I was persuaded to go away with a bunch of guys for a long weekend of hillwalking in Wales. I wasn't sure I was up to it, but it turned out to be exactly the right thing to do. To get away and get out into the countryside. And I met someone, and . . . we haven't even slept together yet. But there's something there.'

He looked at Will, and a sadness welled up in his eyes. 'I'm not trying to pretend that everything is fine, Will. I know that things really came to a head a couple of weeks ago when I took those pills, and that there's still a lot of stuff that I need to sort out. But it's also true that I feel somehow alive in a way that I didn't before. And it's not because I've met someone. I was getting this upsurge before that. It's the whole thing of going from a position of being overwhelmed by things to realising that I have to do something about them. Not only that I have to do something about them but that I am actually capable of doing something about them. The only thing that needs to change is me. Not my job, or my home, or my friendships, or my family. But me.' He shook his head. 'That's big.'

Will nodded his agreement.

'But not impossible,' said Stuart.

'But not impossible,' said Will.

'Exactly,' Stuart agreed.

As Will waited for his session with Guy, he realised that he didn't know what to do with the information that Emma had given him about the man she claimed was her brother. It was clear that she had access to certain information in the world that was not obviously possible for her to know, and yet she knew it. So, what sense could he make of what she'd told him about Guy. There was no precedent for how to process this knowledge. There was no precedent for how to proceed, period.

When Guy arrived, he looked pleased.

'I haven't seen my sister since I saw you last week,' he said. 'It's fantastic. I don't know what you've done, but I'm really grateful.'

'Has anything else changed in your life?' asked Will.

'No, it's all the same old stuff. I picked up a girl, though, and brought her home at the weekend – and there wasn't even a peep from my sister. It was amazing. I'd almost forgotten what it could be like to be alone with another person.'

Will was pensive for a moment or two before speaking.

'I'm interested that you always call her your sister, rather than by her name. You mentioned to me last time that she was called Jo. Was that short for Joanna? Or Joanne perhaps?'

Guy looked a little startled at this. 'I just called her Jo, that's all.'

'You mean Jo as in a girl's name, or Joe as in a boy's name?'

'Hey, this is creepy. How did you know that I called her Joe with an E?'

'It was a guess,' said Will. 'I mean, it's a generic name, isn't it, like Guy? I presume she wasn't christened Joe?'

'No,' said Guy.

'What was her name?'

Guy was squirming, which prompted Will to wonder who he was doing this for. Not for Guy, that was for sure. Will started to feel more like a policeman than a therapist.

'Forget it,' Will said quickly and a little apologetically, 'you don't have to answer that.'

Guy shrugged and looked serious. 'No, it's fine. I don't mind telling you. Her name was Emma. I never called her that, though. She didn't like me to. She thought it was too ordinary, or too dainty, somehow.'

Emma! But then, there were a lot of women out there with that name.

'You mentioned when we first met that you thought that Emma was "haunting" you. I wonder if you have any thoughts as to why she might have stopped doing so?' *Apart from the fact that she seems to have moved on to me.*

'Joe,' said Guy, 'not Emma. And I have no idea.'

'Quite often when a person is haunted by someone – haunted in a psychological sense – there is a sense of guilt that triggers the feeling of being haunted. A person might feel bad about something that has happened or that they have done, and then their guilt can manifest in quite startling ways.'

Guy looked pensive for a while. 'Do you mean that maybe I've worked through some stuff about me and Joe and that, now I've done it, I'm becoming less haunted by it?'

'I don't know,' said Will, 'I'm not trying to tell you anything. I'm trying out a suggestion to see if it resonates, that's all.' *Liar!* he thought to himself. He was trying to check out the validity of Emma's assertion that he kidnapped her, tied her up and nearly let her die. They sat for a while, until Will could no longer resist. 'And does it resonate?'

Guy didn't answer straight away, and then in a quiet, wistful voice, he said, 'Maybe . . . in a way.' He looked out of the window, then back at Will. 'There was nothing dainty about Joe. She was too assertive to be dainty.'

'Assertive?'

'One of the last times we went anywhere together, we went

to the London Eye. We had this thing about me having vertigo and she tried to persuade me to go on it with her. She had a new camera with a great telephoto lens and she wanted to take some pictures of London from up high. But I couldn't do it. Go with her, I mean. She made it seem as if I was doing it deliberately to annoy her or something and caused a bit of a fuss. That was her all over, not seeing things from another person's point of view. She wanted me to go with her, and it didn't bother her at all that I suffer from vertigo. She couldn't put herself into my shoes at all. There was no point me going. I would have had to sit there in the pod with my eyes closed . . . and so, she went on her own, and took a picture of me as the pod was beginning to get some elevation, and I'm looking up at her, upset, but okay at the same time. Actually . . .' He reached into his pocket for his phone. 'She sent it to me later on, so I must have it here.' He scrolled through some screens and then leaned forward to show it to Will. 'It seems to sum up our relationship somehow,' he said. 'Upsetness and okayness.'

The picture was eerie. There was Guy, standing on the riverside, looking up at the Eye, just as Will had done. It might as well have been him, given the angle and elevation from which it was taken.

Will was mesmerised by Guy's story. And the vertigo thing . . . well, it was more than eerie. He felt a flutter of it in his stomach, and a trembling feeling of danger.

On his way home, he realised he was still in a state of confusion. This woman, who claimed to be Guy's dead sister . . .

He'd seen her, with a camera, taking a picture of him from the London Eye, just as she'd done with Guy, from the same angle and everything. Was this a weird inverted premonition, a revisiting of a significant moment? He shivered at the thought, at the mystery of it.

When he got in, he noticed two things. Firstly, that Lara's coats had gone from the hooks in the hall. And secondly, that there was a bunch of flowers in a blue glass vase on the kitchen table. When he went in, he noticed that there were two notes, and a florist's card. The card said *Mexican Riot – blue larkspur, tulip and rose*. The first note, in unfamiliar writing, said, With love from Emma. See you next week. The second note, with a little arrow pointing at the first, had an exclamation mark on it and a quick scrawl: Picked up most of my stuff. L.

Will felt a lurch in his stomach and, yet again, a feeling of having been violated. It wasn't difficult to imagine what Lara would have made of Emma's note and flowers. How dare she! And how had she managed it? What a waste of time and expense to have had the locks changed.

He went into the kitchen and opened a bottle of wine then took a glass through to the sitting room. He took a gulp and looked out of the window over the slightly dilapidated late-Victorian semi-detached houses across the road. He needed to get some clarity here. He needed to think logically!

So . . . what could he say about all this for sure?

Emma was trying to make him see her on a regular basis at his practice. He was refusing. What power did she have to make his life problematic for as long as he continued to refuse?

Considerable! To what extent had this become an ego thing for Will? Massively! He didn't want to lose on this point with her. No, that was a major understatement. He'd said no, and to back down now would be . . . what? A failure? A humiliation? Was it some sort of manhood thing? Probably that, too.

What would it mean to enter into a dialogue with her? He didn't know, but he was aware that there was a hard part of himself that simply couldn't consider it. He didn't care that she might be asking for help because she also seemed to be intent on ruining his life.

Well, maybe he *would* go to the police. He could report her, as Lara had suggested. Get a restraining order. After all, she really was stalking him. But what would he actually say to the police? That she seemed to be able to walk through locked doors? That she kept turning up in his flat inexplicably? That she was haunting him? They would want to know how he knew her, and what would he say to *that*? No. It was impossible. They would think he was out of his mind. And perhaps he was . . .

But then, she'd said she would leave him alone, if only he would agree to see her.

He would refuse to take her on as a client, but perhaps there were some things he needed to know – to ask. About why she was doing this. And *how* she was doing it.

The following day was Saturday. He sat listlessly in the flat, alone, feeling bereft. It seemed outrageous that Lara was not there. He felt empty – literally, too, as he hadn't eaten anything and didn't feel inclined to.

The phone rang in the early afternoon. It was Jamie.

'What's this I hear about you and Lara living apart?'

'How did you know about that?'

'I leant Lara a book on the restoration of Somerset House and texted her to ask if she'd finished with it. She texted back to say that you've left her for someone else.'

Will took a gasp of breath. Was it shock or indignation? He couldn't tell. 'That is so not true. The whole thing has been a complete misunderstanding. She saw me with a rather deranged prospective client and came to an understandable but completely incorrect conclusion.'

'But presumably you explained this to her?'

'Yes, although I suppose, in her shoes, I'd probably have felt the same. This person who wants to be taken on as a client deliberately made it look like we were having some sort of relationship. To hurt me, probably, or at least to make life difficult for me for refusing to see her.'

'This person sounds dangerous.'

'Yes, I think she is.'

'What are you doing about it?'

'I think I'm going to have to ask her what she wants from me. She's more or less stalking me, and so I'll ask her what she's doing and then I'll do whatever is necessary to make her leave me alone. After that . . . well, after that I'll do whatever I have to do to get Lara back.'

'I presume you've been to the police?' said Jamie.

'No, not yet.'

'If you're being stalked then you need to get them involved. It sounds like you're already suffering some major consequences of this. Just go to the police.'

'I will. Soon. If I need to.'

Will felt a little bit more sane as he talked to Jamie. Thinking that made him laugh. 'Are you free this evening? Do you fancy meeting up?'

'I've arranged to go out,' said Jamie. 'I could cancel it, though, if you feel it would help to talk some more about this?'

'No, no. You go out and have a good time.'

'I'm still worried about you, Will. I can't put my finger on it, but there's something that you're not telling me – or that you're not clear about yourself – and . . . well, it's worrying me.'

'I'll be okay,' said Will. 'But maybe you can do something for me?'

'Of course.'

'Tell Lara that I am not being unfaithful to her. I love her and would never do anything to jeopardise our relationship.'

Will had told Jamie that he was okay. But he wasn't. The weekend passed fast enough in a haze of wine, take away pizza and movies, but he wasn't okay. Those two days were sad, depressing and confusing. Then the weekend was over. Monday morning arrived and he went to his practice hoping to be grounded by his client work. He wasn't due to see Guy that day. He'd started a training course on Mondays and so had moved his session time to later in the week. But no one else came during the day, either. Each of his usual sessions passed and no one turned up until Stuart arrived for his 7.30pm slot. He seemed rather more pensive than in the previous session.

'Something very different is happening,' he said. 'I told you last week, I've met someone new. Well, it feels very different. I don't feel that I'm bringing the weight of my past into this new friendship, and only now do I realise how weighed down I've always been by shame.'

'Shame at the unspoken secret? The "terrible thing" you've done, that is so bad you haven't even told your therapist.'

'Exactly. It's as though I felt it was inescapable. As though this shame was a part of me. It was who I was, someone who would never be good enough. The amazing thing is that I don't seem to have to get rid of it. All I have to do is experience a single moment when it is absent to realise that it isn't true. It isn't me.'

Will leaned forward in his chair. 'Do you need to keep it a secret anymore?'

'I'm not sure. In a way, perhaps that's not the most important thing. I thought I would be better – "cured" – when I was able to tell you what I'd done. Tell you without shame, I mean. Now, I'm not sure. And I realise that it doesn't matter that I'm not sure.' He smiled sadly. 'The price I have paid for carrying the shame that I have carried is that I have experienced separation from everyone I have ever loved.'

Will phoned each client who hadn't attended their sessions but spoke to no one in person and left voicemail messages. What had he felt about this other Will the previous week? Admiration? Envy? But now it seemed ridiculous. He didn't know enough to be envious. Envious of what, anyway?

Tuesday came, with no clients, then Wednesday and Thursday. What had happened? What had the other Will done in that lost part of the group session? What had he said or done to make his clients stay away? And what had happened between the end of the session and waking up, fully clothed, in bed at half past midnight? As well as being disconcerting in the now-familiar sense, it was also potentially disastrous financially. He had thirteen clients, which was a basic minimum – twenty would be better. But to go from thirteen to two and to not know why was more than disconcerting.

On Thursday evening, Will prepared for the group session, but with little hope that anyone would come. He had texted Stuart earlier in the day to say that the group session had been cancelled. He couldn't countenance a meeting with Stuart and no one else and with no way of explaining why that was the case. In fact, he realised, he was rather fearful that people *would* come, and then he'd have to face another scenario in which he wouldn't know what had happened and he would have to piece it all together as he went along. But no one came to the group, and so he sat for forty-five minutes before quietly letting himself out of the building and walking home.

THE LOST SESSIONS

On Friday morning, Debbie missed her session yet again. In the afternoon, there was another session booked for Emma. Waiting for her was an unsettling experience. He was clear that he could never be her therapist, because of Guy and what she knew about him, if nothing else. But it was equally clear that demanding that she leave him alone was something he couldn't enforce.

He waited in his room; he couldn't face Becky in reception, as she would undoubtedly ask him where all his clients were and he didn't know what to tell her. At midday, Becky called through to say that Emma had arrived and he went through to get her. She was in her usual clothes but also wore a small black shoulder bag.

'Hello, Will,' she said, 'how are you?'

'We need to talk,' he said.

'You mean you're agreeing to take me on?'

'No. But I do agree to talk to you, here in this room. On the condition that you leave me alone elsewhere. You know why I can never take you on as a client.'

'Agreed. The distinction between client and therapist here is meaningless, so let's drop it.' She looked out of the window at the sun-dappled wall and the laburnum tree and then back at Will. 'I take it Guy didn't admit to having kidnapped me?'

'Look . . . I'm happy to talk about anything but my confidential client work.'

She looked dubious. 'Well, I'm going to have to do something about that, I suppose. Watch this space.' She leaned down and picked up her bag, taking a large bronze-coloured aerosol canister out of it. 'Do you know what this is?'

'No,' said Will.

'It's hairspray. I'm not sure whether that will become relevant later, but it might.' She put it back in the bag and waited for him to speak.

They looked at each other for a few moments. Will realised that it was not his prerogative to wait for her to break the silence. She wasn't his client.

'Right . . . Who are you? Why are you here? And what are you trying to do to my marriage?'

Was there a hint of triumph in Emma's eyes? He wasn't sure. 'What do you think the answer is?' she asked.

'I have no idea.'

'Really?' she asked.

'Really,' he told her.

She pondered this for a few seconds. 'Do you believe me when I say that I am Guy's dead sister?'

'I don't know. You know things about him – and about me for that matter – that you couldn't possibly know unless you had access to information that an ordinary person wouldn't have. And you had access to my flat even when I'd changed the locks. But whether that makes you dead . . . I don't know.'

He watched her face for a reaction to what he was saying, but she remained impassive.

'Perhaps I can ask you a question?' he said. 'If you're Guy's dead sister, why pick on me to haunt? Why not pick on him?'

'You think I'm haunting you? Well, I suppose you would. But

before I answer your question, I must ask you one of my own.'

Will looked at her, impassive in his turn, unsure whether the emotion he was feeling was hostility or acquiescence.

'Okay,' he said.

'Do you trust me?' she asked.

'No, of course I don't trust you. What possible reason have I got to trust you?'

'Perhaps because I am completely true to my word. What I have said I will do, I have done. I asked to have a chance to come into dialogue with you and you kept pushing me away. I needed to do whatever was necessary to get you talking.'

'By ruining my marriage?'

'Ha, ha! What I'm inviting you to do is to trust me. I don't know how long that will take, but when you can trust me, I'll show you the answer to your question.'

'Show me?'

'Yes. It's not really something I can tell you in words.'

Will was nervous about his next session with Guy. The whole Guy-Emma thing was getting too weird. The question of whether he should be seeing Guy at all was also an issue given that Will knew confidential information about him. But Will didn't have time to consider this further as, when Guy did arrive, he was white with shock.

'Are you alright?' asked Will at once. 'I mean, do you need a glass of water?'

'No,' said Guy, 'I'm alright. I've had a shock, that's all.'

'You've seen your dead sister. You've seen Emma – or Joe.'

Guy went even whiter. 'How do you know?' he gasped.

'I can't think of anything else that would be so shocking and so scary for you.'

'She was real! I mean, I even touched her!'

'You mean, you've really seen her, rather than pretending that you've seen her because you feel haunted by her?'

'Yes,' said Guy, a little sheepishly. 'I suppose you could tell that I was making it up when I first saw you?'

'It's not my job to try and work out if people are lying. Did she say anything to you?'

Guy hesitated, then nodded.

'Perhaps she told you to come and confess to me the part you played in her death?'

Guy gasped. 'I suppose because you're a therapist you can tell that from the way I've behaved – that I feel, well, responsible for her death . . . to some extent.'

'No, this has nothing to do with me being a therapist. It's an unusual situation all round.'

'I don't know what you mean.'

'Nor do I, really,' said Will. 'But what I can say to you is that whatever you do and whatever you tell me, you must tell me because you want to and not because you've been frightened into it.'

Guy fell silent. Will watched him.

'But, Joe's dead. She's dead, and so she's not real. She couldn't come back to haunt me. What I am being haunted by is my own feeling of guilt and shame which has . . . manifested. You said last week that guilt can manifest in startling ways. Well, I guess this counts as startling.'

The look of pain and vulnerability on Guy's face at that moment caught something in Will. A whisper of a memory. *Oh!* Now he saw it! They were both haunted by a feeling of responsibility for the death of a sister.

'What?' Guy had clearly picked up on Will's expression.

'It's nothing. Or at least it's nothing to do with the work we're doing here.'

Of course! A warm flush of recognition spread through Will's body.

'The thing is,' said Guy, 'that it's really hard to reveal something that you've held so tightly as a secret. I want to tell you, but . . . I can't.'

Will looked at Guy, as he teetered on the brink of confessing, before pulling away.

'Why is it so difficult to say?' Guy asked.

'Because telling your story will lead to change,' Will told him, 'and there's a part of us that will always resist change.'

Guy considered this quietly for a moment. 'I loved her. I really loved her. If only she'd been a willing participant! But she wasn't. She resisted me every time. I knew that what I was doing, I was doing because I loved her. But she hated me for it. *Really* hated me. Well, I can see why. No one wants to be physically overwhelmed like that, do they? It's humiliating for a start. But at least I know that I was doing it for her own good.'

'For her own good?' Will tried to keep indignation and

disgust out of his voice, and so it came out a little croaky.

'Yes. I'm sure it didn't seem that way to her.'

'Say it. Say what you did to her, then it will be in the open and we can look at it.'

'I . . .' Guy looked down at his feet, and kept his head bowed. 'I can't. I feel you're pushing me.' He sighed. 'It's not even as if I did anything wrong. I mean, if you did something for the love of another person, then it's not wrong, is it? Even if they end up killing themselves?'

'We all need to take responsibility for what we've done.'

'Yes, that's true, and I guess that's why I'm here. I want to take responsibility.'

'Well, you can start now,' said Will. 'Let's stop evading this. You tell me you didn't do anything wrong, because you loved Em–'

'Joe.'

'You loved Joe, but you have to take responsibility for the fact that you were the one who traumatised her to the point that she took her own life.'

'You have no idea what I did,' said Guy. 'You sound so critical and censorious, as though you're trying to make me feel that I *did* do something wrong. Well, I didn't. I loved Joe, that's all. Perhaps I loved her too much, but that's not a crime.'

'I have a very good idea what you did,' said Will. There it was: that tone of disgust and anger again.

Guy shook his head. 'If you're so sure, then tell me!' he challenged. 'What did I do?'

Will took a deep breath. 'You kidnapped her. You tied her

up and kept her prisoner until she nearly died, didn't you? And then she killed herself.'

Guy went completely ashen. He seemed to stop breathing for an unfeasible length of time. 'I . . .' he began, but he couldn't speak. Tears welled up and he opened his mouth again but nothing came out. Then he stood and fled the room.

Will looked after him. He'd broken every therapeutic boundary in the book – and not in a good way. But what sort of boundary is appropriate when both the therapist and his client are apparently being haunted by the client's dead sister? Dead, but in some ways very much alive.

Will sat quietly. He did not write up any client notes. He realised that he'd stopped writing notes on his client sessions after he'd stopped being in supervision.

Something was slipping.

Twelve

That weekend looked set to be another twilit weekend of immobility and uncertainty. Will had no real sense of what to do, which was disconcerting as there wasn't much time left in which to do anything. He might bump along the bottom, financially, for a little while, but he was already living perilously close to his credit limit and that was unnerving. He knew that to do nothing would be to fall into despair, and so he looked around for something to occupy his attention. Sending pleading texts and emails to Lara, particularly when drunk, was counterproductive, he knew. But to do nothing felt worse.

He received a text from Dan, his old friend from university, asking him round for a meal. *If you come round at lunch time, we could go for a bike ride, too. Lara can join us later.* How impossible it seemed to say anything meaningful when he responded. He was aware that Dan always grounded him and made him feel alive and dynamic. But he couldn't accept the invitation without explaining about Lara, and he had no idea himself what was going on there . . . Instead, he sent a short reply saying that things were pretty hectic at the moment and that he'd text soon to sort something out. Dan responded: *Mark will be coming that evening, too. He'll be disappointed not to see you. He's only down in London for a few days.* Mark was a friend from their Edinburgh days and Will felt a beat of disappointment at the thought of missing him. He wondered how long this unsettled limbo period would last and realised that it was beginning to have consequences that reached into every corner of his life.

In fact, he'd received messages from other friends recently, asking how he was and wondering why he'd gone so quiet and he'd answered everyone in more or less the same way. As he sat in the sitting room on Friday evening, he could feel his whole world shrinking. He noticed that the flat was becoming shabby, and had been for some time. So, on Saturday morning, he went out to get some paint to redecorate the sitting room. It was worth the extra expense to be doing something that Lara would appreciate. Once he'd done the walls, he realised that the skirting boards now needed to be done. So, he did them too. The decorating took him the whole weekend, but by the end of Sunday evening it looked good and had the clean, heady smell of newness about it.

On Monday morning, he had the unexpected realisation that he was beginning to cope with the strangeness of his life, if not be happy with it. There was another session booked in with Emma and he wondered what it might bring, and although he wasn't looking forward to it, at least he wasn't actively *not* looking forward to it.

As he came in, Becky asked him directly what had happened to his clients.

'It's all going according to plan,' he said. *Although I'm not sure whose plan I'm talking about.*

It was an inadequate response but Becky didn't pursue it. She looked at him dubiously, though not without sympathy, and kept quiet as he went to his room.

Emma arrived in her usual attire, with her bag, and a newspaper folded open to an interior page.

'Look . . .' She handed the paper to Will. 'Guy killed himself.'

Will looked. There was a brief story of an as yet unidentified young man throwing himself in front of a bus on a busy street in Kennington at lunchtime on Friday.

'He did it immediately after he left you. He walked straight out of your room and threw himself under a bus.'

Will felt a thump of shock that was accompanied by vivid memory – of how Guy had looked, so pale and panicked, as he'd left the room on Friday. 'Oh no . . .'

He realised that he hadn't even thought about how Guy must have felt as he left the room. Will hadn't expressed his thoughts verbally at the time, but perhaps if he had done so, he might have said something like, 'you heartless monster!' Now he felt a welter of self-recrimination. The purpose of boundaries in therapy was to stop judgement getting in the way of helpful therapeutic work, person to person. All Will had seen in that last session was a criminal who had killed his sister. But in fact, he knew, Guy was also a young man wracked with pain and guilt, a young man who was suffering and who needed to be seen.

'I know what you're thinking,' said Emma. 'You're thinking, "I showed him no kindness, no empathy, no unconditional positive regard. It's my fault that he killed himself." But don't worry, Will. Everything is happening exactly as it was meant to happen. You did all the right things. You'll see.'

'You seem very sure of that,' he said. 'Almost pleased.'

'Pleasure has nothing to do with it. This is how it has to be. It's an interesting situation. As far as the funeral is concerned, there's no close family who would care. Certainly not our parents. He doesn't see them, but I guess the police will have told them as next of kin. They'll do the cheapest funeral possible and hope to inherit something. It's a bit of a cracker, though, isn't it, to have both of your children take their own lives? But not really surprising given the way they treated us. Maybe they'd need a good bit of therapy to come to terms with what they've done, if they'd ever admit to it. Not that they would ever consider therapy – unless it was offered free on the NHS. Which it probably would be, in a small and insufficient way.'

'What *do* you feel about your brother killing himself? You seem very hard.'

'This is exactly what I'd hoped for. I believe you understand murderous rage, at least in principle, and I'm sure you can understand why I might have felt it towards him. I knew I could trust you to break your boundaries and act inappropriately at exactly the right moment. Your boundaries have been rather indistinct for some time, haven't they? But you don't have to worry. You may have caused my brother to kill himself, but that was all part of the plan.'

'You're trying to make me defensive,' said Will.

'I'm asking you to listen to your heart,' said Emma. 'I don't need to tell you that you behaved badly. You know that already. You acted in anger and you behaved towards him as an unthinking idiot would. You didn't bracket your own feelings off. Instead, you acted on them when you shouldn't have, and then he went straight out and killed himself.'

'If you wanted that to happen so much, why didn't you kill him yourself?'

'Because, sadly, that's not how it works when you're dead. You need a living person to deal with living people.'

'So, you used me? You deliberately manipulated me so that this would happen?'

Emma shrugged. 'You can try to blame it on me, but did I make you feel the way you felt? Did I control the way you behaved with Guy? You don't like me, Will. In fact, you hate me, don't you? You're beginning to feel rage. Especially now.'

Will looked at her but didn't say anything.

'It's as well you're not in supervision. How would you even *begin* to unpick this one? Let alone the fact that your clients have stopped coming to see you for reasons that remain unclear.'

Will still didn't say anything.

'You're a mess, Will. Admit it.'

Will seemed to be empty of everything, including rage, and was unable to reply to Emma's assertion.

'Say it,' she said.

'You want me to say I'm a mess?'

'Yes.'

'Why?'

'Because saying it is important.'

'I'm not a mess. My life may be a mess, but my life is not me.'

'Oh, well, if you're going to make impossible distinctions like that, then this will go nowhere,' said Emma. 'Your therapeutic practice is a mess. Where are your clients? You only have one client, if you don't count me. One client who is recovering from a suicide attempt. The other client you had has just killed himself by throwing himself under a bus. And you are partly responsible for that. You know you are. And your marriage is a mess. Where's your wife now?'

Will remained silent.

'You see, you *are* a mess, because everything has fallen apart and you have no idea what you're doing or where you're going. So, you might as well say it.'

Will stared at her. She'd told him that he hated her, and in that moment, he felt it. He *really* felt it.

'I'm not a mess. Why are you trying to make me say it?'

'Maybe you'll work that out sometime. But right now I want you to come with me. I want to show you something.'

'What do you want to show me?'

'You'll have to trust me.'

Will smiled with derision. 'Trust you?'

'I've told you before . . . I've always been true to my word. You may not have liked what I do or say, but you can't accuse me of being untrustworthy.'

'I suppose I can trust you to make my life . . . difficult.'

Emma laughed. 'To make your life a mess, you nearly said!'

'If my life is a mess, it's your doing.'

'Look, Will . . . it's not my intention to make your life difficult for you. Unless I have to, to get my point across.'

'So, you want to make a point? Why can't you make it here?'

'Say it.'

'No!' He had a brutal sense that the only power he had left was this anger. 'It's not me that's a mess. It's the whole situation that's a mess and you're the one who's caused it. You're the one who's ruining my marriage, whatever you're trying to imply. And you're the one who's ruining my livelihood.'

Emma was watching him with a benign half-smile on her face. And suddenly there it was, another adrenaline rush of anger. Will could feel the annihilating nature of it, the murderous quality of inchoate rage. It rendered him speechless and he looked at her, frozen in his chair. He could feel his hands clutching the arms.

Emma's inscrutable look turned into a grin. 'Here we are,' she said.

'Where?' he croaked. 'What do you mean?'

'Your anger, Will. Your rage.'

It was familiar, but old. He vividly remembered being in

Edinburgh as an undergraduate, drunk, standing against the stone balustrade of North Bridge wanting to fight, wanting to be beaten up – wanting to be hospitalised. That was the last time he'd knowingly felt rage like this, and it was so clear right now that although the conscious response was to disown it, to project it onto someone else, it was in fact his own.

He looked out at the sky, at the sharpness of the sunlight as it picked out the yellow blossom that was coming out on the laburnum, making it radiant.

'I wasn't angry with them,' he murmured. 'I was angry with myself! That's why I wanted to be beaten up all those years ago.'

'But why?' she asked. 'Why did you want to be beaten up?'

It was there, the answer, just below the horizon of his consciousness. Like an indistinct object shrouded in mist, it gradually came into view.

'I was looking for the punishment I thought I deserved,' he whispered.

'Good,' she said, softening. 'All I wanted was to hear you say it.'

They sat in silence for a few moments.

Will's rage subsided. It didn't disappear, but it ceased to have a focus. It had been directed at Emma, then at himself. Now, it had no object, and from that perspective it made no sense.

'Let's go,' she said.

'Where? Why?'

'Because I have to show you something and it's a couple of blocks away.'

Will thought for a few moments. Something hard in him had softened and he felt suddenly more capable of rational thought. 'Okay, I'll come and see what you have to show me. But I have to tell you . . . this had better be worth it.'

'Oh, it will be.'

He followed her into the hallway and out of the building. They walked across the bustling high street and down a lane that led to Kennington Park. There was a small newsagent on the first corner. As they came up to it, an Asian man came out carrying two bin liners of rubbish in one hand and some flattened cardboard boxes in the other. As he went around and into the alleyway to the side of the shop, the cardboard slipped and scattered onto the pavement. Will moved immediately to help him but the man waved him away.

'Don't worry, mate,' he said.

Emma went into the shop and Will followed her in. Once they were inside, Emma went back to the doorway and looked out. She checked up and down the street then came back in.

'Right,' she said. 'Watch carefully.'

She leaned over the counter and picked up a disposable lighter from a display case by the chewing gum. She opened her bag and took out her can of hairspray. She took the cap off and as she started to spray the canister she clicked the lighter and lit the plume of spray. Instantly and with a roar, it was ablaze like a small flamethrower. Will leaped forwards, grabbing at her arm, but Emma was ready for this and turned the flames on him. He felt a furious blast of heat in his face, which made him stagger back a few steps, blinded, caught by the agony of it, the stinging in his eyes and the caustic fumes in his throat and lungs that made him cough so hard that he retched. After a few seconds he tried opening his eyes but found they were in a kind of chemical agony. In the brief moment that he could see, though, he was aware that she had been playing the flames along the rack of papers and magazines, which were taking immediately in the heat, a blaze already underway. He closed his eyes again and retched as he heard the roar of flames beside him. Emma grabbed his arm and pulled him from the shop. He stumbled along beside her and when they stopped he took a deep breath and threw up on the pavement. His lungs burned and he could still barely open his eyes, which watered profusely.

When he finally managed to open them he could see through a bleary mist that she'd marched him across the street and a short way up a narrow mews. Looking back, he could see the shop. There was still no sign of the newsagent, who was presumably at the back sorting out the cardboard. It seemed incredible, but only two or three minutes had passed. Strangely, there was still little sign of the fire from where they stood. The door and the windows were covered with posters and signs and so the flicker of light and the billow of smoke in the shop were hardly visible, though clearly that was about to change. Through his blur of tears, Will saw the edges of the posters in the window beginning to curl with heat.

'Why the hell did you do that?' he managed between coughs.

'We'd better go,' she said. 'I know you didn't do it, but they're not going to be able to pin this crime on someone who's been dead for over five years.'

When he didn't move, she took his elbow and leaned in towards him with a movement that might have seemed affectionate in a different context. Actually, she was applying her full bodyweight into getting him moving.

'No,' said Will, 'I need to go and help.'

As he said this, the shopkeeper came out from the alley and saw that his shop was on fire. He stopped in shock for a moment and then, with a yell of anguish, pulled the door open. Flames billowed out and he staggered back.

'There is nothing you can do to help,' she said. 'He'll call the fire brigade. You couldn't do it any more quickly.'

'You're mad,' Will said. 'No, not just mad, you're criminally insane.'

'And you look like an arsonist.'

He put his hand to his fringe and felt the frizz of burnt hair. His cheeks were throbbing from the flames that Emma had turned on him. He felt the accelerated pulse along his clenched jawline. He could guess how bloodshot his eyes were.

'You don't want anyone seeing you looking like that,' she said. 'You'll be arrested.'

She started walking away. He stood where he was.

'I'm not going anywhere with you,' he called after her.

'That's okay!' she called back. 'Remember . . . for as long as there's something to burn, you'll get fire!'

He watched her receding figure and then turned away, looking over to the blazing shop. Flames now roared out of the doorway and licked up over the roof. It was a one-storey building with a flat roof so there was nothing above it and the flames were already sending a roiling column of black smoke up into the sky. Although he was standing away from a clear sightline, it was obvious that if anyone looked directly his way, they would see him and 'know' that he had started the fire. He started to walk away. It was only a short mews. Emma was already out of sight and he was relieved that he couldn't see her. He could still feel the thump of his heartbeat.

What was that? He thought.

Back at the practice, the reception was unmanned. He could hear Becky's voice down the corridor, talking to one of his colleagues in the kitchen and so he slipped past and into his room. As he sat down, he heard the distant sirens of fire engines.

He still hadn't had an opportunity to even start processing his reaction to Guy's death and his experience of rage. He was in shock, and so all of that had become muffled. And he had clients to wait for. They weren't confirmed in the practice diary, but he still hoped that, at some point, at least some of them would start to return.

Twenty minutes after his second no-show, he left, saying a brisk goodbye to Becky. As he left the practice he took a detour home, walking past the scene of Emma's crime to see what damage had been done. It was over two hours since he'd parted from her by the burning newsagent. He saw that the interior was completely gutted. A fire engine still stood outside, but it was lifeless. The firemen had finished doing what they needed to do to get the fire out and were now inside the building checking things that firemen check.

Will felt impotent, unable to do anything – unable to act as a witness, for example. After all, what could he say about the perpetrator of the fire? He wondered if it had been captured on CCTV. If so, it would be clear that he'd tried to stop Emma. But, in his heart, he knew that it wouldn't have been caught on CCTV. That wasn't how Emma's world worked.

When he got home, he was flushed and sweaty so he had a shower, and it was only when he got out that he noticed that his eyebrows and lashes were singed almost out of existence. His wild, curly fringe was almost gone, burned away by the flames that Emma had turned on him.

My God, he thought, *I really do look like an arsonist!*

He took a pair of scissors and tried to cut out the frizzed hair at the front but it only made things worse. Then he remembered that he had a pair of electric hair clippers and he went to look for them. He found them, eventually, at the back of the cupboard in the spare room. The half-finished paintings in there haunted him with their abandoned proficiency and promise.

He had no option but to cut his hair back to a Number Two crop all over. When he had finished, his singed eyebrows and lashes didn't look quite so noticeable, but he still hardly recognised himself. His cheeks and forehead were bright red for a start. They had that zinging feeling that young burns had and he didn't know if they would blister. He looked down at the shorn locks on the bathroom floor and felt perhaps that he had cut off more than his hair. He hadn't had short hair since his one attempt with these clippers nearly ten years previously. He understood that he was leaving something behind. He looked . . . well, he looked *hard*. Hard but vulnerable at the same time. It was odd and unnerving. He didn't recognise the person who stared back from the mirror. His blue eyes had an icy quality that stared back at him with an edge of . . . an edge of . . . he couldn't put a word to it, but if he'd ever seen it in a client, it would have worried him. A lot.

He sat for a while and felt the pressure building up. The rage was returning. It was old and familiar and, in an unnerving way, almost comfortable. He remembered it from his time in Edinburgh – inchoate and ungraspable. He tried to rage at Emma, at the absurd pantomime she'd made him witness when she'd torched the newsagent. But he couldn't rage at her. He knew the object of his rage and it wasn't her. His whole body prickled with it, like midges crawling on his skin, and suddenly it was impossible to sit still. He went into the hall, picked up his coat and turned to leave the flat, catching his reflection as he did so. He looked hard and angry and on the lookout for trouble.

The first bar he went to wasn't half as rough as its reputation suggested and as he stood at the bar and downed a double scotch, he barked a mirthless laugh. This was insane! How totally ridiculous he was to be out here like this. What possible benefit could there be in coming out and looking for trouble? When he'd been in Edinburgh, at least he'd had the excuse of being a troubled youth. Now it felt pathetic. The people around him deserved his unconditional positive regard, not his fists.

He returned to the flat, picking up a bottle of whisky on the way. He'd never been a great drinker and it didn't take long to get drunk, downing shots and slamming the robust glass down on the kitchen sideboard after each gulp. It took him half the bottle to really see the self-pity that stood behind the rage. There was a moment when he saw himself as another therapist might, lit up with the energy of it, almost revelling in it. He could imagine that therapist saying, *Admit it. You're enjoying this!* He was in an ecstasy of self-pity. The word *ecstasy* stuck. It really was a kind of ecstasy, a whole body sensation that was excited and energised. It was weirdly euphoric, too – or if not euphoric then elevated to an absurd degree. *I'm in an ecstasy of rage*, he told himself, *against myself.*

As he neared the end of the bottle, the nausea began. It built swiftly to a crescendo of vomiting in the toilet. He knelt on the bathroom floor, head hanging into the bowl. Here was another thing he hadn't done for years: drinking until he threw up. There was an apposite, if not fully grasped, metaphor in having got drunk on whisky, as though he was vomiting his faux-Scottishness down the toilet, that inauthentic, constructed Scottishness that had come from a point of inarticulate rage against the circumstances of his unhappiness. The self-harm in it was so obvious that he might have smiled had he been able to control his facial muscles.

The next day he phoned in to say he wouldn't be coming in. He sounded rough enough not to have to explain himself. Surprisingly, he only had a moderate hangover – he'd drunk the whisky so fast that he'd probably thrown most of it up. Still, there seemed no point sitting in an empty therapy room in the hope that someone might turn up.

'I'm not expecting anyone,' he told Becky, 'but give me a ring on my mobile if someone does come along.'

He sat at home and drank coffee and looked out of the window. What could he do with his day? As he thought this, the phone rang. It was Steffi, the manager of the Claygate Centre.

'Hello, Will. I thought I'd give you a ring to check how you are. I'm not sure what's happening at the practice for you, but Becky tells me you've stopped working with almost all of your clients.'

'That's true, in a way.' His voice came out husky somehow and as damaged-sounding as he felt. 'Temporarily.'

'What does that mean?' asked Steffi. 'Becky says you've been talking strangely to her – in ways that she doesn't completely "get".'

'I haven't stopped working with my clients, Steffi. We're doing project work together, that's all.'

'That's fine, Will. So long as you're having effective supervision and everything that you're doing is properly scrutinised and approved, then it doesn't matter if it looks a little unusual from the outside.'

'Exactly,' said Will.

'Becky was a little concerned about how you sounded when you phoned in earlier, but I can hear that you are unwell. And, please, don't mention that I called you to ask about it. She spoke to me about it informally. I thought I'd give you a quick ring to check that you are getting on alright. The practice diary does look quite empty for you right now. Give me a shout if you feel you're desperate for a referral or two. And, under the circumstances, perhaps we can prioritise the next few referrals so that they come to you.'

'Thanks, Steffi. That's really kind of you. I'm fine with the level of work I'm doing at the moment but I'll let you know if that changes.'

'Good, good,' she said.

They exchanged a few pleasantries, and, as she was about to go, Steffi paused.

'Your concussion?' she asked. 'That has cleared completely, hasn't it?'

'Yes. It's cleared completely.'

'Good.'

After the call, Will felt a sense of risk, as though he was on the edge of a precipice and might fall off. The sensation was neither pleasant nor unpleasant, experienced as an unadorned and impersonal fact. Were they suspicious of his behaviour? Had Becky decided that he was behaving so strangely that she wanted to raise it as an issue or had she made a passing comment by the kettle?

At that moment, he heard someone coming into the flat. He braced himself for Emma, but it was Lara, who started.

'Oh!' she gasped, 'Will, I didn't expect to see you.'

She came into the sitting room, obviously embarrassed. Will smiled and got up, pleased to see her.

'What have you done to your hair?' she asked.

'I've cut it, that's all. 'Don't you like it?'

'I loved your long hair. Now, you look, well, sort of . . . bare. And what about your face. You look like you've got the worst sunburn I've ever seen.' She looked around her. 'And there's something different about this room.'

'I've redecorated,' he said.

'Oh, yes, so you have.'

'Lara, I'm so pleased to see you. Now you're here, maybe you could stay for a coffee and a chat. There are so many things I want to talk to you about. About everything that's been going on. Honestly. Truthfully.' He raised his depleted eyebrows at her, trying to look hopeful.

'No,' she said, 'I can't stay. I need a couple of things from my drawers in the bedroom.'

She left the room and Will stood looking at the empty space where she'd been standing. Lara was gone for a short while and then returned, stuffing a couple of items into her bag.

'I see by the clippings on the kitchen floor that you've cut your hair yourself.' She stopped, and the hard expression in her eyes softened for a moment. 'Are you alright Will? I mean, you're not having a nervous breakdown or something, are you?'

'I don't know.'

For a moment she seemed undecided, but then her expression closed off, quite suddenly, leaving him very much outside. 'At least you're in the right profession to get the help you need. And you know what I need from you before I'll have a proper conversation with you.'

'I can only offer you the truth. I've only ever told you the truth.'

'Right . . . I'm off. Bye.'

And she was gone. Will silently watched her go and he felt his powerlessness in that moment. Asking her to stay obviously wasn't enough, and pleading would have been worse. He had to hold the idea that she was out there. She might not be well disposed towards him but neither did she obviously hate him.

And that had to be be positive – hadn't it?

It was this thought that made him realise, with a thump, how far he had travelled from the state of mind he'd been in only a few weeks ago. Being pleased to realise that his wife didn't hate him. That was . . . well, it was tragic.

And that was the overall feel of the rest of the week. Tragic. He realised that he'd lost all his confidence, as a therapist, as a husband and as a human being. Steffi had asked him whether he was getting good supervision and he'd answered her indirectly. He'd certainly implied that he was. But of course, he wasn't.

He remembered his course leader talking about self-supervision. That, after a time, it was possible to internalise your supervisor and know what they would say in most situations. All Will knew was that his supervisor would say something like: *This is really messed-up, Will. Stop it immediately!* But, even though there was a part of him that could hear this in his head, by way of self-supervision and as a sensible reaction, another, louder part of him, was saying – shouting, actually – *When did you last have a client who claimed to be dead? Convincingly! Who could get through locked doors and into your apartment?* The answer to this was, of course: *This means that you're psychotic, Will.*

But he wasn't psychotic, he tried to convince himself – or at least not in the usual way. Not in the way that he'd seen in some of his clients.

Psychotic people always deny that they're psychotic, Will. And psychotic people argue with themselves in their heads!

Self-supervision was clearly a non-starter under these circumstances. He tried to sit calmly and, yet again, go through how things stood.

He had conducted sessions with clients while concussed – his lost sessions – of which he had no recollection. All he could say with certainly was that he had screamed at them, fallen asleep at their feet, taken his clothes off . . . He had somehow known information about them that he couldn't possibly know. He'd instigated a client group, most of the content of which he could not remember. He had a 'client', who certainly wasn't a client in any traditional sense, who claimed to be dead, but who had managed to pretty well remove his eyebrows with a makeshift flame-thrower. He had a client who had just committed suicide, and he was certainly culpable in that. He had acted unethically, if not illegally. He had been actively judgemental, treating him as a kidnapper and criminal rather than as a human being. He had a client who was recovering from a suicide attempt, whom he'd visited – appropriately, he thought – in casualty. But he had consistently relied on that client to bring relief from his more arduous clients. Every single member from the group he'd formed had disappeared from his practice, for reasons he did not understand. And then there was his private life, in which he had painted pictures without even knowing that he'd done so, that were . . . well, beautiful. His wife might have left him because she thought he was having an affair with someone who was, as far as he could tell, dead.

So, his self-supervisor said, *to summarise: you are so tenuously attached to 'reality' that you should take yourself to the nearest psychiatric hospital and check yourself in.*

And yet, somehow, over the last few weeks, he had felt more alive than he had ever felt before.

He thought once more of Guy. Wasn't it true that, perhaps in subtle ways, he'd always been like this with his clients? He'd paid lip service to the fact that he was non-judgemental, but in fact he was far from it. Guy had been a young man in distress. What were his responsibilities under those circumstances?

He remembered a session during his training when a scenario was presented to him and his fellow students in which a potential client reveals that they are a drug dealer who waits at school gates to sell drugs to children. Obviously, this was a scenario that was chosen to invite judgement. Will, who didn't have kids, could see beyond this one and wasn't drawn into it. After a great deal of vitriol had been expressed by a handful of his colleagues, particularly the mothers in the group, in which they said they couldn't possibly work with such a monstrous client, the second part of the scenario was presented: that this person then says, 'I feel so bad about it. Can you help me to stop?'

Will had been so smug at not being drawn into that debate. But wasn't that exactly the judgement that he'd passed on Guy? He hadn't sought to explore with Guy how he'd felt about what he'd done to his sister? Clearly, he was haunted, but did he regret what he'd done? Did he want to understand it or atone for it? Will hadn't thought to ask . . . And now Guy was dead.

Will found it impossible to describe in words what he felt when he thought of this. Shamed? Yes, that was part of it. Failure? Yes, that was part of it too. Rageful? He had been triggered into experiencing his rage by Emma. The rage had passed, but clearly hadn't been dealt with. It was lurking, waiting for an opportunity to ambush him. In this moment, it seemed inevitable that Lara would have left him. There was something very ordinary in this thought. It didn't have the anguished melodrama of self-pity about it. It seemed utterly matter of fact.

Under the circumstances, who would want to be married to him?

On Thursday evening Will had a call from Jamie.

'Have you spoken to Lara?' Will asked him.

'Only briefly. I told her that I was sure you hadn't been unfaithful. It's not that it's impossible, but you're not a liar, Will.'

'What did she say?'

'She's confused. We both are. You haven't been yourself recently. I mean, objectively, and by your own admission. I still worry about your head injury and the aftermath of that. Lara's just confused.'

'Thank you for saying that to her,' Will said. 'It's a strange situation. If only I could get her to sit down with me and talk for a while, I'm sure things would start to get back to normal.'

Even as he said this, he wondered what he actually meant. Probably, that he wanted to go back to a time before the accident. Before meeting Emma. Before the lost sessions and everything that had happened since then. He'd taken it all for granted, that stability, security – that ease.

'It's just as well that I don't know where Lara's staying at the moment,' he told Jamie, 'otherwise, I'd be on her doorstep waiting for her. I know that would be counterproductive but doing nothing active to get her back is killing me.'

'Waiting as patiently as possible is not doing nothing,' Jamie said. 'And it's what you have to do. I know how hard it's going to be for you. I'm around, though, so let's see a bit more of each other over the next few weeks. I've got quite a few free evenings coming up.'

Will noticed the nuance in Jamie's tone and laughed.

'And quite a few evenings that you won't be free, I guess,' he said.

Jamie laughed too. 'I might as well come clean . . . I think I'm in love. I'm sorry I haven't seen you for a while, especially when you're having a difficult time, but that's what's been going on.'

'That's lovely,' Will told him. 'I haven't even had a chance to start worrying about you.'

'I know, I know. It's quick off the mark, even for me.'

'So, who is he? How did you meet? And are you rescuing him?'

Jamie sighed. 'It's true that he does fit some of my old patterns, but I think there's something different this time. Perhaps I'm too fed up of making the same old mistakes. I don't know, but he's very different in some ways to people I've been out with before. He's older than me for a start. By some way.'

'How much older?'

'Eight years. He's forty.'

'How did you meet him?'

'In Snowdonia. I thought it was time to climb a mountain again, and I discovered that my gay outdoors group was off up there, so I went along. He's not a mountaineer, as such, but it's an auspicious sign, I think, for me to meet someone on a mountain.'

'Oh my God . . . what's this guy's name?'

'Stuart. Why, what's wrong? Do you know him?'

'Yes.'

'How do you know him?'

'I'm not able to say.'

'Which means that he is, or was, one of your clients.'

His only client! As far as he knew.

There was a short silence.

'What does this mean?' asked Jamie. 'Does this mean I have to stop seeing him?'

Will laughed. 'No, Jamie, it means that *I'll* probably have to stop seeing him.'

'Oh, Will, I'm sorry,' said Jamie. Then after a pause, he added, 'Oh, no. You must know all kinds of things about him. I mean, confidential things. Like whether he's good boyfriend material or not.' He laughed. 'This is awkward, isn't it?'

'Some things are awkward and some things are *awkward*,' said Will. 'This is just awkward. Believe me, I have experienced things recently that make this feel positively straightforward. I'll have a chat with Stuart about it when I next see him.'

'Should I have a word with him first?'

'Are you going to be seeing him before Tuesday?'

'No.'

'Then, perhaps we can leave it at that. The less we talk about it the better, and I can bring it into my next session with him. I'm sorry I've outed him as being in therapy like this.'

'No, it's okay,' said Jamie. 'He's mentioned it to me. I would never have told you about it, though, because you would have worried that I was up to my old habits. Which perhaps I am. Given the circumstances, you're probably in a better position than me to say whether this is a good idea or not.'

'And that statement is a perfect example of why this should be discussed as little as possible.'

'Point taken,' said Jamie.

After the call, Will felt lifted by the happiness that he'd heard in his brother's voice.

Thirteen

When Will went back to the practice on Monday, Becky did a double-take when she saw him.

'God, Will! I didn't recognise you for a moment! You look so different with your hair like that.'

Will tried to look casual about it but, judging from Becky's expression, he failed. He didn't respond and went straight to his room to while away some hours.

Much later, when Stuart came for his session, Will felt so kindly towards him that he couldn't help smiling.

'Wow,' said Stuart. 'Your hair!'

'Hello, Stuart.' Will sobered as he spoke. 'I'm not going to start today's session by asking how you are. I have to start by having a chat with you about something that has cropped up. It might affect the work we're doing together.'

Stuart looked worried.

'It's nothing bad.' Will smiled. 'It's just that the man you are falling in love with happens to be my brother.'

'Jamie?'

'Yes.'

Stuart caught his breath. 'Oh . . . Oh!'

There was a short silence as he absorbed this.

'He said his brother was a therapist, but it didn't occur to me that it was you. He's got an English accent and you're Scottish.'

'Actually, he's the one who's Scottish,' said Will. 'But it's not my place to give you information about my brother. Especially not in a therapeutic context. What we have to do today is to decide what to do about it.'

'How do you mean?'

'Well, I'm afraid it's probably not possible for us to continue in a therapeutic relationship.'

'Why not?'

'Even if you stopped seeing Jamie today, what would happen if you wanted to bring aspects of your relationship with him here, into your therapy?'

'Oh . . . I see what you mean.' He looked at Will. 'Oh, God! You know all about my suicide attempt. You know I hold something that I feel I can never be forgiven for.'

'Perhaps we can agree something about this,' said Will. 'I can't unknow these things. But I can hold them. We can't be sure if we'll be meeting in a social context, but if we do, perhaps we can set some ground rules. For a start, I can guarantee that I won't deliberately disclose any information from our time together. Similarly, I would expect you to keep confidentiality regarding my practice as a therapist. Particularly with regards to some of the . . . odd happenings after my head injury last month.'

Stuart nodded. 'Although there's some unfinished business there.'

'Which will have to remain unfinished, I'm afraid,' said Will.

It was with considerable sadness that Will said goodbye to Stuart and, once he was alone, he realised that he now had no clients at all. Or at least, he had no clients that he could be sure of. There was no longer a single genuine session booked for him in the practice diary. There was a meeting booked with Emma, but that wasn't a client session. It was something else.

Over the next few days, Will spent some of his time at the practice, more to give him something to do than because he actually expected anyone to turn up. He went to the kitchen every now and again to get himself a coffee to take back to his room where he would drink it and eat biscuits or chocolate. He might as well use the room, he thought ruefully, seeing as he was paying good money for it.

On Friday, he sat in his comfortable blue chair and looked around him and felt affection for this space in which so many emotions had been expressed and felt – his as well as his clients'.

But what now?

There was no hurry to do anything. No reason to go home. No reason to stay here. Both places were in their own way bereft – as well as expensive. Lara hadn't paid her half of the rent this month and he was pretty well at the limit of his credit. He wondered whether to write up his final session notes for Stuart from earlier in the week, but there were such holes in the recording of his client work since his lost sessions that it didn't seem worthwhile, and so he sat for a while looking pensively out of the window. At 2pm, the phone on his desk rang. It was Becky.

'Your two o'clock appointment is here.'

He wasn't expecting a client, but he took a breath and said, 'Thanks Becky.'

He gathered his thoughts for a few seconds and then went to get whoever it was. It was Guy. Will was shocked and bewildered, and he almost stopped breathing. It occurred to him suddenly that Guy was dead and had also come to haunt him. He looked normal, but then, so did Emma. He gestured for Guy to follow him to his room where he sat down.

'Hello,' he said as neutrally as he could manage.

Guy didn't respond at first. Will was happy for once to retreat into silence and wait for Guy to speak. He needed the time to collect himself.

'I wondered whether to come here today,' Guy said, eventually. 'I think I might have lost a lot of trust in you. You behaved so badly to me last week, and I wanted to come back and challenge that.'

'I thought you were dead!' Will blurted out. 'It was in last week's paper.'

Guy looked confused. Will crossed to his desk and picked up the paper. He handed it over and pointed to the article. Guy glanced at it and then unfolded it.

'This isn't last week's paper, it's six weeks old. Who gave it to you?'

Will stared at the date that had now been revealed. Guy was right.

'Someone . . .' said Will.

'Whoever it was, they were having a sick joke at your expense,' Guy said.

Will took back the paper and double-checked it. How had he missed it? When she'd showed it to him, Emma had folded the paper so that the date couldn't be seen. He sighed heavily.

'That makes sense,' he said. He sat back in his chair, took a long deep breath and looked at Guy. 'I'm glad you're here, because I want to apologise unreservedly for my behaviour last week. It was unforgiveable. Unhelpful judgement got in the way, I'm afraid, and I've thought a lot about that over the last few days, and I have regretted it. Not many therapists have the opportunity to make an apology of this kind, because a client wouldn't usually return after a session like that, so thank you for being here.'

Guy considered that for a moment without any apparent reaction. 'I thought I was going to face some hostile cross-questioning today. So this is helpful, if a little surprising.' There was a pensive frown over Guy's drawn face. Will felt that he was seeing Guy as if for the first time. Or at least, the first time in this way. He could see the tension around his eyes and the suffering that it implied.

'I can see that you have suffered,' said Will. 'I can see that clearly and I want to respond to that and nothing else. That's the truth of this situation. You have suffered and you need to be seen in that suffering. I can witness that in you. I couldn't do that last week for my own reasons and I apologise again for that. Maybe we can move on from last week's session and maybe we can't, and I am happy to take responsibility for that.'

Guy seemed to ponder what Will had said. 'Okay,' he said. 'Let's see.' He rubbed his hands briefly against his trousers as if feeling the sensation of the cloth against his fingers, before looking at Will. 'Perhaps I can tell you what really happened?'

'Of course,' said Will. 'Please, go ahead. I'd like to hear whatever you feel able to say.'

Guy closed his eyes and leaned back a little further in his chair, gathering himself. Will waited respectfully. When Guy reopened his eyes, he looked composed, intense, and very alert.

'I didn't kidnap Joe,' he said. 'I didn't kidnap *Emma*. Or, well, I guess I did, but it didn't start out that way.'

He took a deep breath.

'You never met Joe, so you don't know what kind of person she was. But she was very troubled from an early age. We were twins and so we were very close in some ways and knew each other well. By the time she was fourteen, I was beginning to get really worried about her. I was the one who flagged up to my parents that she had anorexia – not that they cared. They just thought she was thin. But look at me, I've got the same constitution as her. She needed to starve herself to stay thin. I caught her a couple of times being sick when my parents weren't in the house, which is how I discovered she had bulimia.'

He looked down at his hands, and kept his gaze lowered.

'We both went to the University of East Anglia – UEA – in Norwich. I hoped I'd be able to keep an eye on her, but she avoided me most of the time. We'd joked about going to university as far away from each other as possible but, in our twin-like way, ended up both going there. I studied Economics with Accountancy and she took Philosophy, Politics and Economics. On the surface, the courses looked quite similar but they were very different, though they played to our strengths – me being more practical and she having a sharper intellect. In the summer after our first year, we went home for the holidays. Joe had completely run out of money. I went home too because I was still concerned about her and to help dilute the effect of our parents.

'A friend of mine lived with his dad in an old thatched cottage near Cromer. I was going to go there to stay with him for a fortnight. In the end, my friend got the chance to go to New York on an internship for the summer. His dad was having an affair with a violinist from Norwich who was addicted to various drugs, and so I was offered the cottage while he spent some time with her.

'I had this idea that I would invite Joe to come along with me. Which she agreed to do. And then . . . well . . . I suppose I did kind of . . . kidnap her. Though that's not a word I would ever use to describe it. This cottage was on its own and I had the keys. And I locked us in together. Or, at least, I didn't at first. At first, I made sure we stocked up with plenty of food from the supermarket by the station, and then I tried to persuade her to eat, which she did. But then I had the problem of how to stop her from being sick. When we went to bed that first night I only half slept. And at about half-past one, I heard her getting up and creeping to the bathroom. I got up and caught her with her fingers down her throat.'

He paused as if recollecting the scene.

'We had a bit of a screaming match then, which was incredibly unpleasant for both of us. I told her I loved her, that as my twin she was a part of me, and that I was worried that she was going to die. The next day, I wouldn't let her out of my sight – literally, except when she was in the bathroom. Then, I insisted that she keep the door open and I stood outside so that I could hear what was going on. A bit humiliating for her, but that was nothing compared to what came later.

'She refused to eat. Just refused. The next day, I force fed her. It was . . . well, it was hideous. She bit me quite badly, but I managed to twist her arm up behind her back, which worked, and she eventually ate what I gave her.'

He sighed.

'I loved her. I could see that she would die if she went on like that. It was a nightmare. For both of us. But after three or four days of this, of not sleeping and of keeping a constant vigil, I eventually tied her to the bed, so that I could sleep and be sure that she wouldn't get up to be sick.

'That went on for a few days, me tying her up at night. But she wasn't eating anything and so she had nothing to sick up. After that, when she looked like she was really ill – that she might die anyway – I gave up. I hadn't slept at all in that time, even when she was tied up, and I was feeling terrible. Joe was crying all the time. And I . . . gave up. I said to her, "Look, it's your life. You've got to do with it what you want to do with it. I realise I can't help. I thought I could help you, but this isn't help, is it?"

'And then I drove her home. I told her that I loved her and she could do what she wanted. She could tell my parents what I had done. She could tell the police, if she wanted to. I wouldn't deny anything. But Joe didn't say anything. When we got home, she smiled, and my mother asked why we were back early, and Joe said, "The house was ghastly and I got a bit ill". And that was that.

'Our shit family life went on. My relationship with Joe had the outward appearance of being the same, at least in front of our parents. But it was completely different. We didn't speak when there were no other people there. And it changed me. Completely. I realised then that there are some things in this world that I have no power over. None at all. I loved Joe, but I couldn't save her. About a week after we went back to Norwich, she took her life. I knew it was going to happen. I also realised that it was partly my fault. I had forced something on her in a traumatising way. In the weeks and months after that, I read quite a lot about eating disorders and came to understand that they mostly come about as a result of trauma. In traumatising her in the way I did, I made things worse than they already were rather than better. But anyway, whatever the truth of it is, I'll never know for sure what my father did to her.'

He paused at that, as if taking in what he was saying for the first time. He looked still and shocked and went silent for a while before he spoke again.

'I'd always known it, really, but I'd never acknowledged it until later on, when I understood that eating disorders don't come from nowhere. In a way, it doesn't matter how she was hurt. Forcing my will on her was a kind of secondary abuse. And I did that. I can't even begin to get my head round that. I loved her. I wanted to help her, and yet – in some way that I can't sort out in my head – I abused her.'

After Guy finished, the silence went on for some time. Will didn't need to say anything. He sat and accepted what Guy had told him.

'You were trying to help your sister,' Will said eventually. 'You were trying to save her life, in fact. And what you've ended up with is guilt and shame and a sense of failure. You were unable to fulfil the task that you set out to achieve.'

'How can good intentions go so terribly wrong?' asked Guy. 'Emma is dead, and it's no exaggeration to say that my life has been ruined by it. Ruined!'

Will could see a visceral pain etched into Guy's face. There was a deep moment of connection between them that was humbling for Will to experience. He understood the scale of what Guy was facing and the terrible inertia that could come with it, of not knowing how to begin to work with it. He was in there with Guy and Guy could see that he was in there.

'We can get stuck in trauma,' Will said. 'But that doesn't mean we have to always remain stuck there. The death of your sister weighs heavily on you and it's as if you'll never get beyond the feeling of guilt that goes with your sense of responsibility. But that doesn't have to remain true.'

Will felt a surge of energy, a sort of tingle that rose from his feet to the crown of his head. He realised that he had addressed himself as well as Guy.

Guy was looking out of the window. With a mirthless laugh, he said, 'I'll never wear cowboy boots again!'

Will waited for Emma's arrival with a thrill of expectation. He didn't know what he was going to say, or how she would act, but he knew that there was no way he was going to accept anything less than a full explanation of what was going on. She arrived on time and wore the same clothes as ever. She sat down and smiled at him.

'A couple of things puzzle me that I want to get out of the way,' he said. 'First, you're slim, but a long way from looking terminally underweight.'

Emma's smile was enigmatic. Was she gearing up to respond to a confrontation or was there perhaps a sign that she was somehow at ease, pleased even, that he had spoken to Guy and learned of her story.

'Second . . . how old are you? Twenty-five? Twenty-seven? A bit old to have just finished your first year at university?'

'Poor Will,' she said. 'You still haven't quite grasped how this works, have you?' Was she goading him or was there a note of genuine affection in her voice? 'What you see is how you imagined me right at the beginning. You didn't know how I died or how old I was. Only how I was dressed. The rest you had to create for yourself. I've no doubt it's part of what's upset Lara. She knows what you like . . .' There was the merest flash of the provocative Emma that Will had grown used to, but he sensed that something had already shifted between them. Things were very different now.

'You were abused by someone,' he said. 'Possibly your father, and also by your brother, even though he did it for love of you.' He felt himself welling up. 'And then you killed yourself.'

'Yes,' she said.

'I don't know what to say to you about the pain you have suffered. To say I'm sorry seems so ridiculously inadequate.'

'I didn't come here to talk about myself. And I'm not trying to avoid any issue, by the way. This isn't about me.' She laughed lightly. 'I'm happy to answer questions if you have anything to ask.'

He took a breath. 'Why did you lie to me about Guy committing suicide? Why did you bring that paper in here to deceive me?'

'You deceived yourself. You didn't even look at the date on the paper.'

He felt himself flush.

'You look younger when you blush. With your short hair.'

He wasn't sure whether she was complimenting him or making fun of him.

'Guy was trying to save your life. You presented it as

though he wanted to hurt you. Why did you mislead me?' He felt a frisson of other-worldliness as he said this. He couldn't have asked this unless he had accepted, and believed, that she was dead. How had that happened? How was it possible and, in this context, how could it sound so reasonable?

'Guy himself confessed that he kidnapped me.'

'And now we know why.'

She looked at him and frowned slightly as she gathered her thoughts. It was a look of concentration that belied her previous looks of assertive – even aggressive – self-confidence.

'I'm not going to get angry with you,' he said. 'I can't. I already vomited that out and it seems to have gone, at least for the time being. So now, maybe you can tell me whatever it is that you have come here to say.'

'Of course. There are so many layers to this.' She looked out of the window. 'Maybe I could start by hinting at one of them.'

There was something soft about her expression when she turned back to him.

'I needed you to experience rage. A particular kind of rage. The rage that obscures shame and guilt. And I don't mean the guilt that my brother feels for his sister or the guilt that you feel for yours, but dark, constructed guilt built on misinterpretation and a personal way of seeing happenings and events as being about "me" or, more accurately, a kind of self-obsessed "me, me, me". Guy was never going to tell you about his shame. Yes, I know, he came into therapy. But he was incapable of telling you the truth. I mean, he had to make me up, didn't he? He had to say he'd seen me when he hadn't. He had to invent me as a ghost, and you would have spent all your therapeutic time working on that. Was it psychosis? What did it mean that he was "seeing" me? That was all a smokescreen, hiding what he really needed to look at, what he has finally spoken – with a little help from me along the way.

'And for you, the only doorway into this was rage. That's why you shut it off when you were younger. Oh, you felt the shame alright, but you had no access to the root of it and so you could never get beyond it.'

'And it was the same for Guy,' said Will. 'He needed to feel rage against me to open up to what he really felt.'

Emma nodded.

'So . . . you told me what happened in the way that you did because you knew that I would make certain judgements and then confront him with them. I would feel the anger and then he would feel the anger.'

'Exactly.'

Will found himself unable to take this in on anything other than an intellectual level.

'Why did you appear to me?' he asked. 'If you are Guy's ghost, why did you also become mine?'

'Guy's guilt. Your guilt. Guy's rage. Your rage. What's the difference? None of it matters. It's not authentic. That becomes so clear once you've found a way to look at it. To *really* look at it.'

The next day, Will stayed at home. In the afternoon, he went to Wandsworth Common and walked by the pond, watching the swans swimming gracefully past him, oblivious of his inner turbulence. It wasn't until he got home and came into the familiar environment of the flat – familiar, and yet bereft in Lara's absence – that he could see it.

There were two men: himself and Guy. There were two sisters. Two dead sisters. Two manifestations of blame and guilt.

He went into the sitting room and sat down. What was this? What did it mean? Was this another of the layers that Emma had mentioned?

He suddenly remembered Stuart saying, after he came out of hospital, that the price he'd paid for carrying shame was that he experienced separation from everyone he'd ever loved.

As he sat and considered Guy's shame and guilt, he felt his own thrill of . . . what? Something more like amused embarrassment. It wasn't that the death of his own sister was immaterial or that it hadn't been traumatic – of course it had been traumatic. He recognised, quite suddenly, that there was no longer any reason to feel guilty about it. Or rageful at the world or himself for what had happened.

His guilt had been so convenient for him. At university he'd used it unconsciously with women to seem vulnerable and in need of their healing, so the perpetuation of his guilt had – again unconsciously – served a purpose. It had been important that he portrayed vulnerability, but it was equally important that he should never be healed, because if that happened, what would be left to make him interesting and worthy of attention?

He'd carried his pain about with him, pretending he wanted to get rid of it, but locked into an unhealthy, addictive need for it. Seeing Guy's pain, *really* seeing it, made his own pain seem like an unnecessary use of mental storage. Guy had a major journey ahead before he could get beyond the burden of his pain, but what about Will? What did he need to do to get beyond his? Emma had forced him to look at the wellspring of this pain. Feel it. But could he let it go? And if not, would he continue to experience separation from almost everyone he'd ever loved? He thought of his mother and his father, of their pain after the death of Charlotte. He thought of his other sister, Kitty, and her antipathy towards him. He'd always focussed on his own pain and never really acknowledged theirs.

When he got home he emailed Lara.

I am emailing you because I recognise some things that I haven't noticed before. I am stuck in a pattern of behaviour that I thought I'd escaped. But I haven't.

Then he sent exactly the same wording to Kitty. Lara didn't respond to him that evening, but he got an almost immediate reply from Kitty.

When are you next in Carlisle? I'd be interested to hear more.

That evening, Jamie phoned.

'Hi, Will, I'm having a couple of friends round next week

to meet Stuart and wondered if you'd want to come along?'

Will thought about it and then declined.

'Stuart's fine about it,' said Jamie. 'In fact, he was the one who suggested it.'

'I'll feel comfortable when a little more time has passed,' said Will. 'That way there'll be more chance of seeing each other as people and not as client and therapist.'

Though Jamie was happy with this, Will said, 'Please make it clear to Stuart that it's not because I don't want to see him, but that it's a question of timing.'

'Of course.' Jamie was quiet for a moment and then said quietly, 'I think this is serious, Will. I think he might be right for me. At least for a while.'

'Good,' said Will, 'I'm glad.'

'Ha!' laughed Jamie. 'You said that with such conviction, Will, I know we have your approval!'

'No comment!'

'No comment required.'

On Friday morning, he saw Emma again. This time he felt calm and sat silently with her. He did not start the conversation. Emma waited for some time and then smiled when it became obvious that Will was happy to wait in silence.

'It wasn't deceit,' she said to him. 'It was a question of scale. Even though you would have denied it, you imagined your own suffering to be greater than that of a woman who was kidnapped and who committed suicide. Or as great as the shame that my brother holds for the disastrous attempt he made to save my life. But these things have no scale. Suffering is suffering – to place it on a scale of any kind is to misunderstand the nature of suffering. By dealing with you in this way, I gave you the opportunity to look at your own suffering and I pulled Guy into a real relationship with someone who could help him.'

'So,' said Will, 'what you're saying is that everything you did was an act of kindness?'

Emma gave a small bow of her head in acknowledgement.

Will sighed. 'I think I see. You never intended to be my client, did you?'

She smiled. 'You thought I came here because I needed therapy. Which was natural, of course, and sweet.'

'You were taking me on as *your* client.'

'You spent so much time seeing things as being wrong. But everything was okay all along. All of it.'

'What do you mean by "all of it"? Your death? My bike accident? Lara moving out? My clients disappearing?'

'Yes, all of it.'

'That's not how it feels.'

'What we're talking about here is perspective. You categorised me as a problem and so that's what I've been. If the habit you have – which you would call instinct but which I can assure you is only habit – hadn't been to push me away, things might have unfolded very differently.'

'I've pushed everyone away in my life except Jamie. Even Lara. *Especially* Lara.'

'Separation,' said Emma. 'You feel separate, so you make everything else separate to fit in with how you see the world.'

'I realise that I've caused every separation I've ever experienced. That's not okay.'

'Maybe what you mean by the word *okay*, and what I mean by it are rather different,' said Emma. 'Let's start with okayness as acceptance. Are you okay with yourself? Are you okay with your wife? Are you okay with your clients? Are you okay with me?'

She looked hard at Will to emphasise her point.

'The answer is no,' she said. 'Not because you couldn't be, but because you place yourself in a position of judgement over everyone, including yourself. You have never had unconditional positive regard for anyone. I wonder what would happen if, even for a moment – and a moment is all that's needed – you had unconditional positive regard for yourself?'

He stared at her. She stood up and picked up the foldaway chair that was leaning against the wall and opened it up, placing it a few feet in front of Will. She sat back down and smiled.

'Imagine yourself in the chair. What might you say?'

Will looked at that empty space. It was a long time since he'd been asked to do Two Chair work.

'I'm not sure . . . I feel sorry that things have been so difficult.'

'Say it to him.'

Will felt a prickling sensation and looked at the space, feeling his way into the sense of himself sitting there. 'I feel sorry that things have been so difficult for you. I feel sorry that you can't remember a time when you felt whole. Unbroken.'

Emma leaned forward. 'Say . . . "I have unconditional positive regard for you."'

Will hesitated. 'I have unconditional positive regard for you,' he said.

'Did you believe that?' she asked.

'No.'

'If you managed to say it with conviction, would you be able to have unconditional positive regard for me?'

He stared at her.

'I love you, Will,' she said.

He continued to stare at her, caught in the moment as it opened up into a cascade.

'I remember!' he whispered.

'What do you remember?'

'My lost client sessions. The group sessions. I remember them!'

'What do you remember?'

Will closed his eyes. 'It's not clear. Something about . . . surrender.' He opened his eyes. 'I told them to surrender.'

'What does that mean?' Emma asked.

'It's not clear, the memory isn't clear. It's fading.'

'Surrender,' she said quietly. 'And what are you going to surrender to?'

'To you?'

'You did it just then. For a moment.'

'That's what it was!' said Will. 'It's not that there was

another Will who took over. It was a surrendering *of* Will, a surrendering of mistrust, of the fear that led to over-caution. It wasn't the addition of something – another "person" to be admired – but an absence of someone who was in the way.'

'You broke the rules,' said Emma. 'But what are rules for? They're helpful only if you don't know what you're doing and need guidance. It's like a man diving into a river to save a drowning child. Does he take notice of the sign on the river bank that says *No Swimming?* Of course he doesn't.'

She was right. She was right! 'You're doing it to me!' he laughed. 'You're doing to me what I was doing to my clients in our lost sessions!'

'One more thing . . . for our last session . . . Bring a car next week. Make sure you don't have any appointments later in the day. I want you to take me somewhere. And, by the way . . . She smiled a mischievous smile. 'You'd better get used to the idea of fatherhood.'

As Will was about to leave for the afternoon, Becky smiled at him with obvious relief.

'Christina has booked in to see you tomorrow morning at 9.30,' she told him. Her smile acknowledged him and something of the journey he had taken. Will returned the smile and thanked her.

As he walked back to the flat, he pondered what Emma had said to him and also the session he'd had with Guy. He'd sensed something of surrender in Guy – surrender to honesty and process. He could also see in himself that life was a process. That therapy and his therapeutic training had given him all the knowledge he needed in order to understand why he'd turned out as the person he now seemed to be. But it hadn't taught him how to surrender to the *being* of it. Surrender, it seemed, was something beyond knowledge. It had nothing to do with therapy. It wasn't a thinking thing, it was an *allowing* thing, a letting be. In fact, he realised, thinking could be – at least on this level – profoundly unhelpful.

As he passed the gutted newsagent's, the shopkeeper who had been round the back when Emma had set fire to the place, came through from the side passage. Will caught himself running his hand through his bristle-short hair. The man looked at him and smiled ruefully.

'Is this your shop?' Will asked. 'What a terrible thing to happen?'

'I hated this place,' the man said. 'Business was bad. I was persuaded to make a bad investment in buying it by people who lied to me. I was never cut out to be a shopkeeper, anyway. Now, with the insurance money, I'll be able to go and do something else. I have a brother in Exeter who runs a guest house. I might go into business with him.'

When he got back to the flat, a call came through on his mobile. It was Lara. He waited a couple of rings before accepting the call.

'Will?'

'Hello, Lara,' he said. 'How are you?'

'I got your email.'

'Oh? And?'

'I don't know if it's going to make any difference, but we do need to meet up and have a talk. It was true about the coin, Will. That I was tossing it to decide whether to try for a baby. I don't know who this woman is, but I realise that you were obviously shocked to see her in the restaurant and then in the flat. You didn't fake that. But I want you to tell me the truth. As you know, that's my one stipulation. I know you, Will. Better than you think I do. And you were keeping things from me after you had your accident. If it wasn't because you were having an affair, then I want to know what it really was.'

'Agreed,' said Will.

―

The following morning, Christina arrived. Did she look a little thinner? He wasn't sure. She looked pensive and rather distracted.

'Hello, Will,' she said.

'A glass!' Will suddenly remembered. 'I smashed my water glass against the drawers during our session.'

This brought her right into the room.

'Yes,' she said. 'Maybe we could start there. I didn't know where to start, but that's a good place. You seem to have a bit of a penchant for smashing glasses!'

She looked down at her hands, whose fragile fingers were interlocked with unconscious precision and symmetry.

'I've thought a lot about the glass and why you smashed it in front of me like that. I had to pull a couple of small shards out of my sweater afterwards, which put it in context, as something out of the ordinary. Out of the normal category of interventions that a therapist might make. After the last group session, when you told us to go away and not come back until we had something concrete to report, that was what kept coming up for me. It was an obvious metaphor in its own way ... the metaphor of fragility, of frailty. But I got more of a sense of it later ... the hardness, the transparency and the trappedness. I can see out of my glass bubble. I can see the world, but I'm not a part of it. I am protected from it but I am also separated from it. And then, smash! Could it really be as easy as that? One simple movement – not even a strenuous one. One that someone like me might manage even at my most fatigued, even when I'm so exhausted that I can hardly lift my arm. But smashing what? What is this invisible barrier?'

She looked at Will then as if irritated with him for a moment, irritated and unsure.

'In the last group session, when you asked me to surrender to my eating disorder, I thought you were telling me to kill myself. But, of course, you weren't. You were asking me to step beyond that invisible barrier between me and the world that I have tried to keep myself so safe from. The world that was killing me, or that I felt was killing me. And do you know what? I have no idea whether I'll survive this. When I said to the group that I wanted to die, what I really meant was that I'd rather die than live like this.

'My parents have persuaded me to contact our local eating disorder service. I know you've had that on the agenda from the word go, but after the group it suddenly seemed possible for the first time. I may even be prepared to go residential for a while. We'll see. But I hope to continue seeing you, if that's okay, when I'm around?'

'Of course, it's okay,' said Will.

'This is a little hard to say,' she said, 'but in that session when you broke the glass in front of me, I could see that you loved me. That was confusing because actually I've been a little in love with you all along.'

She laughed with embarrassment.

'Oh, what a cliché, to fall in love with your therapist. How safe! How predictable, when you're keeping the world at bay, to fall in love with someone unattainable. I even asked at the front desk if you were married, and the lady there said yes, but immediately made me promise not to say that she'd told me. She realised she'd breached confidentiality. But it wasn't her fault, I asked in such an innocent way and, in any case, you're wearing a wedding ring.'

She seemed to scrutinise Will.

'Was it the long hair? I'm not sure. This new look that you have seems more vulnerable, but also no-nonsense and military. I think I could cope with you like this a little better because you no longer look like the man I had a crush on. It's like starting all over with a different person.'

'In a way,' said Will, 'that's exactly what it is.'

She nodded and looked out of the window and across to

the church. 'You know, in that group session, it seemed clear to me from the start that you didn't levitate. I don't know what all the fuss was about.'

'Levitate?'

She laughed. 'Yes, it's ridiculous, isn't it?'

And then Will remembered. With clarity. Like a lens coming into focus from a blur. The lost sessions had come back to him only in a general way at first. Now they became sharp, with an immediacy as if they had only just happened. The vague mist through which he'd perceived them when he was speaking to Emma parted to reveal a clearly delineated landscape. The lost group sessions were there, too.

He remembered the session in which he'd asked Emma to leave and her assertion that he was fake – her explosive accusation that he hadn't faced his guilt about his sister's death. It had been an agonising few minutes. What therapist would ever want to be on the receiving end of such profound and shattering truth in front of clients? And he could remember clearly what happened next.

It was like a tableau: Emma leaning towards him from across the group; the rest of them in rapt and slightly embarrassed attention. He could feel a strange sensation, a thrill of restlessness in his body, like an itch. It invited a response that could as easily be resistance or . . . surrender. He could feel a stiffening as he went into fight or flight mode and shifted uncomfortably in his seat. The muscles in his back tightened and he arched backwards slightly to relieve them. For a moment, he felt dizzy and almost weightless, reminded of his dreams of floating timelessly above the bonnet of the car that had knocked him off his bike. This lasted perhaps two or three seconds, but felt much longer, and then his pen and clipboard fell to the floor with a startling clatter.

'Look!' Emma had cried. 'Look at Will! He's levitating!'

There was a thrill of excitement in the group. Debbie let out a small scream. 'Oh my God,' she cried. 'He did! I saw it!'

Will felt a tremor in his body as the taut energy in him released and he slumped, a movement which he disguised by leaning forward to pick up his clipboard. The pen had skittered across the circle. Matt picked it up and came over to Will, holding it out, his hand shaking slightly.

'How did you do that?' he asked, fear in his eyes, 'I've never seen anything like it.'

'It was nothing,' said Will. 'I was stretching, that's all.'

'This is what happens,' said Emma. 'Something like this happens and then Will denies it.'

'Oh, leave it out!' cried Laurence. 'Of course Will didn't levitate. What are you trying to say . . . that he's so special that the laws of gravity don't apply to him?' He snorted and looked up at the ceiling, shaking his head.

'I saw it,' said Emma.

'So did I,' said Anna.

'And me,' said Matt.

'Rubbish,' said Laurence, 'I was looking right at him and

he was stretching his back, like he was yawning or something. He didn't levitate.'

'Laurence is right,' said someone else. 'He didn't levitate.'

'But I also want to be clear,' said Laurence, 'that I agree with the others when they say that things have happened that we need to talk about. I want to know what your secret is and how you were able to be so intuitive and accurate in the session we had after your accident – the one you gave when you were injured. It needs to be talked about, but please let's not pretend that it's anything supernatural. Will isn't anything special, he's just a therapist . . .' He smiled at Will. 'A pretty good one as far as I can tell, but he's not . . . divine.'

The group split into roughly equal halves: those who saw him levitate and those who didn't. Everyone had been looking at Will, so it was a matter of discernment or interpretation. Will could see that it wasn't his job to try to convince people. They'd experienced what they'd experienced and that was true for them. As a therapist running the group, his job was to acknowledge and accept people's experiences, not tell them what was true. In any case, he'd felt such a bizarre tremor in his body that he was just as mystified as everyone else.

'Will levitated,' said Emma. 'Those of you who don't believe it are too closed-minded to allow themselves to actually see something that they believe to be impossible.'

'And you only think he levitated because you're three quarters of the way to believing he's got magical powers,' said Laurence.

'Let's stop,' said Will. 'Let's stop trying to get to the bottom of this. We won't. It's part of the democracy of a group that we agree to differ.'

'Stop trying to get to the bottom of this?' said Debbie. 'Surely that's what we pay therapists for?'

'This is different,' said Laurence. 'I mean, what if I decided to tell you all something completely absurd, like "I'm Napoleon Bonaparte"?'

'I'd be fine with that,' said Debbie.

'I'm sure you would,' said Laurence, 'so maybe that's a bad example. But I still think this is different.'

'Of course it's not different,' said Melissa, one of Will's quieter clients. 'If Laurence were to think he was Napoleon Bonaparte that would be a psychosis or something and we might enter his world to be able to interact with him. But we would all know it wasn't true. Like this. It's like saying the door is open when it's closed. It's a question of fact. There's no point trying to convince a person that the door is open when it's closed. It's just obvious! Will didn't levitate; he *squirmed*. That's the effect Emma had on him – those home truths would make anyone squirm.'

Having gained attention, Melissa suddenly blushed but continued anyway.

'In any case, Will's interaction with me that week – the week that everyone wants to talk about – was a bit lame. It was intuitive, but anyone could have surmised that I needed to make some drastic or dramatic changes. But I'm getting it, as I sit here. I'm realising what's happening. This is a collective psychosis. We're all so desperate for there to be something important going on, something – anything – that will let our little lives seem a little bit less meaningless and futile. But our lives *are* meaningless and futile. That's why I came into therapy, to try and find some meaning in life. And do you know what? I realise that it doesn't matter. Watching some of you believe that Will levitated has made me realise that it doesn't matter that there isn't any meaning. The only problem was that I thought there was a problem. I don't need to scrabble about for some insane delusion to convince myself that life has meaning.'

She looked at Will as though he was cheating her.

'All this money I've spent has been for nothing. Well, maybe not nothing, because seeing that something is pointless is useful of itself. But I think we should all stop – stop trying to fix ourselves. Stop looking to someone like Will to give us meaning. There is no meaning.'

'That's what Will told you to do,' said Emma. 'To stop. Stop! Stop telling yourself a story about yourself that's not true. Will's seeing it at last. He's releasing the burden of the past. No wonder he floated into the air. At least a little. That's what happens when you make something lighter. It floats.' She looked directly at Melissa. 'It doesn't matter what you think you saw. You can't make it not true by believing it's not true. It either happened or it didn't. Belief doesn't change that at all.'

'Stop,' said Will. 'Let's just stop all this.'

'Now,' said Emma, 'I think I'm ready to leave.'

'You can't save me, Will, can you?' said Christina. 'That's what I'd hoped for, that someone else could rescue me. And it's not even something as glib as recognising that I can save myself. Either I can or I can't. There's an internet group that I belong to and it's a hotly debated subject on the forum . . . can we save ourselves? In the end it's a bit of a pointless question. Some of us do and some of us don't, even with all the help on offer, from professionals or therapists like yourself or from the peer support that I have available to me. And if I don't make it, how blaming it would be to say that I could have stopped it, that I could have saved myself but chose not to.'

Will did not say anything. There was nothing he could add to this. They were in this space together and words from him were unnecessary.

'I love you, Will,' she said. 'And you love me. It's not sexual, it's . . . kind. That makes such a difference. It's so beautiful. I don't understand why that may not be enough.'

Will's next client was Rachel. She arrived with intent and Will hardly had a chance to say hello before she started to speak, even as she was sitting down.

'I saw you levitate, Will!' she told him. 'I don't know how you did it, or whether it was a trick but it's had a massive effect on me. It has made me realise that nothing is as it seems. Nothing!'

'I don't have anything to say about whether I levitated or

not,' said Will. 'I don't know what happened, if I'm honest.'

'That's all we need to do. Try to be honest. That's what I've realised I need to do. With myself . . . with others. With you. My husband demonstrated that to me when he told me he'd been married before.'

She looked down at the light cardigan she was wearing and adjusted it slightly.

'And in the spirit of honesty, I want to talk to you about the flirting exercise I did on that first night of the group. I want to talk about what I saw and experienced, and about stopping. I was confused and upset by it at the time and couldn't really put any of it into words.'

Will felt completely ready for whatever might arise. 'Let's start there, then. With the flirting exercise. And with stopping.'

Stopping. Was something stopping? At least, it seemed, he'd stopped fearing what might come up with his clients.

'When we were arguing about whether or not you'd levitated and you told us to stop. I thought you were telling us to stop quarrelling, or to stop being annoyed. But you weren't, were you?'

She looked at Will who didn't say anything.

'It's interesting how sometimes you only "get" things later, but it only clicked at the weekend when I was talking to my husband. I was unclear at first what you meant when you asked us to look for something that *flirted* with us, that caught our attention. But then I noticed the laburnum tree out there in front of the wall. Well, it was coming into leaf then and I remembered that when it is in flower it is so colourful – like it is now. Look, it's so spectacular!'

She pointed out of the window at the resplendent blossom. Will agreed with her. It was spectacular.

'I was reminded of something that my mother said to me when I was a girl. I must have been about eleven. We were visiting my aunt at the time. My cousins were playing in the little sand pit by the garden shed and I was on the swing with this laburnum in full flower in front of me, glowing bright yellow with blossom in the sunshine. My mum came over to me. She was a little drunk, I think, and I told her that the tree was the most beautiful thing I'd ever seen.'

Rachel smiled wistfully.

'My mother said to me, "I was beautiful like that, like a flower in spring." She sounded sad and wounded. "I was a beauty, but you'll never be a beauty, you're not that sort of person. You have no life in you, no talent for excitement. Beauty is not about being physically attractive, it's about something inside, an inner radiance. But you have neither and I pity you. I pity you but I think it's probably for the best. If you have never had something, then you can't regret it when it passes."'

Rachel welled up a little at the memory, but the expression of sorrow faded almost immediately, and Will could see a calmness there.

'You know all of this,' she said. 'Well, not that particular story, maybe, but others like it. And I sat there in your group and looked at the tree and remembered that day in my aunt's garden, looking at the yellow of the flowers glowing so intensely and beautifully in the afternoon sun. And I remembered that they are poisonous. I used to think that it was only the seeds that were poisonous but, actually, every part of the laburnum tree is poisonous to some degree, including the flowers. What a truth there is in that! I was poisoned by my mother's rage at losing her looks – she poisoned me because she'd been poisoned herself by the expectation that her beauty would last. She couldn't help herself. And she was wrong, too. She didn't have an inner radiance, at least not then, and I suspect she never did.'

She sighed.

'But it wasn't that. I'd worked that out for myself over the years, really, through life experience and, later, through my work with you. No, what I realised with my husband at the weekend was that I needed to stop. Stop bargaining. I don't need to forgive my mother, that's not what this is about. Not any more. I need to stop striving to *be* someone, whatever that means.'

She looked at her hands.

'You told us all to go away and work this out. And I realised something important. Something about all of this stuff that I do, this pampering and grooming – this nail varnish. Nothing wrong with nail varnish, unless you think it's going to make you into something or someone that you're not. I got up yesterday morning and enjoyed the colour of my nail varnish for the first time. I saw it, really saw it, the red of it – like seeing the yellow blossom of the laburnum when I was eleven – seeing the beauty of the colour, without any negative association, just for itself. It wasn't poisonous. It was beautiful.'

She sighed and looked up at Will.

'And not only that, there have been other more pervasive kinds of striving. I worked so hard at school, and then at my degree. That was the bargain I struck with myself. If I get good grades, I'll be happy. If I get a first-class honours degree, I'll be happy. If I get a good job, I'll be happy. But it was all for revenge against my mother. "I'll be happy in spite of you!" And yet, I was never happy at school. I was never happy at university because I was working too hard to have friends – not proper friends, anyway. I got my first-class degree and I got my job and revenge wasn't sweet. I think perhaps it never is. Because I wasn't happy. None of it had made me happy. And that was what my revenge was supposed to have been – flaunting my happiness in my mother's face. And, of course, wanting to do that was as sad in its own way as her flaunting her unhappiness in mine.

'And then I met Ben and we fell in love and got married, and do you know the hilarious thing? He'd been through all of this with his first wife. He'd realised that you have to stop imagining that any *thing* will make you happy. He'd realised that there is no point investing in the future, because the present is all there is. And I saw it! Yesterday. We were sitting in the garden together and I heard your voice saying "stop!" and I stopped. I stopped bargaining. "I'll be happy, when . . ." When what? When I've got more money? A better relationship with my husband? A bigger house? When my mother dies? I stopped waiting for the something that I'd believed, childishly, would make me happy. I just stopped.'

A flicker of embarrassment flitted across her face.

'I have everything I could possibly need,' she said, 'and the incredible and humbling thing is to realise that this has always been the case.'

Will remembered the glass, the Jacobite glass that he had smashed on the ceiling during the group session. He had let go of it. He hadn't thrown it. He had opened his hand and it had shot upwards, unbidden. He'd made no effort to do anything. It had happened of its own accord.

What else did he need to let go of?

He let himself into the flat feeling lighter than he had for a long time. He was going to be a father. Emma knew these things, and he didn't doubt her. But what did that mean for him? For Lara? Whatever it might be, the place didn't feel empty, somehow, and he didn't feel the dull pull of loneliness. He got himself a glass of wine and took it into the sitting room.

He sat for a few minutes looking out of the window at the bustle of traffic and people and then at his triptych of paintings. It was clear in an instant that he hadn't seen them properly before. When he'd had a go at fiddling with them a few weeks earlier, he'd been concerned with composition, but without any real idea of what that might actually be. He got up and went through to the spare room to look at the works in progress.

Now, he realised, he'd misunderstood the concept of composition entirely, at least with regard to these pictures. He'd imagined it as the placement of objects or shapes or tonal areas of light and shade in space. But now he remembered painting them, and it had nothing to do with objects, however abstract, or a sense of space. It was to do with composition as in musical composition. It was to do with the juxtaposition of harmony and disharmony. When he wasn't trying to impose ideas of discrete objects, it could all flow.

He took some tubes of paint and squeezed different pigments onto his palette. He picked up a brush and it felt like an extension of his body as he mixed the colours and applied them with swift yet precise strokes.

There were no objects in the paintings! He made a splash of colour *into* the painting, and then everything unfolded as flow, with each additional layer of colour and texture coming as naturally as the next note of a melody.

What a revelation! That something like a painting could apparently paint itself. Will – Will the controller, Will the director – had simply been in the way. He had needed to get out of the way to allow that flow to happen. And now he remembered the happiness of that, the enjoyment of allowing whatever was arising to arise. He had no idea what would happen when he next picked up his brushes, and that was the point. Controller Will would always resist that, the lack of certainty and the lack of agency. But controller Will was expendable, unnecessary. He was redundant, surplus to requirements.

As he was finishing the painting, Jamie rang.

'How about coming out to dinner?' he said. 'I'm meeting Stuart at Belluno's later and maybe you'd like to join us?'

'Great! It's time. I'm ready if Stuart is.'

'One thing, though . . .'

'What?'

Jamie hesitated. 'Could you drop by my place on your way? I know it's a bit out of the way, but I'd like to show you something.'

Sometimes, people asked a favour in a particular tone of voice. Without hesitation, Will said, 'Of course.'

He went into the hallway and picked up his jacket. He paused for a moment and then put the jacket back on its hook. It was the first warm evening of spring. No need for a jacket.

As he was about to leave, his phone rang. It was Lara.

'Are you around tomorrow? Maybe we could meet in my lunch break and we can talk?'

'Lara,' he said. 'I love you. I know you're pregnant.'

He heard her intake of breath. 'How did you know?' she whispered. 'Did Jamie tell you?'

'No.'

'I didn't tell him, but he intuited it. I neither confirmed nor denied it, but he knew.'

Will felt a movement of being and coming into being, and love. Not love for anyone in particular. Just love.

Jamie opened the door to him with a look that Will couldn't interpret. Was it shyness or embarrassment?

'Hello,' he said. 'Come through.'

They went into the small sitting room. Jamie sat on the sofa and motioned Will to sit beside him.

'I was having a clear-out after Joel left. Clothes and books, mostly. I came across some pictures that I kept from years ago. The pictures we took of Charlotte, down by The Lake, before the accident.'

'Oh,' said Will. 'I didn't know they still existed.'

'I've had them for years. I never felt there was an appropriate time to mention them or to show them to you. Except perhaps that time we went up for our family meeting. But even then, it didn't quite happen.'

'How come you have them?'

'I used to use Dad's study when I was doing my A-Levels. I found them when I was looking for his geometry set. Well, I was being nosey, actually.' He looked embarrassed for a moment, then pursed his lips a little. 'Do you want to see them?'

Will nodded slowly. He couldn't think of any words.

Jamie picked up an envelope from the coffee table and opened it. 'I've printed out a set for you.'

There were eight photos. Jamie passed the first to Will. It was slightly blurred, but there was the red dumper. The picture was so skewed that it was half out of shot, but he could see part of Charlotte. Her body was in shot from the neck down, her pale green baby grow had dark green frogs on it that were smiling at each other as they frolicked.

Jamie passed him the next picture. Charlotte's face was visible this time, in the lower part of the picture, and the whole photograph was more in focus. Her face was framed by cherry blossom, which was pale pink, although some of the petals were bruised and translucent, starting to go brown already. Again, the picture was skewed and more than half of the composition was water, rippled with reflections of the sky and the reeds that were out of sight. Charlotte was smiling at the person holding the camera. Her face had the radiance that infants can have, when they light up on recognition of someone they love.

'We were never going to be photographers, were we?' said Jamie.

Will looked at the next picture, which was almost completely blurred, and the next, but none of the others showed Charlotte so clearly. After he'd been through all of them, he said, 'It's that second one, isn't it?'

He went back to it and they both looked at it.

'I'd forgotten what she looked like,' said Will. 'I'd forgotten that she used to smile. That's not the way I think of her at all, but of course she used to smile.'

He looked at that face, the face of innocence, and he felt the sadness. It was a sadness that had no pity in it, and especially no self-pity. It was the sadness of the world. The sadness in the knowledge that such tragedies are inescapable. They happen. As a prickling of tears welled up, he realised that these were tears for everyone, everyone who had ever experienced loss – *everyone* – and not only for himself.

The following day, Will met Lara in a patisserie in Camberwell. He had slept well and knew that he had to give himself up to this, that desperation to get Lara back would only push her away.

'I've only got a few minutes,' she said, 'but I wanted to see you in person. I wanted to look into your eyes when I asked you to tell me the truth.'

'Look as much as you like.'

She sipped her tea and looked at him. It wasn't exactly a stare, but it did have an intensity to it, a desire to know what was going on for him, and a curiosity, too.

'How did you know I was pregnant?'

He returned her look, watching for her response. 'Emma told me. The woman you think I'm having an affair with. Also, I saw you toss the coin that night. I saw it come up heads. Because of what Emma had told me, I knew what that meant.'

He waited to see if she was going to respond. It was difficult to tell as she was being so cautious and guarded.

'I'm going to tell you the truth,' he told her. 'I don't know if this will answer your question in any way, but let's see.'

He looked down at his hands and then up at her and kept eye contact as he spoke.

'I believe that Emma is dead. It doesn't fit my world view,

but the evidence is overwhelming. I denied it for as long as I could, but she knew too many things she couldn't know and had access to our flat even when I changed the locks. She knew about my past, too. All of it.'

Lara's expression didn't change. She still looked at him with what appeared to be neutral interest.

'I can't do this anymore,' he said. 'I have to let go of the past. It is so toxic it's poisoning the present, on and on. The past has been my identity and I have to let it go.'

'When you say *past*, does that include me?' asked Lara.

'No, no! You were part of the solution to my past, not the problem.'

A waiter arrived with two plates of bruschetta and Will looked down at his as if he didn't know what it was.

'I have no strength left in me to prop up the old Will,' he said. 'For as long as I can remember, my life has been characterised by a feeling that I've done something wrong, that Charlotte's death was my fault. But I haven't done anything wrong. Over the years I could tell myself again and again that this was the case. My therapists told me so, too. But it didn't stop me from feeling that I was a bad person and deserved to be punished. A punishment that went on and on. Like being in prison with no possibility of parole.'

He paused and kept eye contact. Lara remained inscrutable.

'And then I stopped,' he said. 'I stopped believing it.'

He searched his mind then, scouting around for the dark inner voice of blame, the internal critic that could spoil everything, reduce his character to something grubby and degenerate. But all he found was silence.

'My sister died and I was partly responsible. These are facts. They carry no shame. They are just facts. There is sadness, but there is no shame.' When he looked at Lara then, he could look at her truthfully. 'My head caught up with my heart.'

He smiled at the thought.

'If I'm going to be a good father, which I hope to be, then I need to be sure that I'm not bad. I don't need to be right, or perfect, but I do need to know that I'm not bad.'

He looked down at Lara's hand, undecided about whether to reach out and take it, then decided not to. He could see her noticing this.

'You can ask me about Emma. I'm happy to tell you the whole story if you want to hear it. I was wrong about her. I thought she wanted to be taken on as one of my clients. That's what I told you, wasn't it? But she was taking me on as *her* client. And I resisted her at every turn! But what I want to say right now isn't about her at all. It's to reiterate what I said about my childhood. That I haven't done anything wrong. It was true of what happened to Charlotte and it's true of Emma. I haven't done anything wrong. What your head and your heart have to say about it is up to you. I can't make you believe me.'

Now, he took her hand. She didn't withdraw it but didn't squeeze back.

'I suspect I can be a better father if we're together. But I'll still be as good a father as I can be either way. It's up to you.'

She was still looking at him. He could see caution there and a softness. He squeezed her hand again briefly and withdrew it.

'You'll be a great mother, too. I look forward to seeing that.'

'Oh Will . . . how did we come to be sitting here like this?'

'We're both facing something that we'd hoped never to face again. You can't bear the idea of someone deceiving you and lying to you. And me? Every woman I have ever tried to love has left me.'

He smiled at her and saw the sadness there.

'But it's okay. Everything is okay. If you come back it will be okay. If you leave me, it will still be okay. Everything was always okay. Always. It's not that I don't love you or want to be with you. I do – more than anything I can imagine. But I can't make something happen just by wanting it and I can't be angry any more about things not being as I want them to be. I love you Lara, and it's okay.'

She sat, silent for a few moments.

'Maybe I needed to be on my own to face this,' he said.

She didn't respond and signalled to the waiter for the bill.

'Don't say anything now,' he told her. 'You need to sit with this and let it settle before you make a decision.'

―

Will drove to the practice in a Ford Focus that he'd hired. He had the windows open as the sun was warm, even at

10.00am. He parked in one of the bays reserved for the practice and went in. Becky smiled.

'Your diary's looking a bit healthier this week,' she said. 'Most of your regulars have booked their old time slots again. Phew!'

'Phew!' he agreed.

He went into his room and sat for a few minutes in his chair, looking out of the window at the vibrant yellow of the laburnum. He could see the riot of colour as a riot of colour. For itself and nothing more. He thought, *I don't feel like a therapist. I don't feel like anything.*

When he went back out, Emma was waiting, wearing a pale blue dress and elegant shoes.

'You look different,' he said.

'So do you.'

They went out and he bipped them into the car.

'Where are we going?' he asked.

'Do you know your way out to the M25 and the M4 towards Swindon?'

'Yes.'

'That's the direction we're going in.'

He set off and they sat in silence for a while as he drove south on the A23, then west onto the M25. Once on the motorway, he turned to her.

'Were you the driver of the car that knocked me off my bike?'

'No,' she smiled. 'That was a serendipitous event.'

He drove on for a while, pensive and relaxed.

'I love my clients,' he said after a while. 'I love Lara. Sometimes that kind of love will be enough and sometimes it won't. It's a mystery. It's a mystery, like the levitation thing. Who knows what that was or what anyone saw?'

'When you unburden yourself,' said Emma, 'you get lighter. When you get light enough, you will float.'

'Like in the dreams I had after my bike accident,' said Will.

Emma smiled. 'Burdens are overrated if you ask me.'

Will glanced at the petrol gauge.

'How far are we going? I'll need to stop off for some petrol at some point.'

She glanced across at the gauge. 'You've plenty of fuel. It's fine.'

It was fine, too. The day was lovely. With the windows open, Will felt the breeze as clean and refreshing. They turned off the M4 and onto the A303. A few miles past Andover, they came over the brow of a hill and saw the whole of Salisbury Plain stretched out ahead of them, hazy and brilliant in the early summer sunshine.

'Is there a town up here?' he asked. 'We need some petrol.'

'Don't worry,' she said. 'Trust me.'

After another mile or so, the car sputtered hesitantly and then the engine died. They were at the start of a long decline and the car coasted on down the hill, its speed slowly decreasing from seventy to sixty, from sixty to fifty, then slowing more rapidly so that with the last of his speed Will only had just enough momentum to pull off into a layby, where the car halted by a gate into a field which had a footpath sign and a style.

'That was stupid,' he said, with exasperation.

Emma smiled. 'I'm afraid I have no idea where the nearest town or petrol station is.'

'I thought you knew where we were going.'

'Listen to me. This is important. When there is no more fuel, Will, an engine will stop. It may not stop immediately because there will be momentum, but it will eventually come to a halt.'

He looked at her for a few moments before he understood what she was saying. 'You made me drive all the way out here, deliberately, until we ran out of petrol just so that you could use that particular metaphor?'

She laughed. 'It's all in the experience, Will. If I'd told you this when we were sitting comfortably in your therapy room, it would have had no power. It would have been a concept, nothing more. And there's a world of difference between a concept and an experience. Now . . . Well, now this has got a certain sense of truth, if you see what I mean? When I say something like *when there is no more fuel, the engine will stop* you might have more of a sense of what I'm talking about. When I set fire to the newsagent's, the reason why it burned so suddenly and so furiously, was because there was so much fuel. Now, out here, right now, after all that has happened, there is no fuel. You don't choose when the fuel runs out. It doesn't wait for a convenient moment.'

She opened the door and got out. Will did the same, stepping out into the warmth of a summer's day.

THE LOST SESSIONS

'You've always thought you were driving, Will. You were always steering this way and that without realising that the steering wheel isn't even connected to the wheels.'

Will pondered that for a moment, but she didn't give him a chance to respond.

'You need to locate a garage, Will. You stay here and do that. I'm going to go into this field to look at these amazing poppies.'

He watched her climb over the style and into the field, then got out his phone and looked up local garages. There were two, about equidistant in each direction, perhaps a couple of hours' walk away. He wondered whether to phone them and get them to come out to him, but it was such a fine day that it would be a shame not to walk.

As he waited for Emma, he reflected on what she'd said. He could see the metaphor up to a point, but their last conversation had been about separation. He instinctively understood that these two things were connected, although he couldn't see exactly how. He looked out across the wheat field beside him, where the green stems had begun to take on a tinge of gold, and at the border of poppies scattered along the side like a seam of lifeblood.

After a while he began to wonder where Emma was. After a few minutes more, his growing impatience turned to laughter. Of course! She'd left him here to fend for himself.

He climbed over the style and into the field and looked out over the poppies. There was no sign of her. He looked back at the driverless car and smiled.

'I love you, Emma,' he whispered.

It was a warm feeling of . . . what? Surrender? He realised that the feeling of love had no object. It was just love. Not for anyone in particular. It didn't need an object.

Well, he thought, *which way should I start walking?*

He had no idea. He took a pound coin out of his pocket and tossed it. Heads he'd go right, tails left. It flashed briefly in the sunlight as it went up but, dazzled by direct sunshine, he had to look away. There was no sound of the coin landing on the tarmac. He blinked and looked around him – nothing. No sign of the coin.

Surrender is not about chance. Or choice. Or coins . . .

In the relaxation of the moment, he found that he'd already started walking West along the road. How had that happened?

You put one foot in front of the other. It just happens.

Acknowledgements

For everyone's patience over the ten years it took to write this novel. To Lulu Russell, Lisa Touzel, Charlie Porter, Leonie Gayton, Richard Gayton, my mother and father (posthumously), Edward Draper, Candace Imison, Keith Elliot (posthumously), Alex Pollard, Kate Perks, Roy Webster, Rhian Bowley, Kate Reynolds, Julia McDermott and Peter Finch for their help with the story. To Seb and Jess Jäger for the incendiary hairspray experience. To John and Tatiana, my course tutors, with appreciation and admiration. To my publisher, Ed Handyside, for his support, advice and excellent editing. And to Vidyadhara for unstinting support, companionship and editorial advice.